Ava Finds Time

Ava Finds Time

A Tale of Medicine and Music in Appalachia

Ann Colbert

Colbez Press

Ava Finds Time
BY
ANN COLBERT

Prologue

"Bringing Meanings to Life." That's the subtitle of the latest edition of *Taber's Cyclopedic Medical Dictionary*. And before I turned the first page of my copy, I took out a red pen and crossed out the "s." The one on the end of meaning, not the possessive. People think Taber's, with its many delicate onion skin pages, is dull and unreadable, but I don't. I believe Taber's saved my life.

My relationship with *Taber's* began when I was a twenty-one-year-old medical student. The compact 5 X 8 inch, two thousand plus page book fit nicely in my backpack and wasn't heavy enough to cause permanent back damage, like some other reference books. I got used to sleeping with *Taber's* beside my bed, ready to open in case of a word emergency.

And there were so many words in the green "Cyclopedic Medical Dictionary." Words that danced on my tongue and defied capture with my pen. I thought my year of Latin and spelling bee credentials would help, but they didn't. There were thousands of terms to describe a disease, a cough, a wound, a finding. And endless lists of syndromes bearing the name of the afflicted patient or, more often, their doctor. The words I found could be either everyday common or adorned with a diacritic and a mysterious aura. All of them were fascinating, and page after page led me toward a better understanding of the internal workings of the human body.

Before long, these intimidating terms became my second language. I became fluent in medicalese. I could tell you the difference between hypertrichosis and hyperhidrosis while playing a difficult piano sonata. I could explain in great detail what causes hypernatremia while playing a game of speed chess. Best of all, I enjoyed building sentences with these elongated words that were, ironically, medical shortcuts. Of course, only a fellow medical person could understand my conversations.

At graduation, since I knew all the words in *Taber's*, I handed my book to a wide-eyed and non-sleep-deprived first-year medical student, telling them to enjoy the journey. I no longer needed my copy. Over the years, I would occasionally pick up a Taber's and chuckle that at one time in my life, I had never heard of things like the Somogyi Effect or Addisons.

But one day, sixteen years later, a *Taber's* fell from a cluttered shelf, and I bent low to retrieve it. I felt a pulsating sensation holding the book, now in its 24th edition. And I wanted to reread the entire book from cover to cover, A to Z.

I didn't know my decision would lead to a momentous year of my life, one in which I found myself in situations I never could have imagined. Nor did I know I would find one complicated word in a tiny font that would change my life in many ways.

What follows is an account of how I started reading *Taber's* one random Friday and changed into a different person by the time I stopped.

Ava Hogan, MD

Chapter 1: Running Late

It was a Friday, Ava opened the spring-loaded door quietly and tip-toed into the room. No one noticed until her backpack, protruding from one shoulder and swinging wide, bumped into an overloaded shelf. The resulting chaos drew everyone's attention and caused chairs to swivel. A couple of people rolled their eyes.

One of the assembled staff, Gwen Mayer, a social worker, leaned toward the woman sitting next to her at the table and whispered, "Don't mind her. That's only Dr. Ava."

Ava knelt on the floor to pick up the scattered books and papers. She replaced them one by one into neat piles. She grasped the last one and paused with it mid-air, feeling her heart skip a beat. She gradually noticed the uneasy, exasperated silence in the room. Ava Hogan hopped up and hurriedly took the closest vacant seat. She tried to ignore the stern looks of some and smiled at her friend Gwen. She was still holding the book.

Settling into the rolling chair, she blurted, "I am sorry I'm late. I got held up at the hospital. What have I missed so far? Who have you talked about?"

It was the care plan meeting of Golden Acres Assisted Living. A time for staff to talk about their patients. GAAL—that's what the facility was nick-named. (GAAL is pronounced in two syllables). Ava liked the people who worked there and usually enjoyed the morning meeting. Today, she noticed an empty box of Krispy Kreme donuts on the table and discarded coffee cups stacked nearby. The room doubled as a lunch/break room, and usually, this meeting of professionals was casual and light-hearted. But today, there was an air of formality.

Gwen answered Ava's question. "Well, we have already talked about Gladys' sister. Let me introduce you to Gladys."

One non-scrub-clad person looked toward Ava. Her crisp, unwrinkled business suit drew Ava's eye like seeing a massive goiter on a passerby. Ava smiled at the well-groomed newcomer and wished she had combed her hair.

Gwen went on, "She's concerned about her sister falling. We've been talking about a plan. The nursing staff recommended a different wheelchair and adjustments to her bed and room. We just explained to Gladys that we don't use bed alarms here. They don't help; the extra noise can make a confused person more agitated. Does that make sense, Gladys?"

Gladys nodded. "I see what you are saying. Now that you mention it, GAAL seems quieter than other places my sister has been in."

Gwen asked, "Is there anything else you are concerned with?"

Gladys responded, "No, I can't think of anything. She loves being here at GAAL. The staff treats her nicely, and Dr. Hogan, she says you're funny." She nodded again at Ava, who blushed.

Gwen rose and helped Gladys to her feet. "Thank you for coming this morning. We are always happy to have family here."

"Thank you," Gladys said to the group. She struggled with the heavy door, and Ava jumped up to assist her. The two locked eyes for a moment. Gladys touched the doctor's shoulder and repeated, "Thank you."

Gwen resumed the meeting agenda: "Next, we should talk about safe storage of medicines. We had an incident last week where a resident got hold of some cough syrup lying out and drank the entire bottle. We have to be more careful."

The staff around the table agreed. It was a danger, but it could be avoided. Two nurse aides promised to watch for problems, and the nurse manager reminded everyone that locking up all medicines was a requirement.

Ava missed this discussion because her attention was focused on the book that was still in her hand. It was green and stubby. Same as her copy from medical school, except maybe thicker. The name hadn't changed—*Taber's Cyclopedic Medical Dictionary.* The corners of many pages were dog-eared and greasy. Multi-colored strips of paper stuck out of spots someone thought were important.

She vaguely recalled a recent Saturday morning when Scott Simon from National Public Radio interviewed a man who had read the entire Oxford English Dictionary. The endeavor took him a year, but she remembered that he said he had fun.

She said to herself, "I wonder what it would be like to read a dictionary?"

Ava thumbed through the book, noticing the first word was alpha and other random words like "iodism" and "Menkes disease." She didn't see the word in small print buried on page 2,479 that would change her life.

Her name was Ava Hogan, and she was a family physician. Ava was her grandmother's name; Hogan was her mother's maiden name. Her parents left out her dad's name. The medical staff always called her Dr. Ava. She would have preferred "Ava".

Startled by a noticeable shift in the room's emotional climate, Ava directed her focus back to the meeting. They were discussing one of her patients, Susan West.

Gwen said, "Next, let's talk about Susan West. I had a long talk with her yesterday. She knows she doesn't have much time left, but she really wants to see her nieces graduate."

The chaplain asked, "When is graduation?"

"It's not for six months. Do you think she will live that long, Dr. Hogan?"

Ava took a deep breath. She sighed and said, "I don't think so. Her kidneys show signs of shutting down. She cannot tolerate thoracentesis and the large volumes we take out. I see a big change in her just in the past week. I don't think she will make it six more months. She would be better off being in hospice."

Susan was a thirty-five-year-old woman with widely metastatic breast cancer. Ava met her two years ago when she began coming to the out-patient palliative care center. Susan and Ava saw each other at least monthly while one endured surgery, chemotherapy, and radiation, and both had weathered a marital dissolution. With Susan's deteriorating condition, she moved into GAAL and became a favorite of the staff. Always upbeat and funny even as her body failed. In recent weeks, her cancer had spread to the lungs and made talking, breathing, and walking challenging. She was staying in bed most of the time now.

Like with many terminally ill patients, there was no way to draw a line separating the time when further treatments might help symptoms and let them live a little longer and the time when additional treatments were futile and may even cause harm.

Ava added, "Jeez, I have known those twins as long as I have known Susan. They would often come with her to her appointments. I think they're the reason she went through so much discomfort."

Some months before, Susan confessed to Ava in an exceptionally dark moment that she was ready to die and would have preferred to stop treatments, but her nieces and her sister weren't prepared. Many loving patients chose this approach—suffering more to spare family members. Of course, at some point, there is no choice.

Today, the mood in the conference room was somber. It was hard for everyone to face Susan's decline. She was so kind and never seemed to let her condition get her down. She wore colorful wigs or psychedelic scarves and conveyed more concern for the staff's needs than for her own, and her hearty laugh echoed down the hallway.

Gwen asked, "Could the graduation be moved up? Maybe a mock ceremony? I remember in hospice, we did that for a young girl with cystic fibrosis. We worked with the school and orchestrated an entire senior prom months before the usual May date."

The chaplain said, "I think that could work. I'll call the school and see what we can do." Other people in the room offered to help arrange the event.

Ava pinched the web space between her left thumb and first finger to staunch the tears welling up in her eyes. She pinched so hard it almost brought a conflicting tear to her eye—one she wasn't afraid of. The lump in her throat hurt.

Glancing at the clock with the sweeping second hand, she realized she would be at least fifteen minutes late for her first appointment. Ava paused to notice the clock attached to a pedestal jutting perpendicularly from the wall. Oddly oversized for the small room with two identical sides, it had a Salvador Dali appearance. Time melted before her eyes. "Interesting."

Ava gathered her things but left *Taber's* on the table, nuzzling it toward the center. Something had passed through her while holding onto the book. Rising, she thanked the group for their hard work and asked them to let her know how she could help with the early graduation plan.

As she passed Gwen, she whispered, "Call me this weekend to take a hike."

Gwen nodded and reminded Ava, "Don't drive too fast to your office."

Gwen was one of the first people Ava met when she came to this small town in Kentucky. They frequently went for hikes or bike rides. Ava exited the room and closed the door quietly without any of her previous drama. The rest of the staff smiled at each other as if sharing a familiar, unspoken joke. They were used to her late arrivals and premature departures.

A quiet aide at the table said, "Dr. Hogan is very close to Susan. It's going to be hard on her when she passes."

Gwen nodded and said, "Yes, she has been through a lot this year. I mean, both of them have been through a lot."

The others nodded in agreement. The chaplain, a big, burly fellow with a long white beard, asked, "But why is she always whistling? I thought a person whistled when they were happy."

Gwen again responded, "I don't know why she whistles, but I don't think it means she's happy."

As she walked down the hall, Ava passed the cozy nooks and hypnotic fish tanks. The colorful bettas tempted her to slow down. The faint smell of nonenal in the air reminded Ava of her grandmother's house. The burbling fish tanks sounded like her ex-husband's exotic fish collection. She considered it an odd intersection of comforting and disturbing sensory memories.

Resident rooms were positioned in a semicircle around a central nurse's station and an outside patio. GAAL was the only place Ava had worked where seed for bird feeders and garden supplies were a major expense on the budget.

A lone nurse stood beside Susan's room, popping a fistful of pills into an oversized medicine cup. Even the most miniature tablets made a tiny ping. Ava considered visiting her patient/friend just to say hi, but she didn't have time. Scurrying past the open door and hoping Susan didn't see her, she gave a silent nod to the nurse, who smiled back sympathetically. Ava wondered how many more chances she would get to talk to Susan. Maybe she could make it back after work.

Ignoring Gwen's advice, Ava drove too fast along the narrow, curvy road to her outpatient clinic in Berry Hill. It usually took about twenty minutes, but she could make it in fifteen if no slow vehicles got in front of her. She used the drive time to listen to medical podcasts. This was the year she renewed her family practice certification and took the board exam again. She felt confident treating patients but not acing an exam. The thought of sitting in the secure testing center for a day answering obscure questions never failed to raise her heart rate.

In the past month, Ava used every spare moment to study. Today, the voice of an expert discussing anti-epileptic medicines was a droning monotone. She caught the word "alpha" and remembered her idea to read *Taber's Cyclopedic Medical Dictionary*.

She said to herself, "Could I read that whole thing? I'm going to call it TCMD, and maybe I could write a book like the guy who read all of OED." There was something comforting about the image of curling up in a chair with the book and a notepad.

Ava barely noticed the sights on her daily trip to Berry Hill; her mind was always on something else. When her mom and dad visited a couple of years ago, she drove them out to her clinic for a tour. On the way, her dad sat in the passenger seat. Her mom chose the uncomfortable back middle seat so she could monitor the speedometer. Ava was accustomed to comments on her speed.

"What are those giant Greek letters in front of that house?" her mother asked on that visit. The house she referred to had about eight cars parked at odd angles around it. There was also an old, broken-down trampoline in the yard and a rusted swing set.

"That's a fraternity, Mom," Ava answered. "From what I've been told, a family used to live there, but one day, a drunk driver passed a stopped school bus in front of their house, hitting a child. The family moved out the very next day. Later, the university bought the house and turned it into a fraternity. That was many years ago."

"Oh my. What's this place on the right? With all the sawdust in piles and huge logs?"

"That's a sawmill, Mom," Ava answered. "Logging is a big industry here, but it's hazardous. Last week, I had a patient from that place come in with three of his fingers missing. There aren't safety regulations at those small mills."

"Oh, that's too bad. Is that a golf course over there on the left?"

"Yes, Mom, that's a golf course," Ava patiently replied. "I have only played there once. It has a very tricky hole that winds up in the forest."

Her dad in the front seat said, "Interesting."

From the back, "Is that a church?"

"Yes, Mom, that's a church," Ava explained, trying to keep her voice even. "There are about ten small churches on this road. All of them are Baptist or some other protestant religion."

"Where are the Catholic churches?" her mom asked worriedly.

"Mom, there's only one, and it's back in town. We'll go to mass there on Sunday. Don't expect it to be like our church back home. It's very different."

"Okay."

Her mom was an inquisitive person. For the rest of the thirty-minute drive, Ava was peppered with questions.

Ava finished medical school in Michigan at twenty four, went to an upstate New York residency, and came to this rural community in

Appalachia. Now, at age thirty eight, she had been practicing family medicine in the area for nearly a decade. Most of her days were filled with seeing patients in the office and rounding on sicker ones at the hospital taking call duty one night a week and every third weekend. She was the medical director of GAAL and the only doctor in the hospital's Palliative Care Department.

On this monumental Friday, she rewound the tape to listen more closely to the parts she missed while daydreaming. She thought about one patient on her schedule and wondered if there were other medicines the boy could use for seizures.

This seven-year-old had a seizure disorder and developmental delays. Ava tried a variety of medicines with him but nothing seemed to work. Both of his parents were college professors and provided Miles with many enriching resources. He attended a small Montessori school near the college with exceptional teachers, but still his unpredictable fits caused stress, physically and socially. The droning expert from the podcast was of little help.

Chapter 2: The Office

Arriving at her clinic, the staff greeted Ava. They were already busy answering phone calls and ushering patients into exam rooms. It was the same routine from day to day, but every patient was different, and with every symptom and illness Ava tried to trace its biological cause—unless there wasn't a clear connection. She was seeing this more and more—inexplicable symptoms, patterns of conditions in certain areas, and certain families. She thoroughly enjoyed figuring out why someone was sick and fretted when she failed.

Diving into the work, Ava saw one patient after another and barely had time between them to catch her breath or use the bathroom. Lunch was a quick gobble of a granola bar as she studied the latest lab reports.

"Mary, can you call the lab and see what happened to Mrs. Brown's stool culture? And can you ask them where her CBC is? I can't find either of them," Ava bellowed out from her office. She added a "please" but wasn't sure Mary heard it.

Time flew by and office hours ended. Ava recorded notes on the last patient and shut her computer down. Sitting back in her chair, she wondered if she had offended anyone today. Ava's sense of humor was not always appreciated, and she probably was too impatient with people.

She often saw the irony of a situation and commented on its incongruity. For example, one of her patients said his symptoms started while driving on the Mountain Parkway. After examining and diagnosing him, she asked, "Why do people drive on a parkway but park on a driveway?" The older gentleman merely stared at her.

Despite not understanding her jokes and the rapid way she gave the nurses orders, people seemed to like her. Today, a patient brought her a handmade sculpture made from horseshoes. It was beautiful and imaginative, but the gift surprised Ava. She found it hard to understand a patient's depth of gratitude when she was only performing a physician's job.

Taking a glance in the mirror as she left her office, Ava fluffed her red hair and stopped to look closely for gray among the strands. She thought of her Irish grandmother whose copper-toned hair had never turned gray, even into her eighties. Ava's mother said Ava had the same green-blue eyes as her grandmother. Today, her eyes looked more green than blue, reflecting the color of her favorite shirt—an emerald T-shirt that felt soft on her skin.

With her haphazard schedule, Ava kept her hair short. It was much easier to roll out of bed and go when she was called to the hospital. She kept it as short as her hair stylist would allow. Today, she got up late and forgot to comb it.

Ava never wore a white coat. Her last one was in medical school, she believes, when a short blazer type was required. Most days, she wore comfortable clothes—pants, sweaters, vests—outfits that were indistinguishable from those of her patients. When she could, like on hospital rounds on the weekend, she wore jeans. One older doctor often mentioned that her clothing needed ironing but no authority figures had ever reprimanded her or quoted work dress codes.

Ava noticed she was leaving the office after everyone else. She turned off the lights as she walked through the empty corridors. Being alone in the office always made her feel uneasy. The quiet and her echoing footsteps felt ghostly after all the earlier frenetic activity. She tried to hurry out of the empty building. As she hurried past the room used for X-rays, a sliver of light shone under the door. She reached a hand in to flip the on/off light switch.

"Hey!" Ava nearly had a heart attack. "I'm in here," she heard a voice call out.

With the light back on, Ava saw it was Pat, the X-ray tech. Pat Evans was tall, generously proportioned, and had thick black hair pulled back in a low ponytail. She had a slight Kentucky accent, which Ava found comforting. She knew everyone in town and could give the family history of nearly every patient in the clinic. Ava considered her a friend, though they had never socialized out of the office.

Pat said, "I knew it was you. Heard you whistling."

Ava said, "No, I wasn't whistling. Anyway, why are you here so late?"

Pat pushed her glasses up.

"I'm studying for the X-ray exam. I only have three more days and can never get any reading done at home."

Pat had a family of three children, ages three, six, and ten, and a husband who worked in construction. She mentioned earlier in the week that her husband had been laid off for the past couple of months because of bad weather and fewer building jobs. Ava knew that all the staff in her office—all women—were the primary breadwinners in their family. They had the double duty of caring for the household and working full time. This seemed common in rural areas, where the opportunities mainly were in either health care or hospitality unless a person commuted one or two hours for one of the higher paying jobs.

Pat had recently taken an online certification course to get her X-ray technician degree, but she had been shooting films for years and knew more than most. The hospital that owned this clinic, of which they were all employees, had required anyone taking X-rays to be certified. Thus, Pat was studying for the exam.

Ava found Pat hilarious. She had the entire office in stitches when she talked about her kids and her husband. Days were always brighter when Pat worked. She lived in a house adjacent to her dad's property. This was also quite common in Eastern Kentucky—family compounds. Ava didn't understand why until she started doing home visits. When she saw how beautiful the properties were and, more clearly, how close families were, she stopped judgingly telling her transplanted friends about some of the nurses who had never even been out of the county. Being well-traveled wasn't as important as she had once thought.

Pat told Ava, "You shouldn't be here so late. It's Friday night. Go home and relax."

Ava responded, "I know. I'm leaving now and plan to go to a nice get-together at my friend Rosella's house. You should come sometime. I think you would like it."

Pat said, "Maybe, sometime." Ava knew she would never come.

Pat added, "Slow down, Dr. Ava. You are always moving too fast."

"I know. I know. Someday," Ava resolved.

Ava wished Pat good luck with her studying and left the light on. She felt easier not being the only one in the office. She continued on her way to the exit, stopping briefly to review a mental list of labs on patients. Mid-thought, the door slammed shut behind her.

Today was Friday, and Ava was off hospital call and responsibility-free (unless one of her OB patients went into labor) until Monday morning. She thought about tonight's gathering at Rosella's house. Ever since meeting Rosella two years ago, she attended nearly every one of these "Friday Night Enlights," as they were called. Ava was planning on throwing together a salad for the potluck.

Ava settled the horse-shoe sculpture and a tin of creamed candy from another patient on the passenger seat and prepared to pull out of the sloped clinic parking lot. She recognized Pat's truck and worried for only a moment about the capable woman being in the office alone. Relieved that the work part of her day was over, she turned toward home, the radio dialed into *All Things Considered*.

As she sped by the turn for GAAL, she remembered her plan to visit Susan at the facility. She made a U-turn and pulled into the facility parking lot. There were no cars in the visitor section. Ava felt sad for the residents left alone on a Friday night but also guilty that she would be late for Rosella's party, contributing, once again, only a bag of chips.

Chapter 3: An Unexpected Visitor At Redbud

Rosella was as different from Ava as two people could be. Rosella, musician and store owner, was tall and lithe compared to Ava's solid, muscular build. She was spontaneous, adventurous, confident, funny (in a non-satirical way) and engaging. People liked her. While Ava had a premature crease across her often-furrowed brow, Rosella's face had lovely crinkles around the eyes. Laugh lines. She'd been married to the same man, Cal, for years.

They had met two years previously when Ava signed up for guitar lessons at the store as a strategy for her post-divorce recovery. After years of lessons as a child, Ava was pretty good at the piano but had never played a stringed instrument and thought the guitar would be cool. She reasoned if teenage boys could learn to play so well, she should have some success. Little did she realize she could never spare the requisite 10,000 hours to practice and lacked a typical adolescent's obsession with playing.

The first time Ava walked into "Redbud Music," Rosella was studying the inside of a concertina. She glanced at the door with the sound of the chime and asked, "Why are you wearing a stethoscope?"

Ava fingered the black tube and regretted not leaving it in the car. She wore this tool of her trade so much that it felt like an extension of her body. Covering it now by pulling her coat collar tighter, she introduced herself to the still-engaged shop owner. Rosella had come highly recommended by other of Ava's friends who either took lessons from her or had children involved in music.

Rising from her stool Rosella approached Ava and explained that she was having no luck fixing the sticky button on this concertina. Ava mumbled that she didn't even know what a concertina was and looked around the store.

She saw every genre of instrument in the sprawling shop and a unique system of organization. Instruments requiring air were grouped together, lined up from tiny to huge. Piccolos, flutes, French horns, trumpets, saxophones, trombones, a tuba, and an old set of bagpipes were displayed here, some in cases, some hanging, some laid down as if they had just been played.

Scanning further, Ava noticed that anything with a string (except pianos) was in another section of the store. There were beautiful fiddles, a cello, an upright bass, and an entire room of guitars. Another sizable area to the side held pieces of percussion—two baby grand pianos, a beautiful Yamaha upright, numerous electric keyboards, and an array of drums. From this initial cursory look, Ava could tell there were small rooms in the back and lots of amps, cords, headphones, and other accessories.

Facing Rosella and feeling energized by the potential for making music, Ava asked, "Where do you keep the accordions? With the winds?"

Smiling and nodding her head, Rosella led her to a multi-shelved area with accordions of all sizes: compact Irish button accordions, heavy keyboard ones, and some just the right size for a kid. On the top shelves were more antique-ish instruments. Ava had been to Elderly Music in Lansing, and this place reminded her of that eclectic spot. How Rosella could maintain an inventory like this in a small town puzzled Ava.

While strolling around the store, Rosella picked up a thumb piano and began picking out a tune. She settled into a comfy-looking leather chair and motioned for Ava to sit. They had arrived at a cozy space with chairs of all configurations scattered in the semblance of a circle. Amps, cords, guitar stands, and an unobtrusive music stand dotted the Persian rug in the middle. Ava chose a straight-back chair across from Rosella and remarked, "You have quite a place. I like the name."

Rosella laughed and said, "Yes, I love this place. The best part is I never know who will come in. Every day, new people show up, like you. Oh, and when I moved to Kentucky, I had never seen a redbud before, but they were all around here in the woods and along the highway, amazingly. I figured it would be a good name for a music store."

Rosella's manner was inviting. In just a matter of minutes, Ava was captivated by both the woman and Redbud Music. They arranged to start half-hour lessons on Ava's afternoon off next week.

She sheepishly admitted that she did not actually own a guitar and asked, "Could I look at some in the store?"

Again, they traversed the length of the building, Rosella in the lead, with Ava trailing behind.. Rosella went directly to a wall of acoustics but suddenly turned to Ava and exclaimed. "I never even asked what you wanted to play. I figured acoustic, but maybe you want something different."

Ava had done a lot of research on what kind of guitar to buy as a beginner. She knew the advantage of electric strings being easier to depress and less difficult to learn on. She had read numerous reviews of different styles and brands of guitars. In her mind, she could hear herself playing like Tommy Emmanuel or Kaki King. But she had no clue how to go from a rank beginner to their level, and even as she stood looking at the guitars, her confidence waned. "What am I doing? When will I have time to practice? Would I ever have the confidence to play in front of people or even in the practice rooms here?"

Rosella must have recognized the hesitation but trusted that the instruments would be more persuasive than any words of encouragement.

She simply said, "Take all the time you want with them," and walked back towards the counter to pore over the broken concertina.

Ava looked around and was relieved to find no other customers in the store. She felt better with no one watching her. Sitting in the guitar room, it was as if the wood hypnotized her. The slight, unaccountable smell of hay confused her. The array of colors and designs reminded her of the various skin types she saw on her patients, especially those with tattoos.

She picked up one guitar and strummed the strings. The sound was tinny, not at all full like she had imagined. She gingerly took another one off its hook but soon found it was too big to fit comfortably in her lap. The prettiest one with a starburst pattern seemed out of her league,though she admired its beauty.

She was ambling past the row of instruments like a kid in a candy shop. She considered each one's size, color, and brand name and finally picked up a small Recording King. She strummed up and down on the strings and muted the lowest hesitantly. "Wow, I am playing the guitar!"

Ava liked the sound and the way it vibrated through her fingers and body. Something clicked inside her. She had never felt such a strong connection with an instrument as she felt holding this guitar. Catching herself in this uncharacteristically almost spiritual moment, she pushed the guitar away and clinically inspected the body as if she knew what to look for. A memory of her mother came to her.

<<<<<<<<<<<<<<<<<<<<<

It's 1988; I am seven years old, taking piano lessons from the church organist. Once a month, she lets me play the pipe organ at church. My feet barely reach the row of pedals on the floor. When Mrs. Ingram is in a good mood, she lets me stand on the narrow wood strips, and deep bass notes ring through the church. Otherwise, we sit side by side on the wide bench, our backs to the altar, playing simple duets. There is a complicated system of pulling out the proper stops to open different pipes, and the results sound like magic to me. Two side mirrors are positioned so the organist can see the priest, but I'm so short I only see the top of a crucifix.

Later, my teacher was the very proper Mrs. McAlary, who lived in a beautiful home on the other side of town. I sat at the grand piano each week while my mother, Margaret, waited on a couch in the next room. Mom usually knitted, but sometimes I caught her sitting quietly, contentedly, listening. For a few short but tortuous months, we waited together on the sofa while my brother took his lesson. Ted didn't last long with the piano. He later took up the trombone and found that brass was his forte.

My last piano teacher was the frightening Mrs. Burkhalter, and I went there without Mom. Everything about it was scary, even the house. She lived in an old Victorian three-story mansion on a cobblestoned street in a secluded part of town. The stairs creaked as the old woman descended, and I feared a crash with every step. Mrs. Burkhalter had survived the holocaust but never spoke of her past. She rarely talked except to reprimand me for my phrasing or fingering. I was terrified of her, so I worked harder that year than ever before. The goal of my senior year was to play a problematic Mozart sonata for the Solo and Ensemble Competition.

<<<<<<<<<<<<<<<<<<<

Rosella heard a low whistle as she approached Ava. She stood aside quietly. Soon, Ava noticed her and smiled.

She asked quietly, "How do you like it?"

Ava was speechless and only nodded. She found the shop owner reassuring and, for once, did not feel embarrassed by her ignorance. She felt that Rosella did not judge people as Ava herself often did and was glad she had chosen her for lessons. Rosella continued, "It's odd, but that is exactly the guitar I would have suggested for you. It has a wonderful sound and is a good place to start."

The ease of the selection process surprised Ava, especially after all her online research and fretting about getting the best instrument.

Ava chose a gig bag, tuner, and a selection of picks at the sales counter. As she turned to leave, a group of high schoolers tumbled into the store. Exuberant and boisterous, they headed for the room with the cords and chairs. Each girl toted a black case on her back, varying in size.

Ava took a moment to watch them unpack an acoustic guitar, a cello, an electric violin, and an electric bass. They laughed and joked as they tuned their instruments. Another member of the mob started sorting through the cords and arranging the amps and effects pedals lying in the space. The bass player ran through a funky blues progression with ease.

Ava looked at Rosella in a questioning manner.

Rosella explained, "Those come in after school nearly every day. They play around."

Ava said, "I wish I had done that in high school." She left the store buoyed by her new venture.

Ava returned every other week on her afternoon off for a lesson. Rosella was a gifted instructor who could not be blamed for Ava's slow progress on the guitar. Rather than building fretboard prowess, the two developed a friendship during their sessions in the cozy shop. Rosella often joined Ava and Gwen when they walked in the woods. Rosella's dog, Hannah, usually came. She loved to swim if they walked at the lake. After these outings, Ava's station wagon smelled like a wet dog and she missed having her own pet.

Ava went in spurts with the guitar. Sometimes, she would practice daily, motivated by a song she heard on the radio or a new artist. But most days, she didn't have the energy to take the instrument from its case and strum. On those hard days, Ava had only enough energy to fix a meal and crawl into bed, falling in love once again with her pillow.

On that same Friday, when Ava decided to read *Taber's Cyclopedia*, Rosella received an unexpected visitor at Redbud Music. The bells on the door jingled, and Rosella looked up to see a newcomer enter the store. This person was dressed casually but stylishly in a short blazer, slacks, and low boots. They carried a weathered shoulder bag and had the air of someone from out of town.

A certain freshness distinguished visitors who were seeing the music store for the first time—people who were inwardly processing such an impressive place in a small town. A familiar feeling came into Rosella's head as this unknown person looked around. Rosella thought she recognized the prejudice she herself once carried. This snobbishness of Northerners, of urbanites. She had heard it so often when she decided to move to Kentucky. "Why would you go there? In the land of rednecks and the uneducated? You're going to Cantucky? You've heard the joke, right? Move to Kentucky, so if the world ends, you will still have ten years to go since that state is so far behind. Don't you know Kentucky is one of the least healthy states in the country? Do you know who their senators are?"

Rosella admittedly had some of the same worries when she moved to this small town many years ago, but all her preconceptions were negated when she befriended her neighbors and listened closely to what was said and how things were done. It was not fair to say the state was backward. Many factors contributed to Kentucky's poor performance in terms of health, economy, employment, and education measures. Like with many colonized foreign countries, the state had been valuable to its own country only for the extraction of natural resources. Coal. Big coal. Rosella could feel her face flush and her ire rise, thinking about the injustice. But in front of her stood this out-of-towner.

"Hi, my name is Tresne. I work for a magazine called *Rewind*. You have to be Ro."

Rosella was not surprised this person knew who she was. Every so often, a stranger would recognize her and ask a lot of questions. Tresne handed Rosella a business card with *Rewind* embedded into a stylish logo. Tresne's full name, preferred pronouns, and contact info were printed in smaller letters. Rosella responded to Tresne, "Yes, I am Rosella (tapping a nameplate on the counter). Nice to meet you. I've never heard of *Rewind*."

While saying this, Rosella motioned toward a modest display stand of music-oriented magazines. Prominent on the rack were the latest issues of *Uncut* and *Guitar World*.

Tresne continued, somewhat breathlessly, "Have you heard of *Prog*? The music mag? *Rewind* is a bit like that but based in the US and newer. We are interested in all kinds of music and musicians. Our audience tends to be younger, trying out new things and novel approaches to playing. Our main office is in New York, but I have traveled down from Cincinnati."

"OK," Rosella said curiously, "So, why have you come?"

Tresne replied, "To interview you if that's alright. I've listened to your band's music for years, and we think highlighting you in *Rewind* would inspire our readers. Would you be willing to let me spend some time with you and write about your life?"

Rosella considered. Since moving to Kentucky, she had been approached several times for interviews. Once, even by the afore-mentioned *Prog*. Each request seemed to be a violation of her brother's memory. Maybe an interview represented the absolute acceptance of what happened to her brother. Something she still wasn't sure she could accept. And at a deeper level, she wasn't sure she could get through the retelling.

However, there was something about Tresne that was different—she felt she could trust them. And she realized that despite her initial assumption, Tresne was not looking at Redbud Music with an urbanite prejudice. It was more an expression of glee—an entire world of music.

Usually, Rosella mounted an immediate resistance to intrusive inter-viewers, but with this person, she sensed openness and enthusiasm, and the idea of sharing her story with a younger audience appealed to her. As was her focus at the music store, she was all about the youth. Turn-ing back to Tresne, she asked, "What would this involve? What kind of story are you planning to write?"

Tresne answered, "I would like to learn about your childhood, your musical journey, what it was like to work with your brother. It would be good for our audience to learn what it was like to be so famous so quickly. From what I have read about you, I think you would have a wonderful insight into fame. "R and Me" songs are still played—your popularity never waned. Plus, we want to know about your obscurity. What is it like living here? In essence, all of you."

So, Tresne spent the next two days with Rosella. Following her around, asking questions, playing tug-of-war with her dog, sitting in on the Irish music jam one night—Tresne played the bodhran. Tresne was a drummer who gigged around Cincinnati and Dayton with their jazz group. They fit in nicely with the high schoolers who came to jam and with the dancing jig rhythms of the Irish group. Rosella was quite taken with the young writer/musician's interviewing and playing skills. She invited them to join Rosella and her friends at "Friday Night Enlight," the first night in town.

The speaker for this night was a retired English professor from the university who studied religions. He was well-traveled and frequently worked on Habitat for Humanity builds worldwide. The professor and his wife, a scholar of primary education, were part of the local Habitat for Humanity branch and planned to start the night's conversation by discussing under housing and housing insecurity. The couple had just finished a book titled, *Unhoused in the USA; Making Adequate Housing a Public Good*. Though Rosella had not read the book yet, she heard a little about the housing situation in the area from some students who came into the music store. At first, she didn't believe how many of the teens were sleeping two or three to a bed in their homes or on a relative's couch, but she gradually became accustomed to the stories and the reality of rural housing shortages. Having lived in some larger cities, she was used to seeing people living on the streets, but the problem was much more hidden around this area. Rosella was very much looking forward to the evening's discussion.

Rosella had grown up in the East, and one summer, her parents took the family to visit Forest Farm on the coast of Maine. This was the last home of Scott and Helen Nearing, a famous couple who were some of the original back-to-the-earth advocates and activists. The visit to their commemorative stone house with yurt and greenhouse made a big impact on Rosella, and she returned many times.

One activity at Forest Farm that Rosella particularly liked were the seminars. Each week, a knowledgeable speaker was invited to have an intellectual discussion, hoping to challenge the community to deal with difficult social issues in productive, creative, and progressive ways. In Kentucky, Rosella lived in a home similar to Forest Farm that could accommodate group meetings. So, she replicated the Nearing's practice and, about once a month, invited a speaker, her neighbors, and friends for supper and discussion.

Rosella's husband, Cal, was a philosophy professor at the college and knew people who could stimulate thought. These gatherings were always fun and worthwhile. This Friday's guests were a varied group. Rosella tried to include people who had moved into the area and others who had grown up in the region. She was quite aware of the distinction. The "transplants" who were looked at with some suspicion often had their own social circles that did not include locals. Her contact with local musicians at Redbud Music helped her to bridge this divide, but she continually worked on including native Kentuckians at her gatherings.

When Rosella first moved to Kentucky over a decade ago, she was sometimes peeved by her invites being ignored. People she knew from the store would decline her invitations, claiming conflicts with church or family. After learning about the culture of rural eastern Kentucky, she accepted that family and home were important to people, even to the sacrifice of socializing with new friends. Family was their social network, and many did not feel a need to expand that circle. It took a few years for her to accept that extensive travel and outsider exposure were not necessary for enjoying life.

Rosella and Cal lived about a mile from town in a spacious home surrounded by woods. They designed the house to conserve energy as much as possible, and it featured passive solar architecture with south-facing windows and a thick heat sink in the floor. The national forest was out the back door and provided easy access for hikes and beauty. Their dog, the big black lab Hannah, loved the location, and Rosella found walking with Hannah in the woods to be her daily meditation.

Cal arrived just ahead of the guests. He and Rosella were distinct personalities. She liked to be around people, and aside from her meditative walks with Hannah, she liked to be in groups. Sometimes, she admitted, the quiet bothered her. She could often be seen walking around the house with headphones on, listening to the latest releases of her favorite bands. Cal, in contrast, liked the quiet. Sounds easily distracted him. His position at the university allowed him an office space to escape from Rosella's noise. While he very much enjoyed the discussions at "Friday Night Enlight," he also had to mentally prepare himself for the infusion of people into his home. Luckily, the couple was aware of each other's preferences and had learned to adapt to each other's living styles.

This evening, the first to arrive was a young couple Rosella knew from one of their children taking guitar lessons at Redbud Music. They had converted from being Amish and, for several years, lived in an Amish community with rules banning electricity and driving cars. They used only hand-powered tools and practiced a strict adherence to church. They had three children born during those years of living in this community. A couple of years ago, they left the Amish and returned to the usual states of society. She taught high school, and he continued with carpentry. They were an engaging couple who had, understandably, a unique perspective on life.

Rosella greeted them at the door with Hannah by her side. The kids loved Hannah and went to the backyard to play fetch with the exuberantly cheerful dog. The adults exchanged hugs, and the couple found places in the back room in a space that resembled the music room at Redbud Music. A variety of comfortable chairs and small end tables were placed strategically for drinks, and there was a small wood-fired stove for warmth. Most people brought their own beverages to these events, but Rosella had ample wine and beer. Beth and Joe brought juices. They still maintained many of the practices of the Amish and either made or found homemade products to consume and use.

Next to drive up the circle driveway was Kerry, a professor at the university who was possibly the most different politically from Cal and Rosella. It had taken some time to convince Kerry to attend these gatherings. She confided to Rosella once that she felt outnumbered. Rosella liked Kerry and appreciated her perspective on issues. Kerry, who was in the business department at school, described herself as a fiscal conservative but social libertarian. She wasn't afraid to speak up and generally kept conversations lively.

As she entered the house, she explained, "My husband couldn't come tonight. He had to work late and was just exhausted. He sends his regrets."

Kerry's husband worked as a nurse at the local hospital and was often scheduled for the night shift. Rosella had only met him a few times over the years and knew that his long work hours were straining their marriage. Rosella gave Kerry a hug and opened a beer for her, ushering her into the back room.

A light-colored Prius circled the drive, and four people piled out. Gary and Bryan, from down the street, and their twins emerged from the vehicle. Sam and Shel, now twelve, were twins the couple had adopted at birth. The biracial kids knew firsthand some of the challenges of living in this predominantly white community. They were brilliant kids, and Rosella loved hearing their opinions during these Friday night discussions.

Just behind this foursome, another car pulled up. A nurse who grew up in the area accompanied by her daughter, who was now a doctor at the hospital, and their friend, a teacher at the high school. Rosella did a mental count of participants and was not surprised that Ava had not arrived yet. She was often late and the last to arrive.

A calm descended as the ten guests, two speakers, and their hosts settled in and exchanged news of their lives. Most had been here in this space a dozen or more times before, so everyone knew the night would be interesting. Though people held different notions, the arguments or debates were always kind-hearted, and many minds had been changed because of the civility of their discussions. Tonight was expected to be no different.

The only new person at the event was Tresne, so Rosella introduced them to the group as the social conversations died down. Tresne was staying at a hotel in town but had arrived before the others to help Rosella prepare for the night and to observe her more for the *Rewind* article. Tresne started by explaining who they were and who they worked for. Rosella had prepared Tresne earlier that the people gathered were quite open and Tresne should feel comfortable sharing about their non-binary gender identity. This had surprised Tresne, who had been a little cautious earlier about how they would be accepted, but looking over the group tonight, they agreed this felt like a safe space.

Tresne started by saying how much they appreciated being invited and how interested they were in discussing people experiencing homelessness, particularly the unsheltered youth. When Tresne was a teenager, they finally told their parents that they didn't know if they were feeling like their assigned gender. This feeling surfaced when Tresne was younger, but with time, they became more convinced that neither male nor female felt right. Tresne asked their parents to use the new name, Tresne, to refer to them. And to use new pronouns. The parents, very devout Christians, could not accept this. As tension grew in the family, Tresne was eventually kicked out. For a while, they lived on the couch of a high school friend, but this didn't work out for long. At age seventeen, Tresne was living in their car in Cincinnati, finishing high school barely, and working a full-time schedule at MacDonald's. There were many scary nights on the street and no one to turn to.

Tresne had always been a drummer. As early as three, they were playing rhythms on the highchair. This was their entry into the musical magazine world. *Rewind* advertised for a music reviewer, and despite Tresne's lack of credentials, the owners of this start-up gave them a chance. That was the beginning of a more stable life, the eventual apartment rental, and slow healing from the experience of homelessness. They ended this retelling with a namaste gesture.

The group was silent after Tresne's story. The sound of a closing door interrupted the reverent moment, and Ava rushed into the room, apologizing for her lateness. Rosella motioned to an empty chair and introduced the speakers for the night.

Chapter 4: Stories From The Past

Ava spent the weekend in recovery mode. She slept in on Saturday morning, lingered over a New York Times crossword as she drank her coffee and made eggs and toast for breakfast—all the things that took too much time on a weekday morning. She looked around her smallish house and thought about cleaning but texted her friend Gwen instead to ask about taking a walk. There were many uncrowded hiking trails in the area that they had a choice of several close by.

Gwen was the first person Ava met when she moved to Kentucky. The two women shared many experiences. Their weddings were within a month of each other, they both dropped out of the Catholic church about the same time, and they both enjoyed being outdoors. Gwen was free to walk because her husband was out of town.

Just as Ava laid down the phone from her text conversation with Gwen, a car pulled up the driveway, and she knew before looking that it was Jack, her ex-husband. She heard his old Subaru roar up the street. Last week, Ava told him he could come by today, but she wasn't looking forward to their conversation. Hurriedly, she went to the door and stood on the porch, trying to keep him outdoors. He had a stack of papers and nuzzled past her into the kitchen.

Jack was a limber man who always wore his black hair in a braided ponytail. He had chiseled cheekbones that he proudly attributed to a presumptive American Indian heritage. Today, he was wearing a tight-fitting sweatshirt with shorts and had undoubtedly just come from the gym. He was an avid gym rat and Ava acknowledged that he had successfully taught her the proper way to lift weights—not the greatest of outcomes from a relationship, but one she appreciated.

Ava said, "How are you? It's a beautiful day, isn't it?"

Jack replied, "Oh, I hadn't noticed. My car barely got me here. My neighbors were shouting at me as I left. The gym was packed with new people."

Ava brusquely said, "That's too bad." She didn't want to hear about Jack's troubles. At one time, she would defend him against the people who wronged him, but now that they were divorced, this wasn't her job anymore.

"How's your new job going?" she asked, trying to change the subject.

Jack turned away and responded in a quieter voice, "Oh, that job didn't work out. They didn't know what they were doing. I tried to tell them ways that would work better, but they didn't want to hear. I have a few other opportunities."

Ava listened politely but counted in her head how many times she had heard these excuses and this same refrain. When they were married, Jack must have held fifteen different jobs, all ending with him saying they didn't listen to him.

Jack was an alcoholic. A diagnosis that Ava hadn't made until too late in their eventual five-year relationship. Their first date was at a bar, the Brass Eagle. Their second romantic outing was at an all-night pig roast involving copious amounts of alcohol. Her first clue to the problem was when they went on picnics. Jack was frantic until he had purchased and prepared a six-pack of beer in a cooler with just the right amount of ice. If there was a time when he didn't have his fix, the event was horrible. When he did have the requisite drinks, the activity was often marred by his drinking too much. Ava recalled most of their time together as a roller coaster of emotions. So much so that when they finally divorced two years ago, the stability of her life felt odd. She had lived through so many ups and downs; she felt a little empty.

That was when she began to see a therapist and realized that daily or weekly swings from anger, arguing, and betrayals to loving apologies and niceness were not healthy, nor was it love.

Ava remembers some years of their marriage in detail, like the sugary lemonade served at the Al-Anon meetings. She also remembers the space of time when Jack hit rock bottom—after his third DUI. She regretfully remembers cooperating with his scheme of driving without a license. She would pick him up at the county line so the local police, who knew him and his noisy car all too well, wouldn't pull him over.

She tolerated the missed events, the long nights of worry, and the embarrassing social situations because he gave her some comfort when home. After an equally long night of call, it was nice to curl up to a warm body and go limp. And because nearly everyone she knew, all her family, thought it was a mistake to marry him. To divorce him risked those people saying, "I told you so." And because she didn't have the energy to spare after long clinic days to sort out her life with Jack.

They met at an Alzheimer's 5K fundraiser. The two of them crossed the finish line dead last, and a mutual friend introduced them. Ava had been focused on her dream of being a doctor for so long that romance had never been given much room in her schedule. She dated rarely and was more often suffering in the throes of unrequited love. When Jack persisted in pursuing Ava's love, she was powerless to resist.

Jack differed significantly from Ava, and this probably accounted for his appeal. He was a veteran who wasn't patriotic. This appealed to Ava's sympathy for the downtrodden. He was outgoing and didn't care what people thought of him. Ava, meanwhile, was always worried about how others perceived her.

On the surface, Jack seemed to get along with everyone, and it was only later that Ava discovered the many lifelong grudges he held toward former friends. He was not book-smart, as the saying goes, but he had practical experience and learned a lot about specific topics. He had a blue-collar job but pursued a master's degree, leading him to a better job for a short time. Most of his friends were artists. He lived in a log cabin in a beautiful and remote county area, so remote that when Ava spent the night at his house, she had to walk up to the main road to get cell coverage.

For a while, he treated Ava like a queen and declared his love in words and actions. In retrospect, Ava never felt she deserved this love. "Why would he love her? And did he really love her or just like that she was a doctor and made a lot of money".

Like with many couples, the good times were sublime, and the bad times were hell. Their most harmonious period was likely when he worked away for a summer, and they exchanged only letters. Ava was always better at expressing herself in writing than in spoken words; apparently, the same held for Jack.

When they decided to get married after living together for two years, Ava knew that their union would end in divorce even as she said her vows. She was more enthralled with the idea of being married than the reality of being married to this man. She planned an outdoor wedding that all her family and friends could attend in Kentucky. They held it in June when the hills were at their most beautiful.

Jack was divorced, so they couldn't get married in the Catholic church. This was most disturbing to Ava's mother and, on some level, sad for Ava.

She remembers the conversation with her mom about marrying Jack.

"Why do you want to marry a man who's been married before and is older than you with kids of his own?" was the first question.

Ava wasn't sure of an answer. She offered the most recent nice thing Jack had done, "Because he brings me M and M candy when I've had a rough night of call."

Margaret wasn't convinced this was a good reason. She probed further, "But what else? Are you sure he's not taking advantage of you and your position? He doesn't have as much education as you and doesn't seem able to hold down a job."

Ava bristled. This wasn't the first time Margaret had asked this question about the intentions of someone Ava even casually dated, but it was a question she asked herself sometimes.

She replied, "I don't know. How does anyone know?"

From then on, Ava avoided talking to her mom about Jack. And her mom stopped asking questions, although she wrote a long letter at one point listing all the reasons she shouldn't marry Jack. Ava threw it away.

Around their third year anniversary, Ava took a two week camping trip by herself. When she returned she found the energy to call it quits.. To her mother's credit, she never said "I told you so." The divorce was messy, and it cost Ava a lot of money to be free of Jack. They were civil to each other but spent as little time as possible together.

On this beautiful Saturday morning, he made himself at home at the kitchen table and pulled out a car repair bill.

Jack chuckled and smirked. "So, I see you still whistle."

Before Ava could respond, he went on, "I wonder if you could help me with this bill? I promise I will pay you back, but my bank made a mistake, and they say I don't have any money in my account. I will send you the money as soon as I get that straightened out." He unfolded the bill and laid it on the table.

Ava took a deep breath and remained standing. She clenched her fists behind her back and kept her voice steady.

"I can't help you anymore, Jack. I am not giving you any more money, no loans, no nothing. I've told you that. Don't ask me. You'll have to figure it out yourself."

Jack persisted, "But I know you have the money. What else are you going to do with it? All you do is work. You don't spend money, and you're rich."

"What I do with my money is my business, not yours. There will be no more loans. And it's time for you to leave."

Ava had difficulty saying no to people, which was confirmed during their marriage. When Jack lost one job after another, she supplemented him with a monthly stipend. Recently, though, she had promised herself she would no longer fall for his excuses.

"Okay, okay. You don't have to get mad. I won't call on you again, even if I'm dying. And by the way, your whistling is still annoying as hell."

He folded the bill, replaced it in its envelope, and walked toward the door. With his hand on the knob, he added, "My friends always said you were a bitch."

Ava held her breath and shut the door firmly the moment he was clear. She did not watch his car drive away. That word "bitch" cut like a scalpel. The harshness of that innocent combination of letters was so vehement, the sentiment so apparent. Hearing the word anytime was dreadful, but directed at her, it made tears well up in her eyes.

But she remembered what the therapist had said about this being his problem, not hers. She was free of him. She hoped this would be their last unpleasant encounter.

Gradually, her heart rate slowed, and she made herself breathe. Seeing the guitar case open on the table, she picked up the instrument for comfort. She also thought about the last conversation she had with Gwen. They talked about their marriages. Gwen expressed some minor complaints about her husband, but he was nothing like Jack.

Gwen commented that day, "I don't like how my husband leaves the bathroom door open when he uses the toilet. I have told him many times to shut the door."

Ava usually listened to these comments with only an "umm" reply. They seemed so minor. And she knew Gwen just needed to get them out of her head. Ava reflected that when Rosella was walking with them, they didn't talk about their husbands or ex-husbands at all. Cal and Rosella seemed to have an ideal marriage. But underneath the surface, there was something big that plagued Rosella. Ava felt like her friend was dealing with more than she let on.

Ava was making progress on the guitar. She found it one of the most relaxing things she did. She knew all the basic chords and was beginning to do some finger-picking. Bar chords were still a struggle she mostly avoided. After the beginner lessons, Rosella helped her find easier chords to accompany songs Ava wanted to learn. Ava had the idea she wanted to write songs about her life. She was working on lyrics about a recent patient she had treated.

A few weeks ago, one of Ava's palliative care patients had been admitted to the hospital with aspiration pneumonia. The patient was a young man who had been in a car accident on the night of his high school graduation and had been cared for by his father. He suffered a spinal cord injury in the crash and was essentially a quadriplegic. His father had to help him dress, eat, bathe, and use the toilet. The father was over seventy and had lost his wife, Daniel's mother, two years ago. Through no fault of the excellent care the father provided, Daniel had aspirated some food and been rushed to the hospital in respiratory distress. His course in the hospital had been rough, and Ava's song was about the day he was finally going to be discharged.

Arrangements were made for the ambulance to transport Daniel while his father would drive ahead home to prepare the house for his return. All was going smoothly, and the ambulance crew arrived to pick up Daniel. They got him on the stretcher and were headed out the door when he suddenly stopped breathing again. This episode was much worse than earlier, and despite immediate CPR and other resuscitation efforts, he was pronounced dead in the ER, where the ambulance crew had taken him when his condition changed. Ava had been there through all of this as she was just finishing up his discharge paperwork.

Ava had to call Daniel's father, who was waiting at home for the ambulance, letting him know in some kind way that his son would not make it home, ever. Getting a call of such magnitude—that was what the song was about. Ava herself had gotten a similar call from a hospital and was trying to put into the song lyrics what it meant. She wasn't sure if composing was therapeutic or not.

Looking up from her guitar at the digital clock on the stove, she realized she would be late to meet Gwen. She packed up her guitar, shook off her residual anger toward Jack, and rushed out the door. They hiked around the lake, chatting about different events in town. Ava's friend was a good source of news since she knew almost everyone. She also had a big heart and cared greatly about the community.

While they walked, one behind the other on the narrow paths, Ava spoke about Jack's visit earlier.

"He was asking for a loan. I got so angry I almost said something I would have regretted. I don't know how I could have been married to that man. Was I just so desperate or naïve?"

Gwen turned around to answer. "You were a lot younger when you met him. Older men have a certain charm, I suppose. Don't blame yourself for what you felt back then. I know Jack hasn't been very nice lately, but at one time he was. People change."

Ava continued worrying. "I wonder how I could have been so blind to his faults. I tolerated so much disrespect and embarrassment. Today, he tried to make me feel small again. I was able to almost ignore his comments, though."

Gwen said, "That's good. You don't have to deal with him anymore. Remember that."

"I know," Ava assured her.

The pair walked slowly and carefully up a hill. The trail here was uneven, so they kept their eyes down, only looking at the surrounding scenery when they stopped. The steady sound of their footsteps on the dry leaves was soothing.

Gwen stopped again, and Ava nearly bumped into her. She said, "You know, you should meet my friend Sara. I think you would like her. She's a psychologist who is in the process of moving here. She's younger but very mature. She's moving from New York City and doesn't know many people here. It's been a bit of an adjustment."

Ava replied, "I'll bet it's been an adjustment."

"I'll introduce you to her one of these days."

By the time the pair had hiked the long loop trail, they were exhausted, and each planned to go home to take a hot bath. Instead, when Ava got home, she started thinking more about her future.

In contrast to Gwen's local knowledge, Ava had another close friend practicing medicine in far-flung regions of the world. Linda Munster was a year ahead of Ava in her family medicine residency in Rochester. Linda was Ava's senior resident for two of those three years, and they worked together on many nights of call. During these often-harrowing nights, the two became quite close.

Linda, like Ava, had a National Health Corps Scholarship, which paid for her medical school if she committed to working in a health provider shortage area. Ava had been assigned to Kentucky after residency. Linda chose to go to Alaska to serve out her four-year commitment. She went to a rural hospital in Nome, where she had a full spectrum practice and often flew to the outreach clinics by plane. Linda was the kind of person who thrived on adventure, and the job in Alaska was perfect for her. Even in residency, she was always seeking challenges, both physically with rock climbing and socially, by organizing an inner-city free clinic. Ava admired her bravery and doubted she could ever do something like her.

Linda recently took a job as a volunteer with a small clinic in southern Belize. She started writing a blog about her experiences. Ava enjoyed reading the posts and hearing what her friend commented on. She was particularly curious because she was considering volunteering some of her vacation time to join Linda in Belize. The thought of seeing patients in that faraway place scared Ava and sometimes kept her awake at night, wondering if she should muster the courage to go there. She remembered how Linda helped her overcome her fears during residency and was almost ready to commit to the trip.

Sunday was another day of sleeping late and relaxing. Late afternoon, Ava recalled her decision to read *Taber's Cyclopedic Medical Dictionary*. "Wasn't I going to abbreviate that to TCMD?" She began to think of how and when. Her first priority was to buy the book. This would require a trip to the scrub store/medical supply store, where she knew there were assorted medical texts and cheap stethoscopes for sale. She would go there after work on Monday. She looked forward to the challenge of reading the tome and formulated how she would write about it.

In her residency, she had been exposed to writing medical narratives. Narrative medicine is a way for physicians to understand the personal connections between themselves and their patients. As a young physician and just as often as an experienced doctor, sorting out one's feelings about interacting with patients was therapeutic to counteract some of the stress of practicing. Ava remembered some of her short stories.

She remembered she enjoyed the time set aside at the monthly "self-help" resident sessions to write. Since residency, Ava had written some, mainly in a notebook, for her own perusal. After her divorce, she often curled up on the end of her couch, writing in a notebook. Seeing a therapist had helped during that time, but she expressed herself more openly in writing.

She went to find those notebooks she'd stuffed in a closet. Instead, she found an old story in a box, one she had forgotten she had written about Leonard long ago. She wrote it for a public event highlighting heroes. That night at the local bookstore, some people read poems, others sang an ode. She read this story and struggled to get through the whole thing without crying.

LEONARD

People influence people. At all ages, in all settings, someone influences someone else. Maybe in childhood, the effect is larger and more memorable. In my childhood, one person stood out. He was our gardener. Not our gardener. Technically, he was the prison's gardener. But since we lived on the prison grounds, he was our gardener. His name was Leonard Minor.

Leonard was a "lifer." His sentence was life in prison. But, as it turned out, Leonard did not spend the rest of his life in prison. He was released before he died. But I don't think he would call those "free" years a life.

My dad, Lawrence, was the warden. That's why we lived at the prison. He knew all the inmates' records but only gave me, my brother, and maybe my mother a vague account of why the trustees working around our house were incarcerated. Leonard's crime had something to do with a barroom brawl and two people dying. I don't know if we ever asked Leonard why he was in there, but we probably did—we asked him everything, my brother and I.

Leonard was over sixty when we moved into the warden's residence. He was a short man with a crew cut of gray hair. My brother used to get the same haircut to match Leonard's. Leonard had a chiseled face, and the corners of his mouth had the brown stain of tobacco. His fingers were stained a darker brown from dirt. I can remember how lined his face was.

Leonard was responsible for the greenhouse and all the flora on the prison grounds. Back then, prison visitors were impressed by the beautiful landscaping and gardens surrounding the walls holding their family members. Inmates, who were never allowed outside the walls, were not the intended audience.

Leonard's greenhouse was about fifty yards from the warden's mansion. On our other side was the high stone prison wall—less than a hundred yards away. He was the only inmate to live outside the walls. He had been in prison for many years when we met him, probably thirty or forty. He was beyond being a "trustee." He had a little room in the greenhouse. My brother and I spent many enjoyable hours in that room. To us, it seemed like a palace, though it was just the size of a prison cell—big enough for a cot, sink, and several strategically placed spittoons. There were many things in that room: books, radios, games, and a little TV. Leonard always had sugar cubes for his coffee. My brother and I ate a lot of those.

Somehow, Leonard was our babysitter, teacher, sage, and biggest fan —all rolled into one. There was always a sense for me and maybe for my brother that spending so much time with this man was not usual, perhaps not even wise by society's rules. My mother was always at home and frequently called out to us from across the yard. I guess she was checking. Thinking back, she was much more trusting than anyone at this age could be.

What did we do with Leonard? Everything. He taught us how to play chess. He carried on a correspondence chess game by mail with someone the entire time I knew him. He taught us about flowers, plants, and shrubs. He taught my brother how to ride a bike. He let us go with him to plant and water. We spent time with him in the humid heat of the greenhouse, surrounded by the smell of carnations and geraniums. Sometimes, we would walk up to an old concrete swimming pool in the woods that a former warden had built for his wife. We helped Leonard erect the life-size nativity scene at the prison entrance: Metal Mary, Joseph, and the Wise Men, all with very sharp edges.

Leonard listened a lot. As soon as we arrived home from school, we'd change clothes and be out the door to see Leonard. Then, we would tell him everything that happened that day. He was always ready to listen. I think he kind of adopted us. He had neither a wife nor children—he was imprisoned before he'd had time for any of that. Through all of this, Leonard taught us patience. Who would be better at teaching this than a man in prison for the rest of his life?

I can remember the spot on the road and the smell of the air on the day my relationship with Leonard changed. It was summer, and I'd just returned from 4-H camp. We were walking down the gravel road from the greenhouse, talking. Leonard said something like, "You've started to develop." That was it. In that instant, I became self-conscious about my interactions with him. I was uncomfortable being in his little room and never again felt free to be with him as I had. Somehow, this fracture was unfair to both him and me.

Leonard was released on parole not too long after that at seventy-five. He moved into town and lived in the only hotel. He tried to work at a florist shop, but his health deteriorated probably because he was not walking the grounds and being as active as he had been at the prison. He might have started drinking again.

I'm sorry to say that my family and I didn't help much once he left prison. We invited him to dinner on holidays, but it was difficult to sort out our roles. After a while, it was just too awkward, and even my mother gave up inviting him. Sometimes, driving by the hotel, we would see him sitting on the porch. No one knew what he thought about being out, being free.

When he died, I was at college and didn't get back. My mom, dad, and brother went to the funeral. They were almost the only ones there. A few old officers who knew him from the prison came. There wasn't much said at his funeral, but there is much to say about this man: Leonard Minor.

Ava remembered writing that story and asking her brother Ted for confirmation of some details. He agreed it was all true, though Ted never knew about the changes occurring when she was a teenager. The story still made Ava sad—another regret from her past.

Pleased with the quality of this piece, Ava felt confident she could write something about *Taber's* that someone would find interesting. With a firm resolve, she planned to start reading once she had the book and take notes about words. She said, "*Inside Taber's* has a nice ring to it," as she prepared for bed. "Or maybe *A Doctor Reads Taber's.*"

<u>Aa-Ab</u>

Notes for *Inside Taber's: A Study of the Medical Dictionary* by Dr. Ava

I have the crisp new book and am about to open the first page while sitting in a comfortable rocker on a beautiful summer day. My backyard has been magically transformed to feel like I am in a Tuscany garden, with a plate of expensive crackers, exquisite Irish cheese, cilantro pesto, and a rare midday glass of wine within arm's length. Let the adventure begin.

I can barely describe my excitement about reading Taber's Cyclopedic Medical Dictionary. Of course, it will be comprehensive by definition. I don't know what new words I will find, like "abarognosis, "the inability to feel an object's weight." Already, I wonder if I have quoted the definition correctly. Contemplating the etiology and consequence of such a condition starts me on a cascade of thoughts.

How seriously ill is a person with abarognosis? Was it just an incidental finding that someone documented? In my everyday activities, how often do I need the ability to sense how much something weighs? Are people born with this deficiency never able to recognize the difference between a stone and a feather? My cascade of questions is mind-boggling.

How long will this endeavor take? Will I abandon the effort once the excitement wears off? I hope it feeds my medical curiosity and genuine awe of the human body and stimulates me to delve deeper. I think I will Google abarognosis and answer some of my questions. (I notice spell check is already correcting these medical terms.)

Abarognosis is thought to be a problem with the parietal lobe on the opposite side of the affected hand. A stroke usually causes it. Interesting.

I did not know there were more meanings to the word areola (skipping ahead to ARs) than that referring to the nipple. Even a wheal has an areola. I also did not know there is a definitional difference between cognitive ability and constructional ability. That makes sense.

Here is the word "ablution." Who would ever think that sacred act would have a place in a medical dictionary? Its meaning—simply "a cleansing or washing"—gives a whole new sense to the act of a surgical scrub or the betadine swab for a blood draw. Would it be good or bad if every one of these routine and frequent procedures took on a spiritual meaning?

Chapter 5: Dangerous Roads

Monday morning began as usual for Ava with a visit to see her hospitalized patients. After parking in the lot with a smoking shelter at one corner, she walked toward the doctor's entrance, thinking about smoking. The shelter was nothing more than a lean-to next to the garbage bins.

The "smoking committee" had tried to ban all smoking on the grounds, but neighbors complained employees were standing on their lawns for smoke breaks and leaving butts. So, the hospital compromised with this shelter. On many cold mornings, when Ava parked her VW Passat, she would see a group of nurses and techs standing there, huddled together in a space that was hardly protected from wind, snow, or cold. After years of wondering why people smoked and being honestly a little disgusted, Ava was changing her attitude. She was impressed with these people's fortitude. They would endure extreme hardships for this habit. Sometimes, she wished she could be so dedicated to a practice.

Of course, she knew smoking was a bad habit and helped her patients to stop. In years past, she had a colleague who sported a bumper sticker on his BMW that read Tobacco Paid for this Car. Or it said, Coal Paid for this Car. Either message was a satirical take on the actual message of the sticker that tobacco farmers and coal miners proudly placed on their vehicles.

Tobacco was a profitable crop for many of Ava's patients when she first came to eastern Kentucky. Families would use the money from tobacco sales for Christmas and other expenses. Even the money paid by the government to not grow tobacco was valuable and an essential source of income for many. The same was true with coal, and the decline of both "crops" was felt in the community. Her colleague, of course, was referring to the rampant health costs of these industries. Both to society and to individuals.

Two of the housekeeping staff stood just inside the entrance. Ava passed them and said hello pleasantly. They watched her figure as she continued down the corridor.

One woman said, "Do you know who that is?"

The other, a heavyset woman with jet-black hair, said, "Oh, that's Dr. Hogan. My mom is a patient of hers out in Berry Hill. She says she's very nice. She also helped my uncle with his pain when he had that cancer."

The first woman, Bonnie, said, "That's good to know. My mom is looking for a new doctor. I wonder if she's taking new patients?"

Bonnie asked the other woman, "Was she whistling?"

"Yeah, I thought I heard that, too. Guess she's in a good mood."

Ava continued down the long hallway, passing the familiar photos of the pioneer doctor who started the hospital. She relished this time entering the facility to collect her thoughts and ease into the clamor of the place. Today, she walked slower than usual and, for once, a little early.

Approaching the third-floor nurse's station, Ava prepared to focus on medicine. She said hello to the staff as she passed them and headed for a small workroom with a few physicians and nurses crouched over keyboards. She pulled up the hospital census and the list of newly admitted patients on the computer. She was relieved to find that no new patients of hers had been admitted over the weekend.

She looked over at Jan Roth, one of her call partners, who was absorbed at the next computer. Ava said, "Thanks for keeping my patients out of the hospital. Hope your weekend wasn't bad."

Jan responded, "I got eight hours of sleep Friday and Saturday, and rounds on Saturday morning only took two hours. Then Sunday hit with a bang. I had ten admissions in twelve hours. All of them were pretty sick. I was in the hospital all day. Even when I lay down in the call room, I kept getting calls from the lab about critical values. It was one of my worst call weekends. Glad to hand off some of these patients."

Jan looked exhausted. She usually dressed well in what Ava would call "church clothes," but today, she wore wrinkled scrubs, and her hair was pulled back in a ponytail. There was such randomness about how busy a call weekend would be. Ava had been lucky last week and could sleep in her bed with her pillow, but she'd had similar nightmare weekends in the past.

Over the speaker came an announcement, "CODE BLUE 4th FLOOR."

All the doctors in the workroom rose and ran through the small door. They rushed to the stairs and pounded up one floor. From the crowd outside room 411, it was obvious which room the code was in. A nurse was further away with her arm around a weeping older woman. An internal medicine doctor was inside the room, surrounded by a team of respiratory therapists, nurses, and pharmacists. They were working with an inert body in the bed.

Ava said to Jan, "Looks like they have plenty of help." They both turned back toward the stairs and slowed their pace. As they descended the empty stairwell, Ava invited Jan to sit for a minute on a middle step.

She said, "Jan, take a rest. You look like you might pass out."

Jan sat down heavily and wiped her brow. "You're right. I am about to pass out. These nights of call are taking a lot out of me. Used to be I could bounce back after a night of no sleep, but now, it seems like it takes me two or three days to return to normal. Then I have call a couple days later. It's like an endless cycle."

Ava agreed, "I know what you mean. The day after call, I know I'm not as sharp. I'm certainly not pleasant."

Jan continued, "I don't know about you, but sometimes I can't even sleep when I get home. I guess it's all the caffeine."

Ava thought for a minute. "You know, I never started drinking coffee. My brain is so busy without it I'm afraid of what would happen with a stimulant. But I still have trouble falling asleep sometimes after a busy call. I worry about the patients."

Jan got up and said, "I better get back to rounds."

Ava pulled her back down and said, "Have you ever thought about how much time physicians spend in stairwells? We always use the stairs when we run to a code, even if it's three or four floors up. Or when the elevator is taking too long. And to be honest, I sometimes use the stairs to get away from people. Do you ever? When I don't want to talk to anyone. Have you ever noticed that visitors never use the stairs? They don't even know how to find them."

She went on even though Jan had a questioning look in her eyes. "One time at this hospital in Maine, the stairwells had these full-length windows that overlooked the Penobscot River. I loved sitting there on the steps, watching the river. And one day, I felt my mind slow down. I felt this connection with the universe. It was weird. I felt almost disoriented and dizzy."

With a startle, Ava shook her head and said, "I am sorry. I have no idea why I told you that. I'll let you go. You've got things to do, and so do I."

Jan stood up and started down the steps. "It's okay. I feel that way about the stairs sometimes, too. Never felt my mind slow down like that, though. Well, I better get going."

Ava got up, too, and walked with her. "Thanks for stopping with me." The two returned to the doctor's workroom in an awkward silence.

Ava had two patients on the census. She planned to discharge both today. Before the code interrupted them, she had asked Jan if there were any changes with either over the weekend and if they were ready to go home. Jan, who liked to include folksy phrases, replied that both were "ready to go if God's willing and the creek don't rise."

Her first patient was Betsy Hitch, a seventy-five-year-old who had had a stroke a couple of months ago. By the time she presented to the ER eight hours after her arm went numb, it was too late to use any of the clot busters. Ava wished she could get the message out to the community to come in sooner when signs of a stroke started, but it was difficult public messaging. Lately, she had been talking to some salons and beauty shops to spread the word. That seemed more successful than radio or newspaper ads.

After her stroke, Betsy was left with a paralyzed left side and a condition called "left-sided neglect." Her brain did not recognize the left side of her body as part of her. It was a bizarre condition. Early on, Betsy would argue that the arm lying on her bed was not hers, and she would become agitated, telling the nurses to get it away from her. She refused to eat off the left side of her plate. She combed only the right side of her hair.

Several weeks of therapy had improved her condition, and she was doing well at home with the help of a very supportive family. Last week, though, she had choked on some food and was readmitted with aspiration pneumonia. Now, on oral antibiotics, she was ready to go back home.

Ava liked Betsy and enjoyed talking to her. She had been a patient at Ava's clinic even before her stroke, and Ava wondered if she could have somehow prevented her stroke. Other than high blood pressure and a family history of strokes, Betsy had few other risk factors. She might have refused preventative screening.

Today, Betsy was excited to be going home and had already gotten dressed in her street clothes. That was the first question as Ava entered the room.

"What time will I get out of this place?" Betsy could be rather feisty and never minced words.

Ava replied, "There's some paperwork to fill out, and the nurse will be in with instructions, but hopefully, you'll be able to leave before lunch."

"Good! Because the food here is bad. My daughter can fix me cornbread and beans when I get home. Been craving that." Ava laughed because she often craved that filling dish but could never fix them as well as her patients, probably because she didn't add ham.

Betsy had adapted to her weakened left side but still walked with a quad cane and used adaptive utensils. Everything else with her cognition and mental function remained intact. She liked to talk about church. Her first outing after her stroke was to attend a church revival. Ava liked hearing her older female patients describe their relationship with religion and spirituality because they portrayed it so personally.

Some of the male preachers she had as patients were so much more outward-focused, always trying to persuade the non-churchgoers to get to church. Until those same holy men were themselves dying, and their brand of hell-fire spirituality didn't work. She had seen them question their faith in their last days. Women tended to die with much more confidence they would go to heaven and be happy. Ava, who was, by this time, at least an agnostic, if not an atheist, kept her thoughts about God to herself. She mostly evaded the question to preserve harmony when asked if she was a believer.

That was a debate she and her colleagues in residency and real practice had had many times. How much of a doctor's personal beliefs should be shared with a patient in the setting of receiving medical care? Whether it was their political or religious beliefs. Because the relationship by nature was somewhat of a power imbalance, some argued it wasn't ethical to express these views to a patient. In contrast, the doctor who had the Tobacco Paid for this Car bumper sticker would pray with his patients. People came to him because he shared their religious zeal. Ava hadn't decided how she felt about this discussion. She tolerated the comments of patients quietly unless they expressed grossly racist or homophobic views. Then she spoke up to say that language wasn't tolerated in her office. But thinking back on some conversations, she realized if the comments were subtle, like a patient not wanting to go to a certain specialist because of their foreignness, she still said nothing. It was a delicate balance. She probably could have asked why they didn't want to go to a doctor from Ethiopia or India. She wanted to assume it was because of trouble understanding an accent rather than the color of someone's skin.

Upon leaving the hospital room after examining Betsy, Ava met the daughter who would fix the cornbread. This family tended toward the heavy side, and the daughter was no exception. She was also Ava's patient. At her visits, they talked about weight management, but they both knew there were many factors to the family's obesity—poverty, lack of safe places to walk or affordable gyms, and family traditions of enormous meals. Probably the most significant barrier was that this daughter had little support from her family to lose weight. Her brothers, father, uncles, and aunts were all the same size. Losing weight would have been a subtle insult to them. Ava was slow to recognize this barrier when she started practicing medicine, but she was learning.

Her next patient was more complex, both emotionally and medically. Bert was a fifty-six-year-old man with chronic obstructive lung disease brought on by smoking and a short history of coal mining. He had progressed to needing oxygen all the time and was admitted to the hospital about every three or four months for an exacerbation that would not clear with outpatient meds. He had the classic barrel chest and leaned over his bedside table, resting his elbows for support, using his whole upper body to take breaths. He spoke in short, gasping sentences. Bruises flowered along his arms from chronic steroid use, and the recent blood draws. It was hard for Ava to see him still struggling to breathe even after several days in the hospital and having all possible meds thrown at him. Beside him sat his wife, who waited on Bert patiently. They had been married for over thirty-five years, and for the last five, he had been disabled with his lungs.

Bert stopped smoking after the second time he caught his oxygen tubing on fire with a cigarette. That time, his recliner caught on fire, and luckily, his son was home to douse it with water. There were scars on Bert's thigh from that near-tragic event.

Ava couldn't help thinking about what Bert and his wife had gone through in the last year. Their second child, Kevin, had followed his father into the high-paying job at one of the coal mines, and in only his sixth month on the job, he broke his back. There was no permanent damage except constant pain, for which he was prescribed pain medicines, and a few months later, he had a substance abuse disorder. The family had tried all avenues to get him to stop, using their savings to pay for rehab, reporting him to the police. A younger sibling, who was a nurse, saved him from an overdose with Narcan once while he still lived at home. Last summer, Bert and his wife lost track of Kevin until they received a call from the police that a body in a rest area in Florida was their son's. Dead of an overdose at thirty. Ava had attended that visitation and watched as another son wheeled Bert up to the coffin. Heartbreaking.

Ava's relaxed mood from the weekend was marred by the adrenaline-producing code and now from talking to Bert and his wife.. She wished she could shed this cloud of sadness.

Stepping outside the hospital into the cool, fresh air helped. She returned to her car for the drive to Berry Hill but cast a much less sympathetic glance at the shivering smokers. She cued up a podcast on hypertension and pulled out. As she passed the university, a student streaked out in front of her on a unicycle, and she had to slam on the brakes to avoid hitting them. She felt the second-morning burst of adrenaline with the sudden stop.

As she pulled back onto the road and resumed her routine drive to Berry Hill, she remembered that her purple unicycle was buried under some tools in the back of her shed. She fondly remembered riding bikes every day, morning till evening, during her youth. She and her brother would make figure eights on the streets, ride over makeshift ramps, and down groomed terraces. They rode without caring. She had two bikes back then. One was a John Deere road bike. The other was this unicycle.

<<<<<<<<<<<<<<<<<

It's 1988. I am seven years old, Christmas morning. Stacked presents reach nearly halfway up the tree, and wrapped shapes spread wide around the base. We are all in our favorite spots. My dad is watching from his cavernous black leather chair, and my mother sits in her floral-patterned upholstery chair, a crocheted afghan covering her legs. I perch on the black chair's footstool, and my brother bounces around the room.

Ted and I are so excited to open gifts that our parents tell us we don't have to wait till after breakfast. I had been wishing for a horse and hoped my mom would ask me to look out the window for a surprise. Instead, she points to one oddly shaped present under the tree. I think it could be an accessory for a horse. Of course, I open it first.

The wrapping comes off easily. First, a white leather banana seat emerges, then a purple tube connected to pedals and one wheel—a unicycle. I don't know what to say. I want to try it out immediately.

As I put one foot on a pedal, my mother exclaims, "Not in here! Not with my Haviland china!" She is deadly serious.

"Okay, Mom. Thank you." I contain my enthusiasm for the new conveyance long enough to open my other less interesting presents and be tangentially aware of the other people unwrapping.

I hear my mother exclaim over and over as she opens her presents, "Oh Ed, you shouldn't have. It's too much." (She always called my dad Ed, though his name was Lawrence.)

She holds each sweater or skirt to her body, donning some but oohing and ahhing over every new outfit. I notice she keeps all the boxes in order and refolds the clothes neatly. I learned later that she exchanged most of the new things. My dad never learned her correct size or preferred style. My poor dad always seemed to get the fewest gifts, but my mom said he bought himself presents throughout the year.

Finally, when the unwrapping is over, and breakfast is eaten, I take the unicycle downstairs to the basement. There is a large walk-in freezer in one room where I sometimes trick my brother into going in. Clocks fill another secluded room. Mostly, the downstairs has little furniture or obstructions and is a good bike path.

My mom comes downstairs with me. Neither of us know anything about the one-wheeled contraption.

My mom offers, "Well, just try to sit on the seat. I'll hold your hands."

I try, but all that happens is the wheel flies out from under me.

Laughing, my mom says, "That didn't work, did it?"

My brother, Ted, runs around in and out of another room. I don't know what he is playing with, but he keeps asking Mom to help.

She looks at me and apologizes, "I'm sorry. You'll have to figure this out on your own. I have to help Ted. You know how he gets."

And so, I push the wheel against a corner and hold onto the intersecting walls. I quickly figure out how to step on the lowest pedal first. Before long, I can balance on the seat. My mom is in the next room and every so often calls out, "How are you doing?"

She is helping Ted assemble a Lego set, and I notice she carefully removes the packaging while he tosses the pieces all over the room. My focus is on riding. I try over and over to move away from the corner. On most attempts, the wheel either shoots out straight or falls to the side.

And with each clunk of me or the bike hitting the concrete, my mom calls out, "Are you OK?" After one particularly loud noise, she rushes in to see. I don't think it's unusual that my dad never comes down.

After a while, I can catch myself before contacting the floor, but I do not always keep the bike from thudding to the floor. Over a couple of days, with this intense practice, I can ride, going forward and turning, then cruising around the pool table and down to the laundry room. My mom is sometimes downstairs ironing or in the room with clocks.

She smiles and says, "You're getting good at that." Buoyed by these words, I make another loop around the basement track.

Soon, I am able to ride outside, negotiating small steps, going backward, and wobbling through the grass. I learn to play basketball while riding. The unicycle becomes my life. In the sixth grade, I enter a talent show and ride across the stage at the school gymnasium, juggling three bowling pins. Off my bike, I am so shy I cry if a teacher looks at me funny.

<<<<<<<<<<<<<<<<<<<<<<<<<<<<<<

Back on the road to Berry Hill, Ava's beeper whined and she returned to the present. She whistled and said, "I've got the theme song to Gilligan's Island stuck in my head." Ava was amazed she had driven ten miles on autopilot and she restarted the medical podcast. Ava pulled over briefly to read the number on the beeper. The message to call wasn't urgent and could wait until she phoned from the office, but she needed to speed up to get there quickly.

Ava pulled back out on the pavement and gave the road her full attention as it became treacherous with pounding rain. The oil-slicked roads were slippery, and the day had darkened to give an eerie feel. She flicked on her fog lights.

There wasn't much traffic at this hour of the day, but every passing car sprayed water on the windshield, and she was blinded for a few seconds. She noted the rising water level and rushing flow as she passed over one bridge. Ava had just finished reading Silas House's book *Southernmost*. It was about a catastrophic flood in Tennessee and the aftermath of people sheltering and reclaiming lives. His descriptions of the rising water and the vulnerability of people living at the river's edge were perfect. The book could have described many of Ava's patients who also lived within a heartbeat of a natural disaster wiping them out and destroying homes, where poverty blew through every crack. A tornado could tear their house apart if they lived on a ridge. Rain could wash it away if they lived in a valley.

As she was distracted looking at the creek, a big log truck barreled by and inched over the centerline as it rounded a curve. Log trucks frequently traveled along this road, coming out of the forests to the local sawmill. These distinctive flatbed diesels held twenty to thirty-foot-long logs stacked as high as possible. Most were equipped with steel beams that held the logs in place with hefty straps. But many did not, and those homemade rigs looked pitifully unprofessional and scary.

Last month, Ava watched one truck tip over on a curve and let loose its load like giant tinker toys. Luckily, no one was hurt, but logs splayed over the road and into the adjacent field, diverting traffic for hours. Like coal-carrying trucks further south in Kentucky, these trucks were a danger both to other vehicles and to the loggers driving them while damaging the road surfaces.

Ava had to swerve to avoid the end of the truck as it whipped around the curve. She found her wheels spinning on the wet pavement and losing their grip. She knew this section of the road well. On her right was a small church with a paved parking lot. Ten concrete pillars were spaced on the edge of the lot just five feet from the road's shoulder. For as many times as she had driven past here, she never understood why they were so close to the road and had often imagined plowing into one. Running along the other side of the road was usually a creek, but it was now a raging river with all the falling rain.

Her wheels continued to spin, and she felt the car fishtailing as the truck finally got past. An even larger water spray followed the truck's wake, and Ava lost sight of the road. She searched for the white line on the shoulder or the double lines separating the lanes, but she saw neither.

Time seemed to stand still. Instinctively from her years of driving in snow up north, Ava did not touch the brakes but took her foot off the gas. Fighting with the steering wheel, she attempted to turn into the skid, but the car was out of control.

Abo-Abr
Notes for *Inside Taber's: A Study of the Medical Dictionary* by Dr. Ava

Early in the book is the word "abortion." I feel my blood pressure rising. The word has leaped from the medical world to the legal to the political, legislative, moral, and religious realms and caused so much passion on all sides.

There is nearly a page devoted to the different types of abortions. I guess the kind that everyone talks about has three entries: elective, induced, and therapeutic. Two of the three have caveats in Taber's related to the mother's mental or physical state and being cognizant of the emotional toll.

The more frequent types of abortions don't get so much press. The spontaneous ab, the threatened ab, the missed ab, the tubal abortion. Those are the abortions that tear a mother's heart from her chest. Especially those who have "habitual abortions"—three or more consecutive abortions. These are abortions, too, not just miscarriages, with the same emotional turmoil linked with an elective procedural abortion. Only without the societal guilt. Bizarre and unexplainable. There has to be a solution to this dilemma.

A rather interesting note is the inclusion of the term "abortionist"— one who performs an abortion. It is a legitimate derivation of a word— for example, socialist, capitalist, hypnotist. It is noteworthy that very few other procedures and the operator performing them are referred to in this manner, like a surgeon or obstetrician. There is no term "circumcisionist" in TCMD. In the next column on page 7, "abrachiocephalia"—"a (disturbing) congenital absence of both arms and head." Seemingly a reason for an induced abortion that all could agree on.

Here we come to "abruptio"—"a tearing away from." And the only sub-entry—"abruptio placentae"—"the sudden premature detachment of the placenta from its normal uterine site of implantation." In other words, the afterbirth is ready to be born before the baby. Just the word makes my heart jump, remembering my many deliveries and my constant worry that either some extra vaginal bleeding or a slowed fetal heart rate was an abruption. With an incidence of 1 in 120 births, it is a real fear and a reality, along with perinatal infections being a major cause of maternal and perinatal mortality worldwide.

Chapter 6: Dangerous Roads Continued

Ava's car was out of control. All she wanted was to pull over on the right side of the road. She saw the towering concrete pillars and managed to keep the car on the road past them. She pulled into the next lot, which she knew was part of a junkyard. The area near the road was a gravel lot that ended in a pond. Ava had been going too fast on the wet roads, and her momentum kept the car moving much further than she wanted, but after long seconds of hearing the gravel crunch under her tires, the car stopped just a few feet from the pond.

Ava sat in the car, breathing fast and shaking. "Wow," she said, "That was close."

The rain poured onto her car top, and her wipers flailed helplessly. She turned the ignition off and checked that her arms and legs were still attached. They felt numb. She could see her fingers gripping the wheel but couldn't feel them touching the sticky leather.

Slowly, she grew aware of the radio broadcasting news about the president and reached out to turn off the noise. Her mind couldn't seem to slow down from its crisis mode functioning a few minutes before. She couldn't believe she had been that close to dying or being severely injured. Had she run into the concrete pillars at the speed she was going, she would be dead.

"Why was I driving so fast?" she wondered. "If I hadn't been think-ing about my unicycle, maybe this wouldn't have happened."

A guilty thought came to her, "If I had died in an accident, I don't think my dad could go through that again."

Ava sat for over five minutes, hoping no one would plow into her in the rain. Gradually, her breathing and heart rate slowed, and she felt she could function. It was too wet to step outside, though that was what she wanted to do. Get out of this near-death trap. Totally unlike herself, she picked up her phone to call her brother, Ted. She wanted to hear his voice and tell him how close she had been to disaster. Unfortunately, her phone had zero bars. This was the section of the road where no cell towers reached, and she had always skirted past here when driving home from the office while on call.

Backing up and away from the pond, she noticed the car was driving fine. There was no permanent damage to the vehicle from this near miss. She wasn't so sure about herself. She couldn't see any cars coming and pulled out to drive the few more miles to her office. Luckily, she encountered no other trucks or cars in the oncoming lane. Her office parking lot was full of staff cars, and they had left their dripping umbrellas at the entrance. The floor was wet, and Ava nearly slipped due to her agitation.

She burst into the hall and told the first person she saw, Pat, about her drive. The telling of the experience seemed to cause Ava to sweat and shake all over again. Pat had her sit down and got her a glass of water. She also brought a towel for Ava to dry off and wrap up in. The patter of rain on the roof was so loud that the two had to speak loudly to be heard.

Pat said, "That must have been scary. Those darn logging trucks. I wish they could regulate them better. They drive around overloaded and speeding and don't care what happens to other drivers. Are you hurt at all?"

Ava answered, "No, I'm all right. Just shook up. I can't believe I made it out of that alive. Wow, I just can't believe it."

Pat rubbed Ava's shoulder.

"Do you want to see patients today or just rest? I am sure someone would drive you home."

Ava said, "No, I will be alright. I can't not see these patients. I have quite a few scheduled today, and I would like to get them seen so they can get home before it gets worse."

Pat sighed. "I knew you would say that. You know, sometimes doctors have to take time off."

Ava smiled and said, "I know, but not today. I'll be alright."

With that, Ava removed the towel and walked into her office at the end of the hall. She stopped in the bathroom, threw warm water on her face, and ran her fingers through her hair. All in all, she didn't look much more disheveled than she usually looked. Her face was still somewhat pale, but she was feeling better.

* * *

When Ava walked away, Pat found Linda, the front office receptionist. The two looked toward Ava's office.

"I worry a lot about her. Something feels like it's going to break," Pat said.

"Me too. You feel the tension around her. Wish there was something we could do, but you know how she is," Linda responded.

"I know. She doesn't let people in."

They both shook their heads and went back to work.

* * *

Ava saw the name on the chart of her first patient and relaxed a bit. Leonard Whitt. She enjoyed seeing Leonard Whitt because he reminded her so much of Leonard, the prison gardener. Like his historical namesake, he was living alone and precariously. No one looked after him at home for reasons Ava did not know.

One thing about a doctor's visit is that both parties only see a glimpse of the other. Ava only saw Leonard in this tiny moment of existence, and while he struck her as kind, patient, and lovable, there was a whole other part of his life she had no clue about. He reminded her so much of Leonard from her childhood; from her first meeting with him, she vowed always to be kind to him. Maybe to make up for the way she treated Leonard, the gardener, at the end.

Leonard wore Carhartt jeans, a wrinkled flannel shirt, and freshly polished shoes. The cuffs of his long underwear peaked out at both wrists. Fleetingly, Ava remembered that the Leonard of her childhood wore green prison-issued work pants.

Leonard loved to read and often brought Dean Koontz paperbacks to the office for Ava because he knew she liked to read. Ten years ago, Leonard was diagnosed with advanced liver disease from too much alcohol and had successfully received a cadaver liver in a last-chance transplant. He had stopped drinking and smoking to qualify for the liver back then but recently, unexplainably, had started smoking again. So, the books he donated to the clinic always smelled of smoke. Ava considered it an olfactory reminder of him each time she raced through one of the novels.

During today's visit, Leonard complained of some leg edema and had lost a few pounds. He admitted to not having much of an appetite for the past couple of months. On examination, there was a hint of jaundice in his sclera—the whites of the eye. Without saying so out loud, Ava began to worry and calmly asked him if she could have some blood drawn. He tiredly agreed but brought up his frequent complaint about how many medicines he swallowed daily.

Transplant recipients must take a long list of anti-rejection drugs. Ava knew Leonard was lonely, poorly nourished, living in a hovel, and most likely depressed. Prescribing an antidepressant would not help his social conditions, but sitting with him a little longer on these visits might show him she and her co-workers cared. She just hoped they would find nothing disturbing about his blood work.

This was a common course for her delicate patients. She would consider the worst or most serious diagnosis for a set of symptoms, then walk herself back to a more benign cause. This she did in her head, delaying the worry to patients until the diagnosis was clear. Of course, many of her more educated, computer-savvy patients had already read about their conditions and were much more knowledgeable than the lay public a few decades earlier.

Routine checkups on her diabetic patients took the rest of the day. Once a month, the nutritionist from the hospital would come to Berry Hill to help sort out meal plans for these patients. Most talked about changing their diet, but their resolve never lasted long. Ava wished there could be a "one size fits all" method for convincing people to change their health habits. So much of why patients were sick was because of something preventable. Trying to prevent illness from occurring in the first place or preventing progression was frustrating.

Ava and her colleagues often commiserated with each other in the safety of the lunch area. Pat, the X-ray technician, added her humor to some of the stories. Hearing Pat lovingly joke about her family and friends always gave Ava a lift, and today, her familiar voice kept Ava from thinking about the morning's scare.

The news had predicted rain for the entire day. There were two ways to go home. Ava could take the highway, which was about thirty miles and took a few minutes longer, or the back road, which was fewer miles and faster but much curvier—the road she had taken in the morning and nearly died on. She took the highway, which brought up memories of her mother.

Since her mother's accident, Ava had been superstitious about driving. She would not drive on a holiday because her mother died on Labor Day weekend. And because the accident happened in Grand Rapids, twenty-five miles from her parent's home, Ava grew anxious whenever she found herself twenty-five miles from home.

She remembers riding to Grand Rapids with her parents to shop and dine. Her father, Lawrence, went to one store there for his suits and liked to eat at his favorite German restaurant—Schnitzelbanks—at least once a month. She remembers sitting in the back seat as a child, trying not to get carsick. When she was old enough for a license and allowed to chauffeur, she flew down the curvy road oblivious to her parent's warnings to slow down. Her speed kept them all from enjoying the beautiful views along the river. Thinking of her mother lying on that same road with only one shoe on was unbearable.

It's 2010, I have just finished my residency. My mom, dad, and I are on a trip to Ireland. We come from different places and fly into Shannon Airport a few hours apart. I am the first to arrive, so I pick up the rental car. There's a mix-up; all the agency has are manual transmission vehicles—no automatics.

I know my mother will be upset. I should have demanded an automatic, instead, I say, "It's okay; I'll take what you have." When my parents arrive, I tell them I can drive.

We sort our way out of the airport, navigating along the unfamiliar side of the road. My mother prays in the back seat while Dad calmly wonders where and when we will eat. We successfully make it to our first B & B. A typical Irish lady greets us at the door and has tea and biscuits ready after we settle our luggage. That night and almost every other night, we walk into town, have dinner and a pint of Guinness, listen to music, and return to our accommodations. Then we sit and talk to the hosts. One night, a famous Irish poet joins us. My parents love it. I less so. Mom is a brilliant conversationalist, and Dad can add interesting stories. I am just listening, wishing I could go back to the pub for more music.

We travel around Ireland, visiting Waterford, where my grandmother and other ancestors were born, baptized, and buried. We take a tour of the magnificent Waterford Glass factory, and Mom buys a small glass dolphin. We visit the town where one side of Dad's family was from. We kiss the Blarney Stone and eat smashers. We spend five days together.

I am to leave Ireland before my parents to travel to England for a few days before starting my new job. I feel bad about leaving them alone. And there is the issue with the car.

My mom is worried about driving a stick shift.

I tell her, "But Mom, you taught me how to drive a stick. You should be fine. Just remember to drive on the left."

She was still worried. Later, she told me they went to the airport the day I left and picked up an automatic to drive for the rest of the time.

Abs-Abs

Abs-Abs

Notes for *Inside Taber's: A Study of the Medical Dictionary* by Dr. Ava

I have often referred to, or rather threatened, the "death triangle" to my acned adolescents when it is obvious they have popped a pimple in the area between their nose, cheeks, and mouth. This triangle, like other infamous triangles, can lead to death. In this case, from a brain abscess. I doubt if any of those patients have heeded my warning to avoid risking contaminating a path from their sinuses to their brain. Luckily, it has also never happened to anyone I have known.

With over three pages of sub-entries for abscesses, I find some of them just plain cute. "Collar-button" abscess perfectly describes the state of pressure of "two pus-containing cavities, one larger than the other, connected by a narrow channel." After reading all the abscesses, I felt like I needed a shower. This is the feeling I often have after being with a patient who has some obvious infectious process.

One day last week, I entered the room of a patient who was near death from cancer. She was essentially comatose, but she was spewing sputum or frothy spit from the back of her throat on the throw covering her. It was one of the most disturbing images I have ever seen because this patient had been meticulous about her appearance, had an exquisite fashion sense, and would have also been highly disturbed by this soiling.

7

Chapter 7: R and Me

Rosella couldn't sleep for the three days Tresne followed her around. Cal tried to be understanding, but he slept so soundly that he didn't notice her absence from the bed. She hadn't been forced to talk about her brother this much for many years though he was always in her mind. People she knew before moving to Kentucky were intimately involved with Roger but few of her new friends knew what had happened. She debated whether to tell Tresne about her experience trying to play music at Roger's funeral.

Rosella grew up in Rochester, New York. Her parents, Liz and Larry, were doctors at Strong Memorial, and they lived in an old, rambling house across from Highland Park. Her brother, Roger, was eighteen months younger. He and Rosella were often mistaken for twins with their nearly identical facial features, including high cheekbones, an aquiline nose, and deep dimples.

Both Roger and Rosella displayed an aptitude for music at an early age, which is not surprising since their whole extended family was musical. They were drawn to the strings and started playing when Liz gave Rosella a one-fourth-sized guitar that she found at an estate sale on her fourth birthday and Larry bought Roger the same-sized guitar at a different estate sale a month later. The rare finds were not so remarkable, considering Rochester was uniquely full of music and musicians.

At first, their playing was all about exploring what the instrument could do. Without instructions, they played the fretboard like a keyboard—sitting on the floor cross-legged, one guitar between them, Roger's tiny fingers at one end and Rosella tapping on the other. Eventually, they found the usual playing positions, but often, their strumming mirrored one another.

Larry and Liz hesitated to declare them prodigies but recognized their passion for music. They tried to expose them to different influences by playing everything from classical to rock and taking them to concerts in the area. The two young children sat entranced by the performances. Living in Rochester, there were ample opportunities with the Eastman School of Music just a few miles away.

When Rosella started school, she explored bowed stringed instruments while Roger was at home concentrating on the guitar. School was fun for both of them because they were popular and did well in every grade, but their favorite time was at night and on weekends when they played together—first, one doodling a melody, then the other. By the age of nine and ten, they were performing at family get-togethers and school talent shows. Rosella alternated between violin and guitar and vocals while Roger played either lead guitar or bass and sang. As they got older, they would take a few lessons from accomplished musicians and absorb techniques, but both had an uncanny skill for hearing a passage once and knowing how to play it almost immediately. Older musicians who worked with them complimented their parents on how enjoyable and inspiring it was.

In high school, they added a drummer, Paul, and started a band. Mainly concentrating on experimental pieces and originals in the jazz, blues, and folk styles, the trio found venues in the Finger Lakes region. They played nearly every Friday night at a small pizza joint on Lake Hemlock. The crowd was primarily young, but the group's fame and unique sound drew some older fans from the area.

In her senior year, Rosella started dating Cal. They had been friends throughout high school, but not until their last year did they kindle a romantic relationship. Cal always had a philosophical take on life and planned to get his degree in that field. He questioned assumptions and shared these thoughts with Rosella. Their conversations fueled her songs, and her lyrics moved from the mundane, trite love songs of her peers to deeper content. That is what was likable about the band's performances. Combining Roger's guitar skills with unusual compositions, the band developed a following. Later on, their drummer, Paul, followed a girlfriend to the west coast, and, for a time, it was just Rosella and Roger playing together.

Rosella remembered being frustrated by Roger when it was just the two of them in the band. Roger was often late for a gig. Rosella took to calling him two hours before the event, then one hour before. This worked but strained Rosella and eventually their music because she resented being his "babysitter." Their mom said Roger had always been hard to redirect.

During the time absent a drummer, they named themselves R and Me. It was a family joke that Roger couldn't say Rosella's full name when he was young and often just called her R. Or sometimes Roz.

Roz and Roger accepted generous offers to attend the Eastman School of Music and continued to live at home through college. Many genres influenced them at school, but the biggest takeaway lesson for Rosella was a sense of how music could build community. Guided by Cal's altruistic tendencies, she mainly wanted to live a life where she could balance performance and community building.

They met Raphael while at Eastman and quickly knew he would be a great addition to R and Me, not just because his name started with r. He was originally from Argentina and played all sorts of drums. His off-beat, syncopated rhythms added yet another level of intrigue to their compositions. Rosella was relieved of some of her timekeeping duties because Raphael and Roger lived together, and Raphael was good at keeping her brother on track.

After college, the trio kept busy with regional tours, and then, as their reputation grew, they went on a US tour. By the age of twenty-two and twenty-three, Roger and Roz had made two full-length CDs and performed in over thirty cities. The pace was breakneck, but everyone was enjoying the ride. Cal pursued his master's and doctorate at Columbia, which is why the band eventually settled in New York City.

Liz and Larry visited them often and helped financially so Rosella and Roger could dedicate time to teaching and having fun with music. Finding the most un-supported music programs at schools, the band would hold a fundraising concert to buy instruments, then drop in for impromptu learning sessions every month or so. They would busk in the parks and encourage music students to join them. With many churches in the city empty during the week because of falling church attendance, they would encourage young musicians to play with them in the cavernous, acoustically majestic spaces. They also invited local artists to perform, exposing their audiences to various styles.

Life continued this way for several years. Roz and Cal married. Roger developed friendships with many people, though his romantic relationships never lasted long. Raphael became like an adopted son to Liz and Larry, and they walked him down the aisle at his wedding to a beautiful opera singer.

One day, Roz noticed Roger had less energy during practice and begged off to sleep at an uncharacteristically early hour. The next morning, he had large bruises under his eyes and along his arms. A phone call to their parents confirmed what Roz had told Roger—go to the doctor immediately.

And that was the end of their charmed life. Later in the day, blood work returned, showing that Roger's white count was sky high, and a bone marrow biopsy the next day confirmed he had leukemia, a rare form of acute lymphocytic leukemia, fast-growing and serious. He was immediately admitted to the hospital and started on chemotherapy. Roz was shaken and walked in shock. She dropped objects and ran into tables—as if her body no longer was connected to her brain. In her mind, she kept repeating, "I can't believe someone so healthy could suddenly be so sick."

Her parents were equally devastated. Liz and Larry took leaves of absence from work in Rochester and moved to New York City. They debated for a long time where Roger would get the best care. Should they go to Strong Memorial Hospital in Rochester, where they knew everyone, or to the city, where their medical connections and influence wouldn't matter? They moved into Roz and Cal's apartment and resolved to trust Sloan Kettering..

The initial days of chemotherapy were brutal, and it seemed to Roz as if Roger shrank—his body, of course, with weight loss and weakness, but also his personality and zip. Every visit to his bedside was harder than the last as he withdrew further and further into a state of bare existence. His oncology team had warned them about how sick he would be before he improved, so this wasn't unexpected, but it was still very hard. His family made a pact that they would never use a sports analogy to describe what he was going through because Larry hated when people talked about cancer as if it was a rival football opponent, as if survival was all about fortitude and grit, implying that a weak player could be blamed for not surviving.

After some time, maybe just a week, though the days felt endless, Roger responded to the induction chemotherapy and regained some of what he had lost. He remained hospitalized and in isolation, but his body seemed to be rebounding. He asked for a nylon-string guitar to be brought to the hospital. Soon, tunes could be heard coming from his room.

While Roz dealt with her own trauma of seeing her brother sick, she didn't realize how hard it was for her parents. They were forced to be both affected as parents and professionally involved as doctors. Every decision about Roger's care hit them as a tear to the heart and a requirement to research the best approach. The oncology team had cared for many doctors' kids and were as helpful as they could be, often suggesting that Larry and Liz let go of their doctor hats. But that wasn't so easy. They had no experience separating the emotional burden of seeing their son ill from their usual response to a patient needing care. Those initial weeks took a tremendous toll on them.

Roger received intrathecal chemotherapy to prevent spread of the leukemia cells to his cerebral spinal fluid, and things looked promising that he could be home soon. His family insisted he move in with Roz and Cal, and he agreed. Meanwhile, all the recording, teaching, touring, and playing activities had been suspended for all these weeks. R and Me's fans followed Roger's course on Instagram. That was a special request from Roger just after his diagnosis, stating that he wanted to make people aware of how illness strikes and use his situation to educate.

As Rosella was thinking back on this time, she had difficulty remembering all the details from the subsequent months. She would register a twinge of pain upon seeing a puzzle after that because there was always a puzzle set up for visitors and patients to work on at the oncology unit. Cal was with her throughout the whole cancer journey. He mostly remained quiet unless she asked about specific dates and procedures.

Much too soon, Roger had a recurrence, and his only therapeutic option was a bone marrow transplant. Roz was a perfect match. He underwent the uncomfortable pre-transplant preparation, and Roz underwent the marrow harvesting. She remembers she wasn't too sore and wished she could have taken on more of Roger's suffering. The transplant was not enough to save his life. He passed away at home in hospice precisely one year after his diagnosis.

Roz remained in shock, feeling like everything in life was a dream. Liz made the arrangements for the funeral and talked to the undertaker. Roz didn't know how her mom was functioning. She could hardly make herself get out of bed.

Liz said, "Roz, I think Roger would have liked it if you would play something at the funeral. Can you do that?"

Roz could see her mom's lips moving, but the words made little sense, as if she was speaking in an unfamiliar tongue or had no language at all. She could only nod numbly.

Liz took this as a yes. "Good," she said. "Can you think of something?"

Roz really wasn't thinking of anything. Her brain couldn't comprehend that all this was happening. That she was being asked to play for her brother's funeral. That her brother was having a funeral.

She blurted out the last song she and Roger listened to the night before he got sick: Pink Floyd's "Wish You Were Here." They talked about trying to learn the song and singing it as a duo. The words didn't mean much when they heard it that night at Roger's apartment, but they liked the guitar work on it.

Liz said, "Are you sure that's the song you want to play? I don't even know it."

Roz just nodded, not knowing what she was doing but wanting to close her eyes and pretend this wasn't happening. She didn't think of her commitment again until Raphael asked how she would play it when they saw each other the next day.

"What? What are you talking about? Play what?" she asked.

"The song. Your mom told me you were going to play "Wish You Were Here." She said you agreed to sing and play it." Raphael answered.

"Oh no. I don't think I can."

"Your mom thinks that's what Roger would want. She said it would mean so much to her to hear you sing at the funeral."

"Oh, Raphael. I don't know. Can you help?"

He said, "Of course, I'll try."

The funeral was a blur to Rosella, but she gathered her guitar and walked with Raphael to the front of the church at the end of the ceremony. She looked only at her guitar and not at her parents in the front row or the rows and rows of mourners.

She began the introduction to the piece with shaky hands and then stopped. Raphael, beside her, ready to help sing, stood silently waiting. The people in their pews waited, holding their breaths. Rosella began to sob, handed her guitar to Raphael, and ran out a side door. Her mother stood up, but her dad held her hand and whispered to let her go.

Rosella exited the church, and soon, her tears mixed with the falling drizzle. She ran and ran, not knowing or even thinking of where she was going. She only wanted to make the pain go away. Later, Cal found her sitting on a bench at the far end of the cemetery. She had missed Roger's burial. He gently led her to his car and took her home, wrapping her in a blanket and letting her sleep. He watched over her for a long time until she was sound asleep.

That was the last time Rosella played in public. She hadn't told Tresne that not only did she not want to play in public, but she firmly believed she couldn't.

After the funeral, life had to go on in some form. Roz and her parents managed their daily living activities, but barely. As well-wishers offering thoughts and prayers bombarded them, the family appreciated the words and concern. Fans posted on the band's social media sites; close friends brought dishes and flowers. Religious friends predicted Roger was surely in heaven—one particularly zealous supporter donated to a church in Alaska that apparently would be named after Roger. The outpouring of sympathy was overwhelming. And short-lived. As is natural. While others went on with their lives, Roz and her family existed without a piece of them.

Practically, Liz and Larry went back to Rochester and resumed some semblance of routine with their family medicine practices. They gradually limited their practice to only preventative care and, without speaking of it aloud, both referred any seriously ill patients to their colleagues. Eventually, they started a consulting service for workplaces in the area, concentrating only on preventative medicine. As communicative as they had been, the couple could not bear to talk about Roger. It was too painful.

Rafael reluctantly took a job with another band while Roger was in the hospital to survive financially. He chose one that played similar music to R and Me. He became a success. Roz saw him often, and when they got together, they reminisced about Roger, watching old videos of the band and recalling funny stories. His new band kept him busy, and gradually, the time between his visits lengthened.

Rosella stopped playing. Whenever she thought about picking up a guitar or fiddle, her heart ached so much that she couldn't proceed. She moved back to Rochester and lived with her parents. Cal was finishing his Ph.D., so he stayed in the city and took the train back to Rochester every few weeks. He continued offering his support, and Rosella relied on him from afar.

But Rosella remained numb. Like when Liz had asked her to play a song, nothing made sense and she couldn't understand what people were saying to her. For many months, she just went through the motions of living. Economically, she had her parents and her savings from the band's successes, so her daily routine was to immerse herself in reading mysteries. She was trying to lose herself. Occasionally, an engaging mystery would distract her, and she forgot reality for brief periods.

One day, while reading the New York Times, she saw a notice for an all-women triathlon to be held on Long Island. Looking closely at the route map, she was surprised the run portion went along a street she recognized. It was the street Roger had lived on. Something clicked when she saw this, and she felt like she had a purpose for the first time in six months. She couldn't explain it because she had never participated in a triathlon before and never considered doing one. Still, instantly, she knew this would be one way of memorializing Roger. From that day until the race, appropriately on the anniversary of Roger's death, she focused on training.

Cal was at the finish line with her parents. The four of them went to their favorite Italian restaurant to celebrate. It was the first happy gathering they could remember in over a year. Later, Cal and Rosella talked about the future. Cal had just completed his studies and was looking for teaching positions. Rosella felt like she could move on from her parents' home. All she knew was music, but she still wasn't ready to play.

Back at Cal's apartment in the city, the two of them scoured music magazines and college websites. A small notice listed a music store for sale in a small town in Eastern Kentucky. Coincidentally, the university in the same town was recruiting for a philosophy professor. The serendipity of these listings caused the couple to plan a trip south the following week. Surprisingly, Rosella quickly bought the music store with her savings, and Cal was offered a tenure track position. A new life was about to begin.

Rosella had almost forgotten about the interview when Tresne brought in a stack of magazines to Redbud Music two months later. This would be their third trip back to see Rosella and spend some time playing with the groups gathered at the store and with Cal and Rosella. They placed a flat wooden box on the counter. It was beautifully finished with the image of a coffee tree etched into the top.

Tresne said, "Open it."

Rosella asked, "But what is it?"

Tresne repeated, "Just open it, you'll see."

Rosella tried to pry the lid off but discovered the top slid off. Inside was the newest edition of *Rewind,* with a cover photo of Rosella. In the picture, she stood exactly where she was right now—behind the counter at Redbud Music. She remembered she had been watching some of the high schoolers set up for their practice in the jam space. With only their phone camera, Tresne had captured the look of contentment on Rosella's face.

Tresne excitedly reported, "They printed my interview with you and didn't change a thing. This just came out, so you are the first to see it. I have more copies, as many as you want. I hope you don't mind, but I found some photos of R and Me. They're in the article. I hope you like it."

Rosella knew she would but asked if she could read it later when she got home. Tresne said, "Of course, but please let me know your thoughts and be honest. That was my first interview, in case you couldn't tell."

The two exchanged hugs, and Tresne went over to see what the high school girls were playing. Soon, they were jamming along on a borrowed cajon from the shelf.

Rosella sighed and closed the beautiful box. As she admired the woodwork, she noticed a tiny inscription on the back. Written in cursive, it said, "Dedicated to the memory of Roger. May he rest in peace and his music live on forever." They were the exact words that Rosella and her parents had printed on the program for his memorial. How did Tresne know? Rosella held the box for several minutes; she felt a loosening in her heart, but the hole was still there. When she got home and after Cal went to bed, she propped herself on the floor with Hannah next to her. She opened the box, withdrew the magazine, studied the cover photos and the other shots of her band, then turned to the interview and read:

<u>**Rosella from R and Me**</u>
<u>**By**</u>
<u>**Tresne**</u>

Many people begin to write songs when dealing with deep emotional trauma. This artist stopped writing and performing instead. The "before life" of Rosella reads like a musical fairy tale. The "Life after R and Me" is more like a tale with something missing. Roger.

I had the chance to spend time with Rosella, the sister in the very popular genre-bending group R and Me. The band started recording when Rosella and her younger brother, Roger, were still in their teens. Raphael, an innovative drummer, joined the duo a few years later. While the band was intact, they produced five critically acclaimed albums, staged three nationwide multi-city tours, and performed in Germany, Ireland, and Australia. All before anyone in the group turned thirty.

Five years ago, tragedy struck at the height of the band's success. Roger was diagnosed with adult leukemia, and despite one hopeful remission, he passed away a year later. Their fans were devastated as they watched in real time his illness play out on social media. But as with much of fan idolatry, their pain was short-lived. Roger's family, particularly his sister, continues to live with his loss.

Rosella has not performed in public since his illness. But her life still revolves around music. I interviewed her in a small town in eastern Kentucky where she owns and runs a well-stocked music store, where she spends as much energy providing musical and cultural opportunities to her community as she once spent playing, composing, recording, and touring with her band.

Rosella agreed to this interview when she understood the intended audience was young musicians. She was generous with her time and wise with her answers. Because there was such a schism in her life before and after, I have split the interview into two parts.

BEFORE:

T: What brought you to music in the first place?

R: That's a difficult question to answer for me. It was as if the music was always there, and, as a young child, both Roger and I found it. I suppose it is like a dancer who has this rhythm ingrained in their body. That was the way it was for me with music. Once I had an instrument in my hands, it found a way to come out through my fingers. I started playing the guitar when I was four or five and never stopped.

T: When you were young, were there any challenges to music? How about as you got older?

R: As a young child, I only remember the joy of playing. The sheer thrill of hearing what was in my head come out in the instrument. I guess the only disappointing part was that sometimes I couldn't replicate the sound in my head. Either the tone wasn't quite what I wanted, or I couldn't match it rhythmically. That's why I played all the time and started picking up other instruments. I liked the bowing of the violin and the range of the keyboards.

As I got older, the thing I disliked the most was having to work on lessons that teachers would give me. Sometimes, the exercises would be pure drudgery, and I remember my wise father telling me someday I would be glad I stuck with the tediousness of scales. Playing arpeggios was fun—like dancing on the fingerboard only using my fingers, not my toes. My dad and my teachers were right. Those exercises helped me later.

T: What do you consider your greatest accomplishment with music?

R: That's another hard question. I suppose I was happiest when a fan would tell me they enjoyed the music. When someone else would take one of our songs and make it their own. A lot of times, we would watch YouTube videos and see people playing our songs and trying to be exactly like us—same phrasings, same solos, same inflections to the words. But I liked it the most when I hardly recognized our song. When the person would improvise on the theme in some new and creative way. I also really liked it when our music was used with another expressive art form. I remember going to the Cincinnati Fringe Festival one year to accompany a dance troupe that used our music for an experimental dance. That was beautiful.

T: I wished I had seen that. I have been to several Fringe Festivals here in Cincinnati—they are always new and different. You recorded a song that I listened to over and over. It was titled "War Peace Musings." What did that song mean?

R: Roger wrote that song, so you would have to ask him. Sadly, you can't. What did the song mean to you?

T: Well, I fought with my parents over my gender choices, so the line "love folded over to hate at a dizzying rate" described what I was going through so well.

R: That makes me feel good. Roger would have liked to hear that. Not that you fought, of course.

T: What about your drummer, Raphael? How did he fit in with your sibling connection?

R: Raphael was cool. Somehow, he melded with us from the start. We knew him from school, so we were friends before he joined the band. Roger and I were always amazed at what he could do with percussion. Most times, he brought just the cajon and made it sound like an entire rhythm section. He grasped any ideas we had and made them better. He was easy to travel with and easy to talk to. He tolerated our occasional family spats, and his presence was probably a mediating factor. I miss being around him very much now that we don't have the band.

T: You have been with your partner, Cal, for over a decade. Any insights for musicians dealing with relationships?

R: Nothing specific to musicians. Cal doesn't play or sing, but he is a very discerning listener, and I value his comments about music. We had to sort out the noise/audio spaces when we moved in together. I liked to play at haphazard times—when the spirit moved me, so to speak. And I can appreciate that a housemate doesn't want to hear someone practicing passages repeatedly at all hours. For a short while, this was a sore spot in our relationship. I felt bad when I played, worrying about bothering him, but I couldn't limit my playing to just when he was out of the house. Our solution, which I know isn't possible for everyone, was to design two soundproof rooms. One was his, and one was mine. I would play in my room if he was in the common areas. If he was working on his classes in his room, I gently closed his door and was free to roam the house with inspiration. It worked out.

AFTER

T: How have you changed since Roger's death?

R: Well, I no longer perform. I no longer play other than for myself, Cal, or to teach my students. Like never before, music carries something other than joy with it now. It is hard to explain, but when I think of playing out, I think of Roger, and it's as if someone threw water on me. I have no desire to make music without him.

T: Do you think that will ever change?

R: Never say never, right? I don't know. I can't see it happening in the near future.

T: What is your musical outlet now?

R: I own a music store, which has become my life. My philosophy has changed from this individual selfish desire to make music for an audience's enjoyment to making music accessible to anyone. Let them play for audiences or for themselves. I can provide the means to make that happen with the music store Redbud Music. That happens every day with youngsters, adults, and everyone. That's what I am doing now, and I am extremely happy doing it.

T: Any words of advice for those musicians just starting?

R: I think most people can Google a list of suggestions for being better or being more proficient. So, I can't add to those lists. I don't have any magic tips. One thing I have observed is the difference between people who commit themselves to a career in music early in life versus those who maybe play music as a hobby but have a source of income separate from the music.

The former group gets really good, but there will be sacrifices unless they make it big, like we were lucky enough to do. For many years, they will scrape by with so-so instruments and conform to the music someone else wants them to play.

The other group, those who play for a hobby and have another job, will never be as good—they just can't put in the time. But they will play what they want and be able to afford great instruments.

I can't tell anyone which is the better approach. I think it is all determined by how strong the music needs to come out.

T: Good observation. That is the last question I have for you. Any final thoughts?

R: Thank you for this conversation. And by the way, you are one hell of a drummer, and you're very young. My advice to you is to quit your day job and play on crappy drums for a while because I think you are going to be big.

T: Well, ahhh... Thanks for saying that, and thanks for taking the time to do this interview. I am sure our readers will enjoy reading about you. Maybe someday we will have a chance to see you perform live.

8

Chapter 8: Slowing Down

Ava couldn't stop thinking of her near accident. She knew she should slow down but without her mom, she was afraid.

As a child, she had taken long walks in the woods with her dog. And as a teenager, she hit a ball against the garage door for hours in a meditative, repetitive manner. She never considered those activities therapeutic; they were just what she liked to do. Entering med school and residency, she had less and less time to spend on mindless things, like walking for hours or swinging a racquet to exhaustion. So, she searched for other ways to quiet her mind.

In her early twenties, before she fell away from the Catholic church, she tried "Centering Prayer," which was described as a way to be in union with God by going beyond thoughts, emotions, and sensations. She had first heard of this by reading Thomas Merton and Basil Pennington. Both were monks who embraced Eastern practices of contemplation and meditation. Ava attempted this form of sitting quietly and repeating a single word. She joined a centering prayer group at her church, St. Peter and Paul, and for a while, this seemed effective at slowing her mind, forcing her to stop worrying about patients, what people thought of her, and what mistakes she had made. But then, she found an excuse to skip the practice for a day, then a week, and soon she stopped going to the group or praying at home.

Upon the advice of a friend, she tried tai chi. Yoga always seemed too competitive for Ava because she could never do downward dog or child's pose as well as the person next to her. Tai chi was slow and contemplative. It also effectively slowed her mind, but like many other things, she tired of the practice and gradually fell off performing the moves.

A practice Ava took up and had never tired of was writing with her non-dominant hand. In her case, this involved using her left hand. She picked up a book about it at Half-Price Books, and one weekend, with no call, no expectant mothers, and no other plans, she read the entire book and followed along with the exercises. At first, just etching out her three-letter name was extremely difficult. Then, she was instructed to pretend she was a little girl and write what came to mind as a child. The most advanced exercise from the book, but the one that seemed to stick, was writing a question with the right hand and answering it with the left hand. Ava continued to use this practice when she considered difficult decisions.

These practices didn't seem like enough for Ava. They weren't helping her to slow down. The only activity that brought her quiet now was reading Taber's. She read a page in between phone calls from patients that night.

The next morning around five a.m., Ava got a call from Martha at GAAL s to say that Susan West was unresponsive.

Martha told Ava that Susan's sister and the nieces were at her bedside. Ava said she would be in to visit soon. Just last weekend, Susan celebrated an early graduation ceremony for her twins. Her beaming face made all the efforts to stage this event worthwhile. At the graduation, Susan and Ava talked like old friends.

Susan said in a weakened voice, "I want to thank you for being there for me over the past two years. I felt better going through all those procedures and treatments when I knew you were watching over things. You were my medical champion."

Ava stammered, "Thank you. You knew what you were doing. I never met anyone as knowledgeable about your cancer as you were. I think you could have held your own even without me."

"Now, don't do that. You are important, and what you did, no one else did. I just wanted to say thank you."

Finally, Ava said, "You are welcome. And thank you for all you did for me. I might not have gotten through my divorce if I couldn't have talked to you about it some days."

They both became overcome with the emotion of the moment. Ava looked around because the graduation was about to start and said, "I'm going to let you enjoy your family. I will see you later."

This morning, when Ava entered Susan's room, one of the nieces was lying beside her, sound asleep. The other girl and her mother were crunched in a chair beside the bed. Oxygen tubing snaked over the side, but there were no other signs that this was a medical site. Ava noted the beautiful quilt covering the sleeping figures. The pattern was called "Double Wedding Ring." Ava knew this one because it was part of the Kentucky Quilt Trail—large painted wooden quilt squares hung on the sides of barns. There was a barn with this pattern on the way to Jack's house, and she had seen it many times. She knew this particular quilt as well because Susan's grandmother made it. Tattered but treasured.

Ava gently touched Susan's sister's knee, and she opened her eyes and nodded. The two had met a few times over the years. Susan's sister always had a lot of questions for Ava and was an excellent caregiver to Susan. However, Ava could tell—from a more relaxed look or some other sense—that the sister seemed like she had accepted the inevitability of Susan's disease. This was the first time she didn't ask questions. All in the room seemed peaceful.

Susan was breathing with slow, erratic breaths. At times, there were some stirrings of her hands but nothing more. The aides told Ava before she walked in that Susan's last pulse was over 100, and her blood pressure was hard to find. The nurse's aide, Angie, said, "We stopped checking her pulse oximetry because it had dropped so low, and her fingers were so cold." Ava could see a swab stick on the bedside table they were using to moisten Susan's mouth.

Ava came to the side of the bed and whispered to Susan.

"How are you feeling? Are you comfortable? Your family is all here with you. We can get you anything you need."

Ava wanted to say more but didn't know how. She wanted to tell her how unfair it was that she was dying, that she was so young, and to ask her to say hello to Ava's mother when she reached heaven.

When Ava felt tears well up, she retreated to viewing the scene as an objective observer and thought for the hundredth time that being here was a privilege.

Susan didn't respond to Ava's icy hands, and during the half-hour Ava was there, her breathing became more gurgly. The sister whispered to Ava, "How long do you think?"

Ava responded, "Within the next few hours, I think. You can tell her how much you love her and to tell her it's OK to go. That's important."

With those words, Ava slipped out of the room. She sat at the nurse's station for a while, aware of how close everyone had gotten to Susan. It was a sad day all around.

Knowing that nature would take its course whether or not Ava stayed, she drove on to her office. This all accounted for her being at the office early. She reviewed the schedule and thought about the patients coming in that day. There were a couple of routine OB checks. They were easy and usually joyful. The first two OB patients were married with other children and pretty much knew what was going on and what to expect with their pregnancy. The next two were challenging in somewhat opposite ways.

Laura Rae was only fourteen years old. Her mother accompanied her at each visit, and she was now about twenty weeks along. The pregnancy itself was following nature's plan for growing a baby but not as the family planned for Laura Rae. She had had sex with her boyfriend before Laura Rae's mother even knew there was a boyfriend. The pregnancy was an enormous shock to everyone, including the girl.

The mother, or soon-to-be grandmother, was dealing well, and Ava was impressed by how fast the family had adapted and reoriented toward supporting Laura Rae. Although disappointed, they never failed to love and encourage both Laura Rae and the boyfriend, who had also become quite involved. She continued at school.

When Ava first came to this town to practice, pregnant teens were told they couldn't continue coming to school and would be placed on homebound. The attitude of many administrators and parents was that a visibly pregnant high schooler would be a bad influence on the other students. Luckily, this had changed over the years, and rather than isolating the pregnant teen, the school had started teaching and talking more about how to prevent pregnancy. The local health department organized a peer program to promote abstinence or safe sex. Since this approach was used, teen pregnancy had declined dramatically. Laura Rae was the first pregnant patient under eighteen years old that Ava had seen for over five years.

The second challenging patient was the opposite extreme from Laura Rae. This patient, named Brenda, was twenty-eight, happily married, and her pregnancy was thoroughly planned and executed. Brenda was a professional realtor, and the pregnancy was to follow a strict schedule as in her work life. She meticulously followed her ovulation cycle and arranged to get pregnant so the baby would be born during the spring so she wouldn't be pregnant in the hottest months. Most challenging, Brenda had a birth plan. Actually, she had a pregnancy plan. She kept a detailed log of weight gained, footsteps taken, foods eaten, and ounces of water drunk. She presented all these figures to Ava during her visits. She also insisted on two-week visits instead of the usual monthly visits. Sometimes, Brenda's husband came with her and seemed just as meticulous as Brenda.

Brenda had a birth plan that involved no pain meds, a special birthing chair that her husband had made, and a playlist for music to be played during labor. Ava found it amusing at one level but worrisome at another. In Ava's experience, women who came expecting labor to conform to their birth plan usually had the worst outcome—requiring every intervention that the person had wanted to avoid. Today, Ava breathed a sigh of relief that she wouldn't need to deal with Brenda's labor for at least another four months.

Ava exited the room after seeing Brenda and looked at the clock. The time showed 10:00, and Ava was surprised she had gotten no calls from GAAL about Susan. Just then, her cell phone flashed an incoming call from GAAL. It was the head nurse saying that Susan had just passed. The time of death was 9:55. Ava noted the time and even reached for a pen to write it down.

She didn't or couldn't allow herself to cry now with so many patients yet to be seen in the office. As she wrote "9:55," she briefly questioned why the time of death and the time of birth were so important—such insignificant facts.

Looking at the next chart, Ava was relieved it was a sports physical—a new patient. Entering, she found a tall, dark-haired teenager with his mother. The family had moved from Ohio last year, where Eric had played lacrosse. In Kentucky, he was going to play soccer. It seemed like a simple visit.

Ava went through some questions on the mandatory form. No, he had had no surgeries or illnesses, and he took no medicines. Then she came to the questions about mental health. "Are you sleeping?"

"No," he answered.

"Are you sad?" she continued.

He responded, "Yes."

Ava finally paid attention. "For how long?"

The boy said, "A week."

Ava pushed the computer away and looked at both Eric and his mom.

The mother said, "His best friend died in a car accident five days ago. He was the pallbearer for his funeral yesterday. He hasn't been sleeping, so I've been giving him melatonin. I know he needs to sleep."

Ava looked at the boy, whose head was down. She said, "That's hard. I can see why you are sad."

Tears came to her eyes as she remembered Susan and the reality that she would never see her again. Still, this was not the time for her sorrow. Attending this patient was her job now.

Ava tried to relay how grieving was essential and how, for every person, it was different. The boy's mother went on about how much melatonin she was giving him and how she had put it in his food. Outrage and frustration at how often people wanted to "medicate away" the pain of losing someone tormented Ava. She tried to respect this mother, who obviously cared for her son. Finally, she just told Eric that what he was going through was normal and that it would take time for him not to feel the degree of sadness he was feeling now. He nodded as if he appreciated this advice.

The next patient was a middle-aged woman who was returning for a follow-up after having her gallbladder removed. Ava had seen her a few weeks earlier when she was having some vomiting and nausea after eating. She had referred her for an ultrasound, which showed gallstones, and then she went on to surgery. She had undergone a laparoscopic cholecystectomy and was feeling much better. She was here today for a brief follow-up.

Ava remembered the most recent blog post of her friend Linda, which she had read on Sunday. The contrast of outcomes was hard to imagine, as was what life working in a foreign country would be like. The blog post was about a woman in Belize who died because she couldn't reach the hospital for treatment of her gallstones.

Ava shook her head and sat in her chair for a long time after reading that post. Linda's writings always shook her up. She couldn't imagine experiencing some of the things Linda talked about, but she also longed to have that kind of excitement in her life. Anything to break the sameness of her typical week. On the other hand, she wasn't sure how she would deal with events like this. Would she click into "doctor mode" and just deal? Or would she "freak out? In talking to Linda, she knew that some volunteers who worked in the clinic were not able to function. Would she be one of them?

Ava's ponderings were interrupted by laughter, and she reoriented herself to her surroundings. Pat, the funny X-ray tech, was holding an impromptu story time. Everyone was gathered around laughing. Ava joined the group and relaxed into hilarity. A dour-face preacher came out of an exam room and cast his usual look of scorn upon the group. The laughing stopped abruptly.

He mumbled, "Is this a professional office?"

Ava considered these moments of fun as the best part of her days.

Driving home after work, Ava turned off on a side road she had always been curious about—anything to distract her from thinking of Susan. The dirt lane veered off the paved route at a sharp angle in a dangerous curve. On the corner was the house she had imagined when she had thought of building her own home. Full-length windows lined the south side, and tall clerestory windows were above. A winding path led up to the front door. Shade trees and a beautiful fenced garden adorned the yard. Everything about the house welcomed her in. With no one about, she slowed even further and looked closely at the structure. She was tempted to pull into the circle driveway but thought about where she was and the approaching dusk.

She drove down the lane that curled through an abandoned tobacco field, then up a hill steep enough for switchbacks. A sharp cliff edge inched close on the passenger's side, and Ava felt a twinge of fear. In the past few years, Ava had become afraid of heights. Bridges were becoming a problem and sometimes she found alternate routes rather than cross long bridges—either walking or driving. This was a phobia she had never had as a child when she climbed trees and jumped from the high dive at the pool.

She continued winding up the mountain through a forest of trees still skirting the cliff's edge. Ava drove slowly and trembled when the gravel spun out under her tires. Halfway up the mountain, she saw a flash of color. The bright orange of a hunter's vest worn by a man with long, blond hair. He had broad shoulders, and she recognized the shape of a rifle across one. Running along beside the man was a beautiful golden retriever. Ava recalled a comment one of her young patients had made about white people having dreads. How bad they looked. This man walking in the middle of a forest at dusk sported long dreadlocks hanging below his orange cap.

As Ava passed, she and the man flashed the two-finger acknowledgment signal. Ava looked back in her rearview mirror and wondered where he had come from since there were no cars or visible houses. The forest canopies let in little sunlight, but she drove on. Finally, she came to what appeared to be the mountain's apex and noticed a small footpath heading off along the ridge. There was a small turnoff on the side of the road with a few discarded beer cans strewn about.

Ava had been to places like this before when she started exploring her new state. Usually, the most obscure paths led to unexpected waterfalls or rock formations. Her patients told her about the sites a few times, but she mostly found them by chance, like this one. She considered getting out of her car and walking on the path to discover what treasure it held. In her head, she said, "Dark path, getting lost, falling, and getting hurt, encountering bad people. What other warnings do you need? Getting lost will not bring Susan back."

Finally, opting for a sensible person's approach, she started the car up and continued along the road. As she knew it might, the road descended along similar hairpin turns until the lights of distant homes were visible. The road turned into asphalt, and she came to a recognizable neighborhood on the other side of town. From there, it was a shorter drive to her house than her usual, more direct route.

When she got home, she checked her phone for messages or calls from a pregnant patient who she expected might go into labor anytime. She listened to just one message from Gwen asking to take a walk soon. She ate her simple dinner of finger foods while sitting on the couch with a notebook, ready to write something profound about the night's adventure and the sadness of losing Susan. Instead, she picked up Taber's and read a page of words.

Abul-Abus

<u>Abul-Abus</u>

Notes *for Inside Taber's: A Study of the Medical Dictionary* by Dr. Ava

How often do I suffer from "abulia"? This is "the absence or decreased ability to exercise willpower, initiative or to make decisions." Maybe that would be a kinder, gentler way to refer to people with addictions. Alcohol abulia, oxycodone abulia, or the condition of abulia manifested in the teenage years.

Reading through this Cyclopedia, it is hard to imagine how words placed so close together could have such different meanings and such disparate associations. The next big word I encountered was "abuse." How to define abuse. And what a contrast between child abuse and laxative abuse. Here is an astounding quote from the book. "Of all deaths occurring in the US each year, substance abuse causes half." At first, I thought this statement had to be a mistake. What I forgot was the outcome of the long- or short-term use of the two most abused substances—tobacco and alcohol.

My thoughts on substance abuse. Recently, a doctor friend told me he had a new sympathy for patients who abused drugs. They were just trying to feel normal, especially those who are already addicted and are without the drugs their body craves. They feel bad. And maybe they started taking drugs because they felt bad enough to want to feel "normal"—their pain so distracting, their mood so low, their nerves so rattled, or their lives so dull.

Another friend uses drugs when he feels good. Some people use drugs when they feel bad to make them feel good. Which is the proper way to use drugs? In medicine, many drugs are OK to take when a person feels bad. Some drugs are perfectly acceptable, like Imitrex for a migraine, Valtrex for herpes, and antibiotics for an infected tooth. All these conditions involve pain, and these medicines have the side effect of pain relief, though not the primary mechanism of action. So why does the class of drugs whose primary mechanism is blocking pain fibers and nerve fibers related to pain, ex. Opioids cause the most problems with abuse. Modern medicine and modern science are missing some integral pieces of this puzzle.

10

Chapter 9: Considering Time

Ava had an easier rest of the week. She had no complaints from her colleagues, and all the nurses she worked with seemed to joke around with her as usual. She was able to discharge all of her patients from the hospital on Wednesday, so she didn't need to round on anybody the rest of the week. Work at the office was steady but not overwhelming.

On Friday morning, Ava started her day with the care plan meeting at GAAL. The staff were still processing Susan's death. She had been such a vibrant part of the facility.

Bonnie, the nurse who had been with Susan when she died, said, "It was such a peaceful death. I hope I die like that, surrounded by family."

Others in the room agreed. Gwen spoke up, "Susan was thrilled she could see her nieces graduate. It meant a lot to her. Thanks to everyone for making that possible."

Ava added, "Yes, I know that meant a lot. She knew it was staged early but said she felt better leaving knowing her girls were moving on. That must be hard to know you won't see them again."

Bonnie exclaimed, "Oh, but she will see them again in heaven. I know she will. I talked to Susan about that, and she had faith in Jesus. She'll see them again!"

Others in the room nodded their heads. Ava heard an "amen."

Ava said nothing else. She felt outnumbered. She glanced at the clock in the room and was alarmed to see it read 8:45 when she had patients starting at 8:30. "How could she be so late?" Her heart raced, and her underarms were suddenly damp as she hurriedly gathered her things. On her way past the aquariums and Susan's empty room, she noticed another clock correctly reset after the daylight savings time change. Her adrenaline charge didn't subside for several minutes, and she needed to sit in her car until she felt safe driving. This had never happened before, so she was surprised and thought maybe she was coming down with a cold.

There was a knock on her window. It was Gwen. Ava rolled down the window.

"Hey, I was just checking on you. Are you alright? You looked pretty stressed when you left," Gwen explained.

"I'm okay. I just thought I was going to be late. Turns out the clock in the conference room was an hour ahead."

"I've never seen you so upset, though. You're often late. Is there anything else bothering you? I know losing Susan has been hard, and what they said about heaven was kind of weird."

Ava reassured her, "No, it was just the time thing. I have gotten used to hearing those comments about reuniting in heaven. I nod and go on. Everything is okay. I better get rolling. Let's walk this weekend. I found a new spot I would like to show you."

"Okay, call me," Gwen said. Ava rolled the window up and headed for her office.

She breezed through her appointments and finished unusually early on Friday afternoon. Walking out the door, she and her colleague, Betty, decided to have dinner at the best Italian restaurant in town. They enjoyed a couple of glasses of wine, laughter, and a good time. Ava slept well that night.

She picked Gwen up early the following day and drove up the mountain to the pull-off Ava had found. No other vehicles or people were around, and they hiked about two miles on the path that eventually led to a beautiful waterfall and rocky ledge. Rock climbers had rigged up anchors on the limestone cliff, but no one was using them while they were there. The walk back was uneventful as the two women talked. Ava took another chance and shared some of her feelings about Susan dying.

"Gwen, besides what happened to Susan, I almost got into a serious car accident. It has been a tough couple of weeks."

"Oh", Gwen said. "I'm sorry."

Ava went on, "I'll miss Susan. She was so close to my age, and we talked about many things in the two years of knowing her.

Gwen agreed. "She seemed special. I didn't know her as well as you, but I'll miss her too. You know, I've never had anyone close to me die. Guess I'm lucky that way."

Ava wanted to change the subject of people dying when she felt her heart skipping beats. She said, "That near-miss car incident has got me thinking I need to slow down."

Gwen asked, "Your mother was in a car accident, wasn't she? You've never told me much about it."

Ava replied, "Yes. A man ran a red light and slammed into her. She never sped and was a very cautious driver. It wasn't fair. She didn't drive like me."

Gwen asked, "Were you and your mother close?"

Ava had to think about this question. She'd never felt they weren't close, but their relationship wasn't like the mother-daughter pairs she saw at the office. She couldn't imagine her mom sharing an intimate moment. For example, she couldn't see her mom in the room with her when she had a baby."

After a few moments, she told Gwen, "I don't know if we were close or not. I never thought about it while she was alive. She was my mother, and I always thought that was her role."

They continued walking, Ava in the rear, talking to Gwen's back.

"I know I loved her very much, and I miss her very much."

Gwen was quiet, so quiet that Ava wasn't sure she had heard. Finally, Gwen said, "You know, as I think of it, I don't know if my mom and I are that close. We live so far apart, sometimes I think my friends know me better than she does. But she will always know where I came from and my history better than anyone else. That would be the sad part of losing a parent, I guess. You lose that person who knows your history."

The pair walked on silently, enjoying the crisp air and the sounds of crunching leaves. Back at the car, Gwen took a chance and hugged Ava, even though she knew Ava was not a hugger. They rode back to town and promised to return someday.

Later at home, when Ava sat at her computer, she was glad that Linda had posted another entry on her blog. It would take her mind off Susan, her mom, the accident, and what to do about life. Linda talked about adapting to a new environment.

Ava thought, "In a way, I am becoming familiar with grief—my new environment."

Time was approaching for Ava to go to Belize for two weeks as a volunteer preceptor. All the necessary documents to obtain a temporary Belize license had been sent. She was trying to read up on what kinds of problems to expect. Linda talked to her on the phone several times and repeatedly reassured her she could handle patients' ailments.

She would stay at Linda's house, and they would do some traveling on the weekends. The only slightly troubling part was the small commuter plane to get to the remote clinic. All in all, though, Ava was quite excited.

Ava took the Cyclopedia and a notepad to the back porch on Sunday with her morning coffee. She vowed to make a dent in the As. She enjoyed reading the book but couldn't help noticing how much more she had to go. Her bookmark never moved because there were so many words on each page. When tempted to skip pages or even a single entry, she would say, "I don't want to miss what might be important in those sections." It felt like a compulsion.

Ava considered whether she might have some obsessive-compulsive tendencies. She didn't have habits like repetitive hand washing or avoiding cracks, the only behaviors society associated with this condition, sadly. But she had her list of uninvited "warnings,": "If I don't turn my pillow over, I'll have nightmares." When she brushed her teeth, she heard a doctor from a long-ago radio program saying, "Always brush for a full two minutes." There were more.

Ava considered one pivotal decision she made—to get divorced from Jack. She considered the pros and cons of such a move for weeks, maybe even months. "Was the marriage worth saving, or was it toxic?" Some days were good, and others were bad. There was no scientific or objective way to balance out her choices. She felt all alone in deciding.

Even though Jack was a crucial player, their conversations about the matter usually turned into an argument in which each blamed the other. Jack thought that if Ava could relax and love and respect him more, then they could work things out. Ava agreed that she had lost respect for Jack, and it was hard to gain back her trust.

Their relationship was suffering, but they were stuck in an endless blaming cycle. At some point, after all of Ava's perseverance, it became obvious the marriage was over. She didn't regret meeting Jack or getting married, but she regretted the months they stayed together when neither of them was happy.

It was like this commitment she had made to read *Taber's*. On a much different level of importance, of course. "Am I happy doing this, or has it become painful? No one told me to read the entire book."

But she couldn't stop. The knowledge gained would probably not help her on her next board certification test. As predicted, when she started the task, she looked up a lot and went into more depth on certain topics. She wasn't sure, though, if the new knowledge was helping her patients. Why was she writing down certain words? She recalled Ammon Shea's reason for including specific words in his book—words that he thought people would want to know about.

Ava, on the other hand, wrote about words she found interesting or connected with—an anecdote or a clinical situation she had seen. After much thought and weighing the pros and cons, she decided that reading *Taber's* was a form of relaxation for her if she could relax and read it.

Later in the day, Gwen called Ava and asked if she would want to go to a place called Yogaville the following weekend. There had been a cancellation, and Gwen wanted company. Ava reminded her friend that she didn't like to do yoga, but Gwen assured her this place was different. The yoga was only part of the experience, and the teachers demonstrated a more gentle, spiritual way of doing the poses. She explained she had been to Yogaville twice, and each visit had been special. Ava told Gwen she would think about it. Gwen offered it might be a path to slowing down.

She looked up Yogaville online and found the advertisement for the two-day retreat Gwen was referring to. They claimed there would be calm days of reflection, simple meals, and morning, noon, and evening meditation sessions. It was the ashram of Swami Satchidananda, an extremely difficult name to pronounce, as Ava found out later. After a few hours of consideration, she called Gwen up and said she would go.

Gwen said, "Great. And you will finally get to meet Sara. She will be meeting us there."

Ava looked forward to meeting Sara after hearing Gwen talk about her, and she was excited about the weekend.

"See you Friday afternoon," she said, and they decided on where and when to meet for the trip.

When the retreat began, Ava realized she had never participated in something as intense. She vacillated between silently scoffing at the activities and being wholly absorbed by them. The beautiful LOTUS shrine was particularly captivating, and when in meditation there each day, Ava felt oneness with the universe, like she had once experienced in a stairwell in Maine.

As interesting as the weekend was, the best part was meeting Sara. She was ten years younger than Ava and came to the retreat with her mother. Sara split her time between her new job in Kentucky and her old one in New York. And just as Gwen said, Sara was enchanting. At mealtimes, when participants could break their imposed silence and learn each other's stories, she was the center of everyone's attention.

Sara had the looks and body of a model. Her facial piercings highlighted her beauty, and she had an intricate tattoo on her chest—the ink was visible just above her sternum. Her eyes were bluish-green with a slight asymmetry that added to her overall beauty.

Ava thought later about meeting Sara and their subsequent friendship and realized that coming to understand the young woman's attitudes and thoughts had somehow shown Ava how conservative her own views were. How naïve she was in the realm of drugs, sex, and relations. And how closed-minded she was about mental illness.

At dinner, Ava asked Sara, "Why would you move to Kentucky?"

Sara responded, "I like it there. Do you ever feel like a place pulls you to it? Maybe because some of my family comes from Kentucky, but when I visit on vacations, I feel welcomed by the place. Not so much the people but the land. It's hard to explain."

"I think I know what you mean. I have lived in Kentucky for a decade and have no plans to leave. Do you think your clients will be different than in New York?"

Sara replied, "I don't think they will be that different. There may be less glamor and money, but similar issues exist with all humans. So far, I have enjoyed working with my new clients. It's just hard to leave my folks in New York. That's why I am taking a long time to transition."

"I get it. You become quite close to patients. I do anyway, sometimes."

They were quiet until dinner ended, and the evening yoga session began.

One session at Yogaville was an exercise of trust connected with helping someone in distress. As an MD, Ava reflected on her lengthy educational curriculum and regretted not having paid more attention to these types of role-playing exercises. They consistently paled in importance to the hard-core sciences and the emphasis on biochemistry, anatomy, pathology, etc. In this trust-building exercise, the leader asked participants to assume one of three roles: the person needing help, a person offering help who is unhelpful, and, finally, an effective helper.

Wanda, the leader, divided the group. Each triad was given a unique setting. Ava was paired with Sara and a contemplative older woman. Their assignment was to help a person who was deathly afraid of water to cross a small stream. Ava knew there were more details—making the situation an urgent scene, but she could only recall her feelings and realizations.

In the first round, the older woman was the ineffective helper, and Sara was the helpless victim. As the third actor, Ava just observed this round. She heard the older woman utter repeated assurances to Sara that it was OK. She loudly shouted that she must hurry. That this was an emergency. She must act quickly. Just breathe. Everything would be OK. The words sounded as hollow as a drum. Ava sadly recognized how often she had said the same thing to patients who were stuck in a frightening situation.

This had happened in labor. She remembered saying words like, "It will be OK, everything is going to be OK, you can do it." The volume increased in direct proportion to the woman's resistance. It happened more often during the second stage of labor—when the baby was being pushed out, and the mother was exhausted and ready to give up.

The labor nurse and Ava would become a two-person cheering section. "PUSH, just a little longer. She's almost there. I can see the head. Push harder." Ava had never experienced labor, so she didn't know how the laboring mother felt about this encouragement.

Back at Yogaville, when the two-minute timer buzzed, the group of three changed roles, and Ava became the one needing help. Sara was the effective helper. A strange transformation came over Ava as she imagined herself at the edge of the stream, paralyzed with fear. She became immobile. Unable to move. This had never happened in her life. She was always expected to function. To respond to the most frightening situation. To patients who had stopped breathing or babies who did not take a breath immediately or codes or bleeding arteries. She had never had the luxury of not acting. In this moment of the fake scene, she realized what her patients with panic attacks were feeling and how they were also paralyzed, how the bland reassurances were of no use.

This is when Sara stepped in and came close enough to Ava that she could feel her body heat. Sara had subtly gauged her nearness by Ava's body language. Sara matched her breathing pattern to Ava, and they breathed in unison for a few moments. Then Sara slowed her breathing, and Ava glimpsed the other's arm, moving up and down in time with her slowed breathing. Sara said nothing but continued her unhurried and fluid arm movements. She whispered, "Watch my arm and not the water." This simple distraction was enough to calm Ava, and she slowed her breathing. And with that, the timer sounded, and Ava's mind returned to the room. This experience of being paralyzed by an imagined threat—Ava realized was how her patients felt. It was real.

After the exercise, Ava thanked Sara for her help and complimented her on her gentleness. Sara explained that panic attacks also often troubled her. She understood the paralysis and the resistance to most people's reassuring comments at the time of these attacks.

When Ava returned from Yogaville, she sat on her couch and consciously wondered where her feet were. This was a technique for centering she had learned at Yogaville. She made herself feel the weight of her own body indenting the cushion, like floating in the womb. She needed to find something that could suspend time like this exercise suspended her body. She had to carve out more time in the day.

Her eyes fell on two objects—her guitar and her *Taber's*. They both gave her immense pleasure, and while she engaged in playing one and reading the other, she lost track of time. That was her answer. Spending more time on these activities lengthened her time. If she couldn't practically cut back on her professional duties, then she would alter how she spent her free time. She would commit herself to reading *Taber's* and practicing the guitar as often and as much as possible. She would start this plan tomorrow. That night, she slept like a log and awoke full of energy and resolve.

Ara-Acm

Ara-Acm

Notes for *Inside Taber's: A Study of the Medical Dictionary* by Dr. Ava

Acardiacus (a'-ka'r-d i'a-kus)—what a beautiful word with a rhythm of its own. This lyrical term describes a parasitic twin without a heart. Sometimes, even knowing Latin does not prepare me for these words.

The term for the order to which many ticks and mites belong rhymes with the small musical flute-like instrument—an ocarina. The "Acarina" has an accompanying list of accessory words—acaricide, acariasis, acarodermatitis, acarology, and acarophobia-which also includes fear of small objects.

Surprisingly, the book questions itself. Under the entry "accident-prone," they report, "the validity of this concept (persons having an unusually high rate of accidents) is questionable." Wow, this book is humble.

I will eventually be bothered by a condition related to "accommodation," how the eye adjusts to focus on objects at various distances. This is a complicated process of changing the curvature of the lens by contracting the ciliary muscles, which causes increasing rounding of the lens. At the same time, the pupil contracts, and magically, divinely, and evolutionally, the optic axes converge to produce a clear image on the retina. Clearly, that is for people under fifty who don't have presbyopia and are still accommodating.

The next section is dull. Believe it or not—all the "a"-something, "a" being the absence of. There is a sadness that so much can be negated with this letter. For example, "acephalochiria"—"a congenital absence of the head and hands." Or "acheilia"—"the congenital absence of one or both lips." The word "ache" breaks up the dryness of this section between the fix-ation on vinegar (all the acetic derivations) and the acids. Ache as a noun seems very medical or clinical, but ache as a verb has universal appeal.

Interestingly, both acme and acne come from the Greek word "akme"—point. I never knew Acme had any meaning other than in the Road Runner cartoon. And I certainly have never described a portion of labor as the "acme." I might start, though.

Chapter 10: Songs And Strategies

Ava arrived early for her guitar lesson while Rosella was in a back room with another student. Now that she had committed to playing her guitar as often as possible, she took weekly lessons for a full hour. She was getting better and felt calmer whenever she picked up the instrument.

Sitting on a stool waiting for Rosella, Ava recognized a familiar piece from Suzuki book #1. Ava lived with one of her classmates and his family for six months in medical school. The oldest daughter was learning to play the violin, and every day, Ava would hear songs from this Suzuki Method book wafting down to her basement room. She hadn't minded the squeaks and off-pitch notes because the setting was so beautiful.

They lived on the shores of Lake Michigan, and Ava's basement room opened up to the beach. Out on the lawn rested a Hobie Cat that the family sailed on most weekends. She developed a lifelong love of the activity there. She never found time to sail in Kentucky.

Looking around the music store, Ava noticed the chairs in the jamming corner were in disarray. Must have been a lively group there last night.

A wall under the shelves of old accordions caught her eye, and she moved some boxes to get a better look. She had never noticed this area before. Several framed photos were hanging in the dark, the shadow of the overhanging shelves nearly hiding the set. She used her phone flashlight to illuminate them. The first was of a young family of four. A smiling woman with a taller man, a boy, and a girl were all captured in mid-laugh. Both kids held child-sized guitars that made an arch in front of the photogenic group. It looked like the photo was taken in a park with purple and turquoise lilacs in full bloom in the background.

The next photo appeared to be the same two children, now as teenagers. The parents weren't in this picture, but the guitars were held in the same upright position, again providing symmetry to the pair. In this one, Ava could clearly see that the girl was Rosella. The same lithe body, same smile. She assumed the boy was her brother, as they resembled each other. Though it was a still photograph, there was a liveliness to it, as if even the paper couldn't contain the two's energy.

The third photograph was of a band with two guitarists and a drummer. She recognized Rosella and her brother on guitars and a dark-complexioned, bushy-haired man on drums. Just visible in the foreground were the backs of heads, presumably fans at the edge of the stage. Again, the energy of the moment seeped out. She would guess Rosella was in her mid-twenties in this picture. There were no other photos on the wall and no captions or explanations. Ava knew Rosella had been a gifted musician her whole life but knew little about her life before moving to Kentucky. She wondered how to ask about the photos since Rosella had never mentioned having a brother. As she heard Rosella finish up with her violin student, Ava moved stealthily away from the wall and flicked off her flashlight.

Rosella and her student walked out of the practice room together. They were laughing. Mary, a girl of about eight or nine, always had her lesson before Ava, so she had seen her in the store before. The school bus dropped Mary off at Redbud Music after school, and when Rosella had an extra few minutes, she drove her home. Ava believed Rosella did this with a good number of her students. Transportation was a significant barrier for some kids to participate in after-school activities like music lessons, so Rosella and other volunteers provided rides. The community of music lovers also made sure those kids had instruments. Not cast-off student rentals but good-sounding ones.

When Rosella heard that a child wanted to play a fiddle or a trumpet, she would contact the child's caregivers. It wasn't always their parents; about half the time, a grandparent raised the child. And often, kids' homes were small, with collections of relatives living in them. So, Rosella would try to assess what would work for each family to allow the student to practice at home.

Many stressed-out families did not welcome the extra chaos of a blaring horn or incessant drumming. Noise control was an issue. Rosella and some other of her staff would do a "site visit" if the family agreed. They talked about simple measures to improve sound dampening in the home or set up a reasonable practice time. Kids lived in trailers in this community and shared bedrooms, so they couldn't always retreat to a distant space. Rosella had a supply of powerful 3M noise-blocking headphones and quality mutes to distribute. But mostly she shared with all of them her love of music.

Ava made her way to the practice room and unpacked her guitar. Rosella soon joined her after giving a few instructions to Jamie, a high school student who came in to help at the store every day after school. Rosella's two full-time employees were on vacation this week, and several boxes of recording equipment had arrived by UPS.

Rosella told Jamie, "Be careful how you handle those boxes. We may have to send them back. I may have overspent my budget." She walked back to the practice room.

Settling in, Rosella asked, "How are you? How has your week been? How did you like the discussion on Friday night?"

Ava tried to answer the questions in order but concentrated on the last. The speakers from FNE were engaging and animated. The same couple who had written the book about the homeless. Their prepared remarks about the unhoused were easy to follow, and Ava learned some things she did not know. She liked how they knew specifics about the local housing situation.

Ava went on when Rosella asked her to explain an unsaid "but."

Ava explained, "Well, Kerry made me uncomfortable. Her attitude that the unhoused should bear all responsibility for the problem made me mad. I had difficulty not saying something to her and stewed over it all evening. I know she has a different perspective, having grown up with her alcoholic father and doing everything on her own, but she thinks everyone can do that."

Rosella listened, then was quiet for a moment.

"I know Kerry can be forceful and righteous about her opinions. Sometimes, I also have to bite my tongue in response to some of the things she says. We disagree on many issues, but I like Kerry and don't think she makes comments from an evil place. She truly feels her approach is the most heartfelt way. I can't explain my tolerance for her, but somehow, I do. If it's any consolation, other people have asked me not to invite her anymore, and I always tell them no. I don't want to be around people who are just like me or think just like me."

Ava replied, "I know you are right, but it is much easier to be carbon copies."

They both laughed.

Rosella had been helping Ava find the best way to play and sing the song "Goodbye" by Steve Earle. She had no idea where the doctor had found this song or the other sad songs she had picked to sing, but she listened closely as she played the opening riff.

Not just the lyrics but the chord sequence was sad, especially as Rosella thought about Earle's son's tragic struggle with addiction. Rosella remembered sharing a stage with Justin Townes Earle with her band. A tear came to her eye as Ava soberly sang the tune.

"I've wondered," Rosella asked as Ava finished the song, "why do you pick such sad songs to sing?" Last month, she had been working on "Just Breathe," sung by Eddie Vedder—another poignant song.

Ava took a long time to answer and mumbled she didn't know why. "The voices mostly. They pull something out of my heart when I hear them. I want to make that sound."

The two sat quietly for a while. Rosella knew that Ava's mother was killed in an accident, but Ava never talked about it. When she first started playing guitar a couple of years ago, Ava talked a little about her divorce and explained that was her motivation for picking up the guitar. She decided to open up about her sadness.

"Have I ever told you why I started running triathlons?"

Ava looked up and shook her head back and forth.

Rosella began, "I had a brother named Roger. He was a year and a half younger than me."

Ava interrupted, "I saw his picture out there."

Rosella nodded. "Yes, I'm surprised you found those photos. I hide them from myself, really. We were very close. We did everything together. We even formed a band."

Ava interjected, "I saw."

Rosella continued, "We called ourselves R and Me. Playing was the best. Then Roger got sick, and he didn't live. He was only twenty-eight."

Ava gasped.

"He had the worst kind of leukemia." Rosella continued, "After he died, my heart ached so much that all I wished for was to feel a different emotion. Something that would overpower the pain, the sadness. Late at night, I would walk along the darkest part of my street where there were no lights. There was a canopy of overhanging trees that blocked all the light. It was the darkest and scariest place I could find, but even this black path couldn't push out my memories, the what-ifs, the regret— the grief."

Ava asked how long it lasted and if it ever lessened. Rosella admitted that a few months after his death, she had signed up to fly to LA and work at a homeless shelter in the worst part of the city—in the most dangerous neighborhood, where volunteers were warned not to venture out of the shelter at night or alone.

"I tried to find the most intense experience to lift this ever-present sadness. In the end, I didn't go to LA," she said.

Ava wondered what made her change her mind but didn't press Rosella for an answer and let her continue.

Rosella's voice was now just a whisper, "About six months after he passed, I saw a notice about a triathlon in the city where he lived. The route passed by his house. Had he been sitting in his chair by the window and alive, he would have seen the race participants stream by. I had never run a triathlon before and had never even considered it, but at that moment, I knew this would bring me peace. At least some comfort. So, on the anniversary of his death, I ran in that triathlon and stumbled past his former apartment."

Rosella described her many weeks of rigorous training and how she endured monotonous lap swimming at the pool and endless arm strokes tracking a path from one lake buoy to the next. She used every Sunday to take long and lonely bike rides on the berm of dangerous, curvy roads. Hardest of all, she built her running prowess with exhausting intervals up and down her narrow street—all the while thinking of Roger. "On the day of the race, as I passed by his house, there were tears, but I had a strong feeling that this was how I wanted to—no, I needed to memorialize him. When I finished, my parents were there and wrapped me in their arms. My mom and dad had gotten so they couldn't talk about Roger—even though he was always on their minds. I think this was as close as we all came to acknowledging the loss as a family."

Ava sat back and breathed. The story was so personal, so deep. She knew of nothing to say and hesitantly touched Rosella's arm. Even as she maintained physical contact with her friend, she thought about how she felt the same way when her mother died. Unexplainably, this thought brought her fear that she would break down and open a wound, a pain so deep she wouldn't recover.

She looked around the room to reorient and felt like an observer of the scene rather than a player. Doubts came into her mind—what should she say, how should she act? Would it be the time to mention her own tragedy? Something stopped her from being truly part of the moment and responding spontaneously.

Everything needed to be calculated. What would Rosella think of her if she said the wrong thing? What could she say that would be the most appropriate? Before much time had gone by, Ava thought about being late. Despite herself, she felt impatient at Rosella for taking so much time out of the lesson. Some part of her recognized the intimacy of this conversation, but her mind could not relax the rules of schedules and propriety.

Ava looked at her watch discreetly and apologized to Rosella, saying she had to go. She had arranged a home visit for a patient, and the palliative care nurse, Judy, was waiting to meet her. Ava was relieved she could place her emotions on hold while she rushed off. Walling off unpleasant feelings was a skill she learned early in medicine.

<<<<<<<<<<<<<<<<<<<

*It's 2005.*I am a second-year medical student, and on my first ICU rotation at the hospital when I met my first patient, Karen. She's the same age as me. We are both twenty-two. Karen was diagnosed with leukemia a few months before I met her and was not doing well. Her platelet count was so low she needed daily platelet transfusions. She lived in the ICU while being treated for sepsis and other complications. Every day was a roller coaster. One day, she would rally; the next, plummet.

Most days, I sit by Karen's bedside and watch what happens. We talk. We get close. One day, she offers me one of her government-issued marijuana joints. Luckily, I don't take it since those pre-rolled sticks are later found to have aspergillus, further complicating Karen's treatment.

While Karen is in ICU bed #10, my other assigned patient is in ICU bed #8. She is also in the unit the whole time I am there. I sit by her bedside, but I rarely talk to her. Most of the time, she is barely conscious. She is an older woman who tried to kill herself with a rifle. She failed but blasted through several major arteries in her abdomen and pelvis. She has undergone an amputation of one leg and many operations and received numerous transfusions. The amount of care and resources provided to this woman is equal to those given to Karen.

I don't get to know the other woman. Her family sometimes comes to visit, but there is a huge contrast between Karen's family and this family. I have little sympathy for this woman who was sick by choice—not like Karen.

Had I known anything about the "Social Determinants of Health" and the effects of poverty, discrimination, and generational trauma, I would have excused this woman for trying to kill herself. During the whole month of caring for those two patients, I wrestle with the ethical dilemma of treating patients who self-harm and those who are sick through no fault of their own. I have a stomach ache every day from this feeling of outrage, sadness, confusion, and helplessness. Sometimes, it's so severe I go into the hospital chapel to lie down. So, I stop having feelings. My classmates did the same thing.

<<<<<<<<<<<<<<<<<

Some girls were entering Redbud and passed Ava on her way out.

One girl asked Rosella, "Why was that woman whistling when she looked so sad?"

****

Ava reached her office to find Judy, her nurse, waiting outside, ready for their home visit. The two asked how each was. They had made many trips to homes together, and Ava looked at Judy like she might be a therapist. Maybe Judy was aware of how important these trips were to Ava's mental health—maybe she wasn't. Someday, Ava vowed to tell her.

The patient they were seeing was a boy who had Lesch-Nyhan Syndrome. Last evening, Ava had jumped ahead in *Taber's* to see how the authors described this rare condition. She learned on page 1226 that it was named for M. Lesch, born 1939, and William Leo Nyhan, born 1926, both US pediatricians. Why one would need to know their birthdates confounded Ava. "An inherited metabolic disease that affects only males, in whom mental retardation, aggressive behavior, self-mutilation, and renal failure are exhibited. Biochemically, there is excess uric acid production owing to a virtual absence of an enzyme essential for purine metabolism." This was another of Ava's palliative care patients with a disease notable for being in NORD—National Organization for Rare Diseases. An interesting list clinically but devastating for individual families.

This boy was cared for by his family in a way that Ava wished all children were cared for. His mother knew everything about the disease and provided full-time care to her son to lessen his symptoms. He could not ambulate, and with the many spasms he had, it was even more challenging for him to be positioned in a wheelchair. At ten years of age, he was getting too heavy for the family to carry him easily, so they designed a track system in their house with help from home health and other programs. A track ran from Daniel's bed to the living room along the ceiling. Ava had seen nothing like this before, but it worked well. They lived in a smallish, three-bedroom home with little room for maneuvering a large specially designed wheelchair, so the track system with a Hoyer worked well. Daniel's mom swung him out to a giant beanbag chair in the living room every morning so he could be stimulated by the family's and his dog's antics. So much love was present in that home.

Judy and Ava walked in to find Daniel having intermittent severe spasms and contractions. They talked at length with his mom about how to manage these. It seemed that every week, Daniel was getting worse despite maximal medications and trials of various approaches. The goal was to keep him out of the hospital and comfortable with minimal sedation.

Daniel had an older sister who lived in the home as well. She helped a lot with his care. She also knew that if she had a child, and it was male, he would be at very high risk of developing this same disease she watched her brother suffer from. A disease her brother would eventually die from. Daniel's mother mentioned that his sister was learning to play the guitar and that having music in the house was surprisingly soothing for Daniel and had seemed to calm him, even while his sister was starting to put chords together. His mom praised the music teacher who came to their home to give lessons because getting the sister, Amy, to the music store was nearly impossible with the care her brother required. Ava asked the teacher's name and wasn't surprised to hear the mom say Rosella.

After leaving Daniel's home, Judy and Ava stopped for ice cream. They talked about how hard it must be to see your child decline. Daniel was perfectly normal until he was about two. Judy had a nice way of appreciating people and the sacrifices they made to care for their loved ones. Ava noted that Judy didn't seem to compartmentalize her feelings the way she did. Without overthinking this, she just enjoyed being around Judy.

When Ava arrived home that evening, she thought about reading more of *Taber's*. She was fulfilling her commitment to reading the Cyclopedia as often as possible. She still found that time stood still while poring over the words. She thought it was helping her slow down. Today, though, she decided to learn more about the original book that inspired her project.

She ordered the book off Amazon and had it on her Kindle within minutes. *Reading the OED: One Man, One Year, 21,730 pages*, was compact, 232 pages with no pictures. Ava began reading and didn't look up from the pages until her stomach was undeniably growling.

The author, Ammon Shea, was funny, and his comments about the physical realities of reading the OED were hilarious. Ava liked the way he blended the word definitions into his real life. His history of reading "word books" from a young age made Ava feel like an imposter. There were people who read dictionaries, encyclopedias, and even telephone books regularly. What did she know about this field?

She could relate to something Shea wrote early on about why he had put off reading the OED. He explained that he put it off for two reasons: one, he wouldn't have the adventure to look forward to, and second, he was afraid of abandoning the effort partway through. Ava thought of this possibility as she made little progress in *Taber's.*

While Shea admitted he wrote down some words that he thought people would like to know about, Ava recorded and commented on words that she knew about. The words that had sparked a memory from her doctoring history. She and Shea may have had different motivations in many forms. Reading on in his book, she made a note that the only intersection of their two fields was when he defined "iatrogenic" (pertaining to symptoms caused unintentionally by a doctor) on page 85 and added the comment, *I cannot think of a single word that means 'cured by a doctor.' This is why I do not go to the doctor.*

For reference, when Ava looked up "iatrogenic" in *Taber's,* there was so much more, including descriptions of using a Foley catheter causing infections and chemotherapy causing nausea, vomiting, and hair loss. There was even a statement that in the US, healthcare errors are among the most common causes of mortality. Clearly, *Taber's* maintained its medical focus.

Ava was happy that Ammon Shea had discovered some of the same things she had about reading such a book. Like any great book, he wrote that the OED elicited reactions like laughing out loud or sobbing. "All the human emotions and experiences are right there in this dictionary, just as they would be in any fine work of literature. They just happen to be alphabetical." He thought, like Ava, that reading the OED was a privilege, not so much a task. And sometimes, when he encountered several pages of unknown or previously unheard words, he thought of himself as a visitor in a foreign country. Ava liked that description.

Ava also wanted to listen again to the interview with Scott Simon that had sparked her interest in this endeavor. Much to her chagrin and surprise, upon searching, she discovered it wasn't Scott Simon who interviewed Shea—it was Renee Montagne, another of the NPR hosts. So, it probably wasn't on a Saturday. She did not know why she had misremembered or imagined the entire interview. At any rate, Shea says in an actual interview that reading the book was a moving experience, and he felt sadness when he finished. Ava sensed that her reading of *Taber's Cyclopedic Medical Dictionary* would also be monumental.

Acr-Act

<u>Acr-Act</u>

Notes for *Inside Taber's: A Study of the Medical Dictionary* by Dr. Ava

The word "acro-osteolysis" is one I have never heard. It has two meanings. The first is "a familial disease causing dissolution of the tips of the bones in the extremities of young children." The second meaning is "an occupational disease of those who come in contact with the vinyl chloride polymerization process and involves, in addition to other findings, bone destruction of the distal phalanges of the hands."

A quick Google search confirms this malady nicknamed "Vinyl Chloride Disease" and alerts me to all the hazards of vinyl. There is even the chance of toxicity from the vinyl in a car and "outgassing." Most of the plants that perform this polymerization are located along the Gulf coast in Texas and Louisiana. In the PVC "kettles," not all the Vinyl Chloride Monomer is consumed, and varying amounts are trapped in every finished product fabricated from PVC resins. I have used PVC tubing for many things over the years, even giving some to kids to play with. The reading implies this is not fully disclosed as a hazard to the hundreds of workers or consumers of these products.

That's what I like about reading this book or life in general. I was thinking about how boring reading had become when this new avenue developed.

Here is another word that breaks the monotony. "Action" and all its descriptors. Bactericidal action that kills bacteria; ball-valve action—

intermittent obstruction of a passageway or opening (like with a clot or thrombus in the heart). The word "activator" has three meanings: 1) a substance that converts an inactive molecule into an active agent; 2) any substance that specifically induces an activity; and 3) (complete non sequitur) a removable orthodontic appliance that is also called a myofunctional appliance. The range of meanings is phenomenal.

14 █

Chapter 11: One Year Earlier

September 3-The Day of the Accident

<<<<<<<<<<<<<<<<<<<<<<<<<<<

My beeper went off around seven and I called the familiar number of the labor floor. I wasn't surprised Delores, one of my OB patients, was in labor. I often had a premonition when someone was going into labor. This was Delores's first baby, so I figured I would be at the hospital most of the day.

Dressing quickly into my jeans (since it was a Saturday), I went to the hospital to check on Delores and visit several other patients. It was Labor Day weekend, so the roads and the hospital hallways were quiet.

I liked the staff who were working. They were all good, no-nonsense types, and I felt comfortable around them. Over the years, we shared lots of patients, stories, and tense situations.

When I arrived at the nursing station on the fourth floor—the labor ward—the head nurse told me Delores was having regular contractions every three minutes, and she was already five centimeters. Everything looked good.

I sat down at the small counter that served as the nursing station. There was barely room for three stools; it was a compact and sometimes crowded area. If I looked up from charting on the computer, I could see the nursery clearly through a large window above the desk. This Saturday, four or five swaddled babies were in their rolling bassinets. An older nursery nurse was watching them and soothing them when they cried. I always found that scene of swaddled babies precious. When I picked one of the bundles up and smelled a baby's head, I longed to be married again. Weird.

I grumbled with the nurses good-heartedly about working a holiday. Bonnie, the RN, and Chris, a nursing assistant, were helping with Delores. I talked to them about Delores's pregnancy and her home life. She was young and unmarried but seemed to handle pregnancy well. Her mother and the boyfriend were already in the labor room and had been at all of her prenatal visits. There was no indication that her labor would be anything but normal.

As I sat there waiting, I thought about how most pregnancies and labor were "normal." But there was always a chance things could change, and in a literal heartbeat, the situation became an emergency. It was an odd situation that always made me feel this undercurrent of stress amid the joy of a delivery.

I had, of course, recognized that the more we monitored and intervened with the natural labor process, the more likely there would be something to worry about. On the flip side, we wouldn't be aware of the problems without the monitoring. I never truly relaxed when someone was in labor.

I went to Delores's room and saw her treated like a queen. Delores's mother was in a chair on the left, and her boyfriend was closer to the hospital bed on the right. Momentarily, Delores smiled and laughed while she sipped iced water. Suddenly, a contraction took over, and the atmosphere changed. Ray, the baby's father, grimaced, and the mother instructed Delores to breathe as they had learned at Lamaze classes. The contraction lasted about a minute. I could see beads of sweat forming on the young woman's forehead.

I stood quietly until the contraction ended, and a small smile returned to Delores's face.

"How are you doing?" I asked, trying to mask the absurdity of the question.

Delores answered, "OK. Man, these things hurt. How long do you think it will be?"

I came to the side of the bed and answered, "You're doing very well with your breathing and having your family right here. It's usually about a centimeter every hour, and you're already past five, so maybe another few hours."

Delores groaned, "So long?"

"Well, let me check and see if you've made progress since the nurse checked you. Is that OK?"

Delores said, "Yes."

I gently examined her and announced, "Wow, you're already seven centimeters, so you're making great progress. Just hang in there. Are you doing OK with the pain? I know you said you didn't want to use medicines if you didn't have to."

Delores shook her head, "I'm OK now. I still want to do it naturally."

Her boyfriend squeezed her hand. I stayed through a few more contractions, then ambled out to the nurse's station. There were no other women in labor. The ward was pleasantly quiet. I thought I would have time to leave the floor and check on a couple of hospital patients.

When I returned a half-hour later, there had been a significant change. Bonnie told me that Delores wanted to push.

She said, "I didn't check because I thought you would want to. I was just about to page you to come back."

I replied, "Sounds good. Thanks. "

In the room, I saw a completely different scene. Delores was visibly perspiring, her bed sheets were soaked, and she was no longer smiling between contractions.

I spoke encouragingly, "It sounds like you have made great progress. Do you mind if I check and we get this baby out?"

Delores nodded. When I checked her, there was just a tiny rim of the cervix left around the baby's head. It was easy to push it out of the way, and I was relieved that the baby's head was positioned just right to move on down and out.

I told Delores, "Everything looks good. It's time to push. Now, the work of labor begins, Delores. Follow what your body is telling you to do."

The nursing assistant, Chris, was preparing things for delivery. She went to the head of the bed and instructed Delores about how to push. Delores was a fit woman and could easily bring her knees towards her chest.

Chris said, "When the urge comes, hold on to your knees with your hands and push down like you are having a bowel movement. It will feel weird, I know, but that is how the baby will come out."

With the next push, Delores tried to push, but she mainly was blowing air out of her cheeks. The next contraction was more effective, and her perineum bulged with each push.

"You are doing great," I said, glimpsing the baby's head.

I asked the mom and boyfriend, "Do you want to see the baby's hair—it's here?"

Neither of them took the opportunity. The woman's firm grip on their hands kept them pretty well confined to their positions beside Delores.

I rushed out to wash my hands and change into scrubs. When I returned, more of the head was visible. The subsequent few pushes made tremendous progress, but with each contraction, the fetal heartbeat dropped, and there was a relatively slow recovery back to its baseline.

I urged, "Come on, Delores, your baby wants to come out; push as hard as you can."

With the next contraction, more of the baby's head was visible. Now, about the size of a child's teacup saucer. With the next, the view expanded to an adult cup saucer size. I fleetingly thought of how many sizes of things in medicine were described as food items—like a normal ovary is about the size of an almond, how we use food terms to describe abnormalities—a strawberry tongue seen with Kawasaki's or a café au lait spot on a baby's skin. There were lots of references.

Bonnie and I positioned ourselves at the end of the bed. The baby was within a push or two of delivering, but I was still concerned about the heartbeat.

"OK, with this push, give me everything you have."

The next push didn't advance the baby much.

I said more emphatically, "Delores, OK, the baby needs to come out. His heartbeat is low, and we need to get him out. With the next push, I want you to give it everything you have."

And with the next push, Delores pushed the boy out.

I delivered the head, suctioned the mouth briefly, and delivered the rest of the baby, noting the cord wrapped tightly around his neck. He didn't cry immediately and appeared stunned. I quickly placed the cord clamps and cut the cord, handing the baby to Bonnie. She whisked him to the nearby warmer, drying him and suctioning more fluid from his mouth.

I delivered the placenta and stepped to the warmer. Bonnie was stimulating the baby, but he was slow to respond, and he had no effective respirations. I grabbed a suction catheter, my heartbeat racing, and snaked it down the back of his throat. In sync with the loud sound of the suction, the baby let out a cry. Everyone in the room took a breath as well. The baby continued to cry and began moving his arms and legs. Normal. The team wrapped him loosely in a blanket and placed him on Delores's bare chest. She was ecstatic. Her mother and boyfriend were relieved.

I went back to the foot of the bed and assured myself that Delores had stopped bleeding and noted on inspection that there were no tears or injuries to her perineum. I helped the nurses clean up the blood-soaked linens. Delores was tucked under a warm blanket and cuddled with her new baby within minutes.

I barely had time to take in the serenity when my beeper announced a call waiting from the operator. I unknowingly went to the nurse's station to pick up the phone.

The hospital operator had received a call from an emergency room in Michigan trying to reach Dr. Levine. Our kind switchboard operator somehow knew the call held bad news and arranged for a pastoral staff member, a nun, to sit next to me when I took the call.

I began in my business voice, "This is Dr. Levine." I expected this other hospital to call me about a patient transfer or something medical. However, I wondered why from Grand Rapids, Michigan.

"Is this Dr. Ava Levine?" the voice on the line said. Then she continued, "This is the emergency room at St. Mary's. There has been an accident involving your parents."

"What?" I uttered. Still not understanding what was happening.

"Your parents were in a car accident. A very serious accident."

My questions began, "Oh no, was anyone hurt? Where are my parents now?"

"I am so sorry, but your mother died in the accident. Your father is alive but injured. He is in the emergency room at a different hospital."

"Oh." I found nothing to say. My heart stopped. The nun sitting next to me put her arm around me. I hung up the phone. I sat in the office chair at the desk, looking out at the swaddled babies, and watched them weigh Delores's newborn. My eyes still functioned, but not my brain.

After a few minutes, I walked to a dark hallway and leaned against a wall, soon collapsing into a heap on the floor. The nun followed me but stood a distance away. Tears streamed down my face as I tried to grasp what I had been told.

I knew I had to go to Michigan and get there soon. An instinct kicked in, and I called my closest medical partner to say I needed to leave town and ask if they would cover for me. I went into the locker room to change. I drove home, where Gwen was waiting. I don't know how she found out so quickly.

I packed quickly, remembering a black dress, and drove away. I drove on autopilot through the night, arriving at my dad's bedside early in the morning. My brother Ted was already there, and we just stared at each other. When I talked to my dad and knew he wasn't going to die, all my instinctive behavior stopped.

I remember little after that. A funeral, lots of people, a burial, a ride down the highway following the hearse, my dad being released after the funeral, and watching the taped version with him.

On the day my dad was to be discharged, he stood up and passed out and was discovered to have a ruptured spleen. He went for emergency surgery, and during the chaos of the medical personnel preparing him for the operation, I held his hand.

Just as he was being wheeled into the operating room, he looked at me and whispered, "I love you." The first time ever.

I told him I loved him.

Dad survived the surgery and went home a week later to a house where everything was the same as when the two of them left for a routine errand the day of the accident. Ted and I went to get stuff out of the wrecked car and found one of Mom's shoes. We talked to the ER doctor who had seen their mom. The doctor told them with tears in his eyes that Margaret had not suffered. The autopsy showed that her aorta had been severed at the moment of impact. He said she felt nothing.

I returned to work, and people told me how sorry they were. It was all a blur. Sometimes, I seemed fine, but then, unexpectedly, I was overcome with sadness. Driving in a car for any long distance meant unbearable heartache. I went to a movie with a funeral scene three months after the accident and had to leave midway. The pain was overwhelming. So powerful sometimes I couldn't breathe. I tried to read books on dying and remember one catchphrase—"hunt the good stuff." None of it made me feel better.

Chapter 12: Making Music At Redbud

One of Rosella's favorite things to do was give tours of her store. Not the physical aspects of the building but rather the contents of Redbud Music. The structure was a brick storefront on the town's main street. This building had been a music store for as long as most people in the town could remember. A family named McClain had owned it before Rosella. They were a very musical family, and their four kids formed a band and traveled on tour during the '80s and '90s. None of the offspring wanted to manage a music store, so the parents sold the business, including all inventory. This ad that Rosella had seen prompted her to move to Kentucky. After meeting Rosella and Cal on their exploratory trip from New York, the McClains were convinced Rosella was the right person to take over the business. They sold it to her for a reasonable price and introduced her to the requirements of the music trade industry. Richard and Lois, Ava, and Cal remained dedicated supporters of youth access to music and continued volunteering with Rosella's projects.

Rosella used the experts who had helped manage R and Me as her business team. Her accountant, Bob, took care of the finances. Roberta, her PR person from the band, was more than willing to help with promotion and successfully brought artists in to perform. Once a month, her favorite luthier, Jonathan, visited to work on instruments. He was available at other times for string repair. Jonathan also made violins and cellos, and over the years, Rosella had sold several of these priceless instruments at the store. Redbud Music had a reputation that extended beyond the small town, and she often had customers traveling from Tennessee, Ohio, West Virginia, and further.

When Tresne came for their visit to interview Rosella, they were given the tour. Slowly, the two of them made their way around the store. At nearly 2,000 square feet, the tour took over an hour. When Rosella bought the business, she read the guides, which recommended buying used instruments at the lowest price and marking them up for resale. She also read the advice that dealing in used equipment was a headache. A better business plan was to open online sales and promote cheaper beginner models of instruments. Rosella didn't follow this advice.

A few months after Roger died, still in semi-shock, Rosella took one of his guitars to a store in Rochester to sell. It was an acoustic/electric round body Ovation that he often played in concerts. Inexplicably, this specific guitar was the most painful for Rosella to see of all the others stacked in her parents' den in Rochester. Maybe because of its unique shape and the multiple stickers he had stuck on the case, she felt a stab in her heart every time she glanced into that corner and saw it standing there.

The day she took it to Old Town Guitars in Irondequoit was heart-breaking. She picked that store because she wasn't known there. No one would have heard R and Me, and neither she nor Roger played there as kids. She found the shop rather sterile, with a couple of older bald, bearded, portly men waiting on customers. She had called earlier to see if they took used instruments, and they replied yes, but the owner would have to be present to decide. She approached the counter and asked to talk to the owner about the guitar. The first man motioned to another, nearly identical fellow, sitting on a stool looking over some papers.

Rosella introduced herself to this man, named Jimmy, and explained she was interested in selling the Ovation.

"Let's see it," he demanded.

She placed the case on a nearby bench and pulled out the Ovation. The guitar was in good shape, with only a few nicks. Rosella had not taken it out of the case since Roger passed, but as she handed it over to Jimmy, she felt something pass through her. Jimmy scrutinized the body briefly, strummed it, turned it over, looked through the sound hole at the label, and handed it back to her—an assessment that took less than forty-five seconds.

"I'll give you 200 dollars for it," he mumbled, not looking up from his papers.

Rosella was surprised, actually appalled, but asked, "Don't you want to know anything about this guitar?"

"Nope," he said. That's an old guitar with some known flaws. Better electronics are available now, and it will be hard to sell in this store. Plus, we have another, the same model, on display, so that is all I can offer you."

Rosella was too emotional to even speak while she placed it lovingly back in its case. She thought of what the guitar meant to her. Trying not to scream, she left the store and turned north towards the lake. There was a beautiful place at Durand Eastman Park where she could sit in a little arbor of trees. She drove to that hidden place.

The guitar meant so much to her and had so much history. Almost spiritual, it had music within its fibers. That must count for some value. She couldn't understand why Jimmy didn't or couldn't appreciate this. At one level, Rosella knew she was being unreasonable—no one could know all that an instrument had gone through except the person playing it or someone quite close to them.

After an hour of sitting and brooding, she found no explanations or solutions. But on the way home from the park, she drove around until she was in Brown Square. When she lived in Rochester, her parents volunteered at a clinic in Brown Square, and as a child, Rosella sometimes went with them to the night clinic. She and her brother would sit in the waiting room and play whatever instrument they had brought while patients walked in and out. For some reason, she thought this would be the best place for Roger's guitar.

She didn't put too much thought into her decision but walked up to the receptionist's desk at the clinic and said she had a guitar she wanted to donate. This, understandably, was an odd donation at a medical clinic, but the very nice woman at the desk said, "Hold on just a minute." She rose and walked into the back area. A few minutes later, a tall man who introduced himself as Frank appeared and said what a splendid gift. He asked what the story of the guitar was. Rosella was so relieved she cried, and Frank ushered her into a small room off to the side. She told him of her parents' involvement and Roger's illness and explained that she felt someone here would appreciate the guitar.

Frank nodded enthusiastically. "I know just the person. Someone who has just lost his wife and is having a hard time. This will be a lifesaver."

Rosella left the clinic feeling much better.

So, on that first visit, Tresne made to Redbud Music, Rosella talked about the instruments scattered around the store. A dark violin with an old-style chin pad had been someone's mother's violin. It was at least 150 years old but was originally a student model, so it was not a famous, expensive type. The woman who brought it in said that her mother had been first chair in a medium-sized Michigan community orchestra. The violin had been hanging on a hook in their home all the while the woman was growing up. When her mother died, she sold it because no one in the family played.

Rosella told Tresne, "I listened to this woman's memories of her mother and the violin and could see how valuable it was to her. I knew it needed some work, but structurally, it was sound. After tuning it, I played it for the woman, and the sound was sonorous, deep."

Rosella continued with the story. "The woman exclaimed that the sound made her think of her childhood whenever her mother played, and she said she was crying for joy."

"With instruments like this," Rosella said, "I ask the person what they think the piece is worth in terms of money."

She went on. "Most times, the amount they quote is what I offer them. I still agree even if the price is much higher than the material value. I know how hard it is to sell a trusted or intimate instrument, and I can't place a value on that. Most of my colleagues think this approach is crazy. 'You'll lose money. You'll never sell it for that amount.' But I can't do it any other way after how I was treated in Rochester with Roger's guitar."

With those final words, she showed Tresne more of her used instruments and told more stories.

Tresne seemed to get what Rosella was talking about. Tresne spent a few days with Rosella on that first trip, but they frequently returned to visit. One day, when they arrived on a Tuesday in time for the Irish Group, they took Rosella aside, pulled a drum out of their bag, and said, "This was the only music I could take from the house when my parents kicked me out. I have kept it all these years, and for a few, it was the only drum I had." They continued, "After hearing you talk about the hidden value of instruments, I thought I would bring it tonight and play it."

The drum was a kid's Remo bongo with a surprisingly rich sound, and Tresne beat out a quick rhythm. The two, now friends, hugged and went to greet the group.

Every Tuesday, a group of musicians met at Redbud Music to play Irish music. Rosella welcomed diverse music and advertised that her space was open to regular gatherings. She provided the room, helped them set up notices about the sessions, and provided other amenities. Over the years, this collection of Irish music enthusiasts had grown, and now a regular group of ten to twelve people usually attended. Rosella gave the leader, Leon, a key to the shop, and they played on into the night, sometimes leaving after midnight. She allowed them to bring their own drinks, which meant sometimes she found empty beer cans and bourbon bottles around the next morning. Other than some of this detritus, they had proven to be very respectful of her store. The group was an excellent source of sales as well. Their demand for traditional instruments explained why Ava had thought Redbud Music reminded her of Elderly Music.

Rosella understood that lending an instrument to an interested player to fall in love with was good for her business, though that wasn't her initial intent. As a small business owner in a small town, she appreciated that sometimes she had to think about the monetary profit and not just personal interests. Her stock of button accordions was for this group, and her attempts at reed instrument repairs were because of this clientele. She also carried a whole line of tin whistles, flutes, and harmonicas. Some of the Irish groups had become statewide celebrities, and some even national specialists in these winds.

She carried several sizes of bodhrans as well, and when no one was in the store, she took down her favorite one and tapped out a rhythm. Few people knew what a bodhran (pronounced like Bow-Rawn) was, much less how to play one. Rosella was often invited to schools to demonstrate different instruments. She always brought a bodhran along, and at least two students had been interested in playing them. Several adults picked up the drum as an introduction to Irish music. Some of them came to the Irish sessions on Tuesday. Leon once asked Rosella to tone down her sales pitch because the group was getting overwhelmed with bodhran players. The intermittent addition of a bodhran to a tune is unbelievably valuable, but multiple inexperienced drummers chiming in on every song can be painful.

Rosella appreciated Leon's comments and helped organize a monthly drum circle at the store. She enlisted the help of the university's percussion instructor and provided a variety of drums—some bodhrans, some djembes, big and small. This was another well-attended event at Redbud Music. Over time, the participants had passed on proper etiquette about the role of drums in jam sessions, which casually carried over to the Irish sessions. By an informal system, bodhran players took turns coming on Tuesday, and everything worked out.

Rosella liked the drumming group and felt comfortable playing along with them. To her, drumming didn't remind her of Roger and didn't feel like a performance. She enjoyed losing herself with the beats. She hosted another group of drummers who were more involved with the spiritual aspect of drumming. Though the leader might not describe this group as shamanic drumming, that would be the best description. The setting was usually arranged with low light, incense-infused air, and meditative poses. Rosella attended the first meeting in her role as shop owner but did not return. She debated with herself whether this practice was cultural misappropriation. Thinking about that term, she made a note to ask her youngest friend, Tresne, about what they thought.

Tonight was the Irish group, and Rosella liked to watch as the musicians came in and set up. She liked the easy banter between them and how their love of Irish music connected them. Leon was often the first to arrive with his array of cases and stands. He played the tenor banjo, mandolin, fiddle, guitar, and flutes. He had a self-devised stand that held all of them in a spinning design. With each new tune, he would spin the contraption and select the appropriate instrument. His fingers moved like lightning, and new players were having a difficult time catching up. It was a running joke about how fast he played everything. Leon had been in several bands in his younger days, ranging from bluegrass to rock, and knew famous people from all these genres. Though he didn't tour any longer, his former band members often visited him and joined on a Tuesday session.

Another regular was Phil, the guitar player. Rosella liked him the best because he was so funny. Everything he said was amusing to her. He was, of course, able to play accompaniment to any song, figuring out chords after one pass through the melody. He had a sonorous voice and could harmonize with others. What Rosella liked most about his playing was his improvisation. Irish music uses improvisation differently from something like jazz. Instead of long passages of individual variation, the players of traditional Irish music put variation in the tunes one note at a time. For Rosella, this was hard to hear in the fiddle or whistle parts because she grew to hear them as just the melody. But with Phil's guitar, she heard the exciting changes he made during repeats of songs. The different chord progressions, the passing disharmonious chord. It was constantly changing. Of course, she probably liked Phil and his guitar the most because it reminded her of Roger. He had played like that, throwing in an unexpected and pleasing passage.

The others who came weren't so regular, sometimes not joining for weeks in a row. Ray was a flute player and always used an iPad to look up songs. Ward was a piano accordion player who also brought his guitar. There were a couple of stupendous fiddle players. One was an older woman who could whip out any tune, adding little turns and trills. She was very low-key and never brought attention to herself. The other fiddle player was a younger fellow who was large and loud. His playing was equally astounding, but he played so fast and such obscure tunes that the rest of the group had a hard time joining in. Rosella tried to learn all the players' names when they joined, but with the group's growth last year, she admitted she didn't know everyone. She trusted Leon would keep them all in line and her store safe.

Thinking of the store, Rosella was reminded of her accountant's review of the financials. Redbud was losing money—not hemorrhaging, but the losses were significant. Rosella was not selling as much merchandise as she had purchased, especially some of the more unique items. She hadn't mentioned the audit to Cal, preferring to figure it out herself. And she didn't want to ask her parents for help now that they had cut back on their full-time practices.

Hoping to push these worries away, she actively listened to the Irish music coming from across the store. She marveled at the twists and turns of one particularly lively hornpipe. Absent-mindedly, she looked at a guitar Jonathan, the luthier, had just repaired. He had done an excellent job on the tricky repair. Rosella was more concerned about the owner.

When the older man brought the guitar in for repair, he seemed confused. A woman waited for him in the car. Rosella recalled having to explain to him several times that the guitar would be ready in three days. She had never seen the couple before, but they drove a late-model Cadillac, and the man was dressed in a shirt and tie. Rosella was curious about their story.

Today, the man returned with his wife. She seemed much less confused and introduced herself to Rosella.

"My name is Shirley, and this is my husband, Carl. Thank you for fixing the guitar."

Carl had wandered off, looking at the guitars and strumming them lovingly. Shirley motioned for Rosella to come closer, and she whispered, "I am sorry if he seemed confused the other day. I shouldn't have sent him in alone. He has a lot of trouble with his memory."

Rosella said, "That's perfectly OK. Obviously, he remembered it would take three days.".

Shirley sighed, "Yes, he did because he repeated it hundreds of times daily. He has, and I hate to say it out loud, Alzheimer's. It is getting worse every day."

Rosella said, "I'm sorry."

Shirley continued, "Did you know he used to be the guitar instructor at the university?"

Rosella said, "No, I didn't." The other woman appeared to need to talk. She looked exhausted, and Rosella offered her a nearby stool to sit on.

Shirley went on, "Yes, he was a phenomenal player. Still is. He hasn't forgotten anything about playing the guitar. I think his playing has gotten even better. It's just that he can't remember much else. He has forgotten how to get dressed and how to use utensils. He can't remember how to say the names of things. I have to guess what he wants." Looking over at her husband, examining the guitar display, she said, "He seems to be more like himself here around the music. I haven't been able to be out of his sight this long for many months."

Rosella glanced over at Carl as well. He appeared to be blissful. She asked Shirley, "Do you think he would like to play one of those?"

Shirley responded, "Oh yes. That would make him so happy. And you can see what I am talking about. He used to play everywhere. He drove all over Ohio and Kentucky for gigs, and his students loved him. Do you mind if he plays something?"

Rosella said, "No, of course not."

They approached Carl, and Rosella took down her most expensive Collins acoustic. She said to Carl, "Would you mind trying this one out? I'm not sure how it sounds."

Carl took the guitar in his hands lovingly and perched on a stool. From the instrument came a beautiful finger-picked melody. He began simply and then added embellishments. Rosella was impressed with how he could make such a simple melody turn into this exotic tune with these intricate additions.

"Wow," she said when he finished. "That was beautiful."

He only nodded and handed her back the guitar.

She said, "Please come back anytime and help me keep these in tune and loved."

"Thank you," he said.

The couple left with Carl's guitar, and Rosella thought again about how much she loved music. And somehow, she would make Redbud financially secure.

Ac-Ad

<u>Ac-Ad</u>

Notes for *Inside Taber's: A Study of the Medical Dictionary* by Dr. Ava

I take issue with the definition of the term "active treatment"—this is "treatment specifically directed toward cure of a disease." What would the treatment I provide in palliative care be considered? Inactive? We are very active in treating patients whose illnesses may have no cure. The same goes for the frequently used term "aggressive" treatment of a disease—usually cancer.

Why does the whole spectrum of treating cancer remind me of gameday jargon? "Battling the disease," "Don't let your cancer beat you," "frontline medicines," "fight against it." I guess it relates to pushing people to finish or stick with their treatment. The danger is when patients "lose their battle with cancer." Sometimes, they are made to feel like they gave up, and it is not that at all. It is just nature.

Here is a word that draws my attention every time I look at the page—"adamantinoma."

This is "a jaw tumor arising from the enamel-forming cells." The root is Greek—adamas—meaning hard surface, and it certainly describes teeth well. Carrying this over to everyday language, the word "adamant" comes to mind, and I have a new image of "putting my teeth into it" when I am adamantly opposed to something.

Chapter 13: A Family Talks

After the accident, Ava's dad lived on his own. Just barely. He was letting widowerhood sink in day by day. He made coffee with the microwave in a Styrofoam cup, and various female friends of Ava's mother made meals for him, so he ate well. Delicious casseroles, pot roasts, and pies. Either Ted, Ted's wonderful wife, Sally, or Ava checked on him every other week and brought him more groceries. In the accident, he ruptured his spleen and nearly died as well. He never recovered back to his previous physical or mental state.

Ava went up this weekend for her father's birthday. Chronologically, he turned sixty-eight, but the past year seemed to have aged him ten. After the party and after her cousins and aunts had left, Ted, Ava, and her father sat on the couch, all three exhausted. Her dad lamented, "These parties aren't the same without your mother. It doesn't feel right."

Ava's parents had been married for nearly forty years before the accident. Her dad was an only child, grew up Jewish on the East Coast, but somehow married her mother, a devout Catholic when they fell in love in Michigan. Marrying a Catholic was not acceptable in her dad's family, so he was ostracized from them. He had focused on his career in the prison system, starting first as a social worker, then as deputy warden, and then as warden. This most senior position required a move away from Ava's mother's family but only an hour away.

Ted agreed, "Yes, Mom was definitely the life of the party. She knew what to say to people, what to feed people. She was always so comfortable with people. Being around this kind of crowd makes me feel uncomfortable. Today's party was tiring."

Ava listened to her closest living relatives now and was surprised she had never heard them say anything like this. She also felt uncomfortable with the crowd, even though they were cousins and aunts she had known all her life. There was something stilted about how she felt she connected with them.

The three were sitting on a screened-in porch at Ted's suburban home. Outside, the frogs were croaking, and the patter of a light rain could be heard on the roof. Ava reflected, inexplicably again, on how hard it is to describe the sound of rain. There are many words to illustrate an image, but only a few for auditory scenes, like the tapping on the roof she heard as a backdrop to their conversation.

Ava said, "I really miss Mom." With a faltering voice, she continued, "I miss coming home and feeling safe. It was so predictable. So easy."

Ted spoke up, "Yes, it was comfortable there. Mom would make my favorite dish or fix hot chocolate. She seemed to know exactly what we needed or wanted."

Ava's dad, now sobbing, said, "Your mother was a wonderful person. I don't think I would have survived without her. She made everything so much easier."

Ava asked, "What do you mean?"

He continued, "When I met your mother, I had just moved west to Michigan and didn't know anyone. I went to work, came home, and sometimes went to the bar. I had some friends from work, but no one was very close. I met your mother, and she emanated joy and confidence. Not long after we started dating, I knew she would be the person to make my life more tolerable and less lonely. More livable. As you know, she was quite organized, which is what I needed. I wanted predictability at home because my job was so unpredictable. Going to prison every day was stressful. It was a struggle to face each new morning. Your mother helped."

Ted said, "I didn't know that you thought your job was so stressful. We have never heard you talk about stress or anything about your job. But that's how I think about my job. There is so much underlying tension at my office."

Ted was a human resource person at a large company. His wife, Sally, like Ava's mother, kept the home predictable with delicious meals and an easy existence.

Ava's father continued, "I have been completely lost without your mother. Even though the stress of the job is gone, I have such a hard time. And your mother and I were going to travel so much when I retired, and I was looking forward to being home with her. Now that is all gone."

He pulled out a handkerchief and blew his nose.

Ava asked, "Dad, do you remember how mad Mom was about your drinking? What was that about? You upset her a lot when you drank."

Ava's dad paused and took a deep breath.

He said, "Your mother didn't think drinking was a healthy way for me to deal with things. Her Catholic upbringing probably contributed to that, but she also worried that I would become dependent on alcohol. She once told me that drinking a martini after work changed my behavior. And the change wasn't in a good way. I would get goofy. I mostly drank alone because your mother never touched a drop, and in my role as warden, I couldn't be seen drinking. As usual, your mother was right. I shouldn't have risked using alcohol. I wish I would have listened to her."

Ava said, "Don't beat yourself up, Dad. You did what you could. She was pretty good at knowing what each of us might be susceptible to. Did you know Mom sent me a card every week I was in medical school? They were just simple letters or store-bought cards encouraging me and letting me know what was happening back home. Sometimes, I didn't think too much about them or how important they were. Like you, I wished I would have thanked her for them. Instead, I was more likely to tell her she didn't need to send them."

Ted chimed in, "Yeah, I regret all those times I yelled at Mom when I was mad at someone from school or worried about something. I remember that she always made me feel good. I don't know why I yelled at her. She didn't deserve that."

The three sat for a while in their guilt. Ava broke the silence.

"Do you think Mom knew the three of us had a hard time being in society? We were all so different from her in a social sense. And while she stayed home and supported us, we all went out and got all this education and good professions. Was she the glue to keep all of us functioning?"

Ted responded, "You know, my daughters think I might have autism. Some of the stuff I have read about it sounds a little like me. Dad, did Mom ever mention that I might have something like that?"

Ava's father sighed, "We never thought you and your sister were different. Your mom just thought you both were more like me than her. Ted, I remember you had a hard time being calmed as a baby, and as a teenager, you were kind of prickly."

Ava added, "Ted, I've been thinking that I might be on the autism spectrum too. Some characteristics I've read about are appropriate descriptions of some things I do. Like people say, they hear me whistling. Even when I think I might be whistling out loud and stop myself, I hear the notes in my head. And I always think people talk too slowly—in my mind. I am filling in the words they search for before they say them."

Ted said, "That sounds like me, too. And your whistling is noticeable."

Her dad also said it sounded like what he felt like.

Ava continued, "I know, Dad, that you and Mom always said I was shy, and I still think I am timid and can only start interacting if it's a 'have to' situation. I don't enjoy talking on the phone. I don't like looking people in the eye. And I often worry about making the right expressions when people tell me something."

Both Ted and her dad nodded. Ava was quiet momentarily, then said, "I just thought of something, Dad. Remember when we were fishing on that dock at the lake, and you had your back to the water while I was running on the dock, and you took a step back and fell into the water? Remember, I couldn't stop laughing. My first response was laughing, even though you could have really hurt yourself. And it happened again with a friend who slipped on a wet ramp and fell. I started laughing. Totally inappropriate."

Ted recalled, "I don't remember that incident at the lake, but I know what you mean. It seems like my whole life, I have been studying people to see what the appropriate reaction would be to different situations. My kids have mentioned something called 'masking.' They have a couple of friends who have autism, and sometimes their friends talk about trying to suppress the natural instinct to laugh or whatever to fit in with the so-called normal people. I think I have learned to mask a lot of my natural tendencies. Maybe you need to work on masking your laughter."

Ava's father said, "Ted, I remember when you were young. We tried changing the foods you ate to see if you would have fewer temper tantrums. We also tried soothing music and warm baths. Your mother had a nurse friend who suggested some things. We even tried massaging your feet at night. I don't know if any of it worked. I wish your mother were here. She would know more. I think she didn't know what to do."

Ava asked, "Dad, do you think your life improved as you got older?"

Her father closed his eyes briefly.

"Having your mother nearby was the joy of my life and made me happy. She made it easy to be around people because she did all the arranging, inviting, and conversing. I could be in the background. So, in that way, it was better. I think that is why it has been so hard since she's been gone."

All of them spoke at the same time, "She held the family together." Sally entered with some cookies and tea, and the atmosphere lifted. It felt oddly good to know that both her dad and her brother were feeling the same way about losing her mom. She went to bed with a slightly less heavy heart.

Early the next morning, Ava started her trip home. She knew the route by heart, and she had pretzel sticks within reach and chocolate-covered peanuts to keep her from falling asleep along the monotonous drive. She usually turned off NPR for half of the trip and thought in silence.

Some thoughts were predictable—like a song stuck in your mind. Like awe when she passed the Pioneer sugar factory and saw the mural of two oxen pulling a cart. And when she passed "Touchdown Jesus" south of Dayton—a church with a statue of Jesus with his arms up like a referee signaling to passing vehicles.

The new thoughts that came to her were about her life and what it had been like without her mother. Since the Yogaville weekend, Ava had been withdrawing from social events to spend more time playing the guitar and reading *Taber's*. She missed two Friday Night Enlights.

Her life wasn't in quite the disarray as immediately after her mom's accident. A year ago when she was on call, she could only get up off the couch, go to the hospital, deal with the problem, then return to lie on the couch. She was on call for Christmas and Thanksgiving that year in a cruel schedule twist. She barely made it through.

She missed what would usually happen on holidays when her mom was alive. She missed going home to her parents, where everything felt safe, and her mom waited on her. She mentioned the cards her mom sent. She missed them and wished she had saved even one.

As she drove closer to home, a flurry of other problems occupied her mind. She had dismissed them as being in a bad mood, but it was happening more often. Her partner, Dr. Frost, had mentioned that one nurse had complained that Ava had been sharp with her. While ordering a blood test, Dr. Frost said that Ava had cut this nurse off when she questioned the order. Another time, one of the nurse managers at the hospital pulled Ava aside and said she was concerned because the nurses on the floor had complained about Ava being impatient.

The manager, someone Ava had known for a long time, added, "The nurses said this wasn't how you used to be, and they're concerned."

Ava brushed the complaints aside, thinking they were more related to the offended people than her.

Dr. Frost asked her one day at lunch if she had ever heard of the "imposter syndrome." And, if she knew much about adult autism?

She went on to explain, "I have this patient who sees me often with a variety of complaints. They're usually mild things like different rashes or nasal stuffiness. Sometimes, she comes in with the feeling that her heart is racing. Other times, she feels as if she can't catch her breath. She is a brilliant math professor at the university, and I always enjoy seeing her, but she comes in frequently."

"Today, when I saw her, she mentioned she thought she might be autistic. Or maybe on the spectrum. From what she had read, she fit a lot of the descriptions. On the autism self-tests, she had scored high for masking." Dr. Frost went on, "This patient often talked about how shy she was as a child and how uncomfortable she was at social events. I didn't know what to tell her since I had never heard of an adult-diagnosed autism. Then she threw out some terms I did not learn in medical school thirty years ago. 'Alexithymia' and 'Imposter Syndrome.'"

Ava responded she knew little about autism in adults but treated a couple of autistic children. The young patients who had been diagnosed with this label were struggling. She told Dr. Frost, "I signed paperwork for them for special accommodations at school, but their parents and the school psychologist designed their treatment plan. The psychologist said that girls are rarely diagnosed with ADHD because they tend not to act out like boys. They suffer in silence. Maybe that applies to your patient."

Dr. Frost said, "I will have to read up on that."

At home that evening, Ava skipped ahead in *Taber's* looking up "alexithymia." She had been reading *Taber's* for many weeks and still found it "suspended time" for her. But between work and having so little energy for extra projects, she found her enthusiasm waning.

The entry for "alexithymia" read, "A clinical feature common in posttraumatic stress disorder characterized by the inability to identify and articulate feelings. Often, feelings are reported to the health care worker as physical symptoms. Patients suffering from chemical dependency and somatoform disorders may also display alexithymia." This definition was intriguing, and Ava googled the term. One listing in *Psychiatric Times* connected the condition more clinically:

"In 1972, Peter Sifneos introduced to psychiatry the term *alexithymia*, which (derived from the Greek) literally means having no words for emotions (a=lack, lexis=word, thymos=emotions). Alexithymia is not a diagnosis but a construct useful for characterizing patients who seem not to understand the feelings they experience and patients who seem to lack the words to describe these feelings to others. Identifying this deficit in expressivity is important because doing so gives the clinician a leg up in making a diagnosis and charting a therapeutic course."

There were so many parts to the mind and body that could go wrong. Finding out about this word re-motivated Ava about *Taber's*, but she also started to think about herself.

In residency, when all the residents had a six-month experience with group psychoanalysis to better understand the psychiatric method, the psychiatrist implied she had "dysthymia." She jumped ahead to look up the term but was surprised to find only instructions to "SEE Nursing Diagnostic Appendix."

That was yet another section of the book located past the word entries. She tried to find dysthymia there, but soon, her head hurt either from the small print or the memory of her stressful time in residency.

The day Dr. Frost asked her about autism, Ava had a hard time falling asleep thinking about the possibility that she had autism. The conversation with her brother and father only reinforced her worries.

Or was she fitting her normal behavior into a set of characteristics of people with autism?

When she pulled into her driveway after the long drive, Ava had a muddled head. She was glad her family had talked. It was the first time she had spoken aloud about the sadness of losing her mother. Ava thought of people near her whom she might be able to talk to, and Rosella came to mind.

Ad-Ad

<u>Ad-Ad</u>

Notes for *Inside Taber's: A Study of the Medical Dictionary* by Dr. Ava

Reading about adaptation, I came across Sister Callista Roy, who developed the Adaptation Model of nursing. The RAM (Roy Adaptation Model) is a conceptual model that sees the individual as an adaptive system, a biophysical being required to adapt to environmental stimuli. There are so many paths of discussion related to this concept it is hard to begin. Basically, human beings are designed to persist. Speaking only to the physiologic realm of human beings, all our body functions are designed to keep us in a homeostatic balance. Our kidneys monitor our internal fluids better than even the most advanced car computer. Our adrenal glands bump up steroid production when there is stress in our body (like right now in my body as I realize how long this is taking), and gastric juices change acidity based on what we eat. Every organ and organ system is finely balanced.

We become sick when an imbalance is induced by an internal process or an external agent, intentional or accidental. This is so fascinating; it gives me goosebumps.

Nurses have long known that treating patients in multiple dimensions is the best way to return to balance. Correcting the physical malady alone won't always return the person to their balance point. There are many other factors. Hence, it makes complete sense that Sister Roy was a nurse. It also makes sad sense that I had never heard of the Roy Adaptive Model.

In the distant past, before the technological explosion occurred in medicine, maybe doctors intuitively had a better sense of the patient as a total being. Maybe there wasn't so much pressure to see the next patient, to hurry and diagnose and cure patients. This urgency to prescribe a medication and make someone "better." In the end, it means spending less time with the patient.

I think of myself as dimly enlightened, but reviewing my day at the office yesterday, too numerous to count times I interrupted either the patient, family member, or nurse who was talking about a peripheral topic to the "disease" in question. The obvious malady (to me, anyway). Each time, I thought about the clock and the work yet to be done.

Chapter 14: Art Lessons

Tresne had come to town for another of Rosella's FNEs. This week, the discussion was going to be about problems with uninsured people getting health care. Rosella had invited the two founders of a free clinic in a neighboring town to speak. She was excited about them coming but wished that Ava was speaking also because Ava was heavily involved with free care in Berry Hill. Ava hadn't been coming to her lessons or joining on Friday nights. As always, Rosella did not press Ava but continued to send her messages about the events. She occasionally called and left voice messages. She called Gwen.

"Hello, Gwen, this is Rosella. Ava's friend."

"Oh, hi, Rosella. How are you?" Gwen answered on the first ring.

"I am doing well. How about yourself?"

"Doing fine. A little busy right at the moment."

"Oh, I won't keep you. I just wondered if you had talked to Ava lately?"

Gwen paused, "You know I haven't seen her for a few weeks. I was away at a conference, so I didn't overthink it, but yeah, we haven't taken a walk for a while. Is anything wrong?"

"No, I hadn't seen her either, and she canceled some of her lessons. I was just checking on her. Maybe I'll stop by her house one of these days. I'll let you get back to what you were doing. I'll keep you posted if I hear from her."

Rosella made a mental note to stop by Ava's on the weekend. Meanwhile, she cleaned the house a bit to prepare for her evening's visitors. The night's speakers started New Life Clinic and were well known for their dedication to providing free health care. Rosella once visited the clinic to bring some donated supplies left at Redbud Music.

Sharing her car with the IV tubing and other medical equipment for the ride to the clinic unnerved Rosella. She kept being reminded of Roger's illness when pumps surrounded his hospital bed. She was relieved to have an empty car on the way home.

New Life Clinic took anyone who wanted to be seen and who did not have health insurance. Rosella knew the founders, Jerry and Judy, would talk more about this on Friday night, but they had told her many of the patients were Amish. She wondered what her friends, Beth and Joe, would say about this since they had lived with the Amish for so long. Though this wasn't specifically about health care, she wondered if there would be a debate or discussion about some of the Amish ways. Rosella herself questioned the education system. Children were not allowed to go to school past eighth grade.

When she became friends with Beth, Rosella read the book *An Amish Paradox: Diversity and Change in the World's Largest Amish Community* by Hurst and McConnell.

She knew that there were a lot of reasons Amish parents did not want to send their kids for more formal education. Their life needs were met with practical experience, not book learning. And what intrigued Rosella was this concept of "pride." Having more education might lead some individuals to think they are better than others. From what she understood, this was an incredibly important value for the Amish—that no one was better than another, even though men seemed to dominate all leadership roles and were the deciders of practices. Rosella was glad she had some first-hand accounts and understanding of the culture from her friends and hoped she would understand more after Jerry and Judy talked tonight about how the Amish used the clinic.

Late Friday afternoon, Tresne breezed into Redbud Music, slightly out of breath, weighed down by a heavy backpack and a ratty old leather briefcase. Rosella greeted them with, "Welcome back."

Tresne laid down their luggage and sighed, "I took the back roads to get here today and hadn't realized how beautiful the countryside was. I stopped at a couple of covered bridges along the way and an Amish store. I bought some cheese and bread for tonight's gathering. Have you ever heard the acoustics in those old wooden bridges? Amazing!!"

Rosella laughed at the young person's exuberance.

"No," she said, "I have never been inside one, though there are several around here that I've seen."

Tresne continued, "Yes, I got out a drum and played for a good half hour inside one. Loved it. Some people stopped who were walking by and listened for a bit. A woman on a horse trotted by and gave me an odd look. This is so different from where I grew up."

Rosella asked, "A horse?"

"Yes," Tresne gasped. "When I asked the people walking, they said many of the folks there had horses and went out for trail rides along a route that featured the old bridges. Different groups in Kentucky had repaired the bridges, making them safe enough to walk through. No cars are allowed."

Rosella responded, "Wow, I didn't know that."

Tresne walked closer to Rosella and quietly said, "I want to record something in those spaces. I'm going to talk to someone in Cincinnati about how to do that. I think it will be phenomenal with the timbers and water underneath."

"That would be cool. A while back, a group recorded a CD inside an old tobacco barn. Like the bridges, the acoustics were terrific. I wonder where I put that CD? You might get some ideas from that. If I can remember the producer's name, I think he bought his equipment here, and our sound expert helped him with the mics."

Tresne nodded energetically. Rosella felt an unfamiliar enthusiasm for this idea.

Since Roger's death, as most people close to her knew, Rosella refused any offers to perform in public. The thought of playing in front of anyone besides her students or Cal made her stomach turn and her heart race. Not in the way of stage fright. She really couldn't explain it. But for the first time in a long while, she could picture herself inside one of these bridges with her violin and guitar. She could almost hear the melody wafting up. She could feel the vibrations of her instrument and the sounds bouncing back to her. A slight grin appeared on her face.

Tresne and Rosella had gotten close over the months since they first met, and Tresne noticed the change in their friend.

"What are you thinking?" they asked.

"Oh, nothing," was Rosella's reply.

Tresne laughed, "I know something just popped into your head. Please tell me."

Rosella still didn't know what her image meant and was a little worried about speaking about it out loud.

"I will later," she told Tresne.

With that, Tresne unpacked their briefcase with copies of the latest *Rewind* issue for Redbud Music. The two then took time to arrange the magazines in the best place on the display rack in the corner. Rosella was impressed with the small-scale journal and usually read each issue cover to cover. She loaned out copies to some of the high school musicians who played at the store, so a few of the older issues were tattered from use. Rosella was glad they were being read.

Tresne looked around and asked, "Where is Hannah? Come here, Hannah. Here, puppy."

"She's not here. She's home with my mom. Mom came to visit this weekend and will be at the gathering tonight. I'm eager for you to meet her."

Rosella recalled the conversation she and Liz had at breakfast. She had come without Rosella's dad this time because Larry was just getting involved with the residency program at the hospital, and this weekend was their orientation. Liz said she was happy Larry was interested in teaching as they thought about cutting back on their clinical practices.

Rosella thought her dad would be a great teacher with his infinite patience and interesting way of presenting ideas. She remembered some of his explanations when, one time, she had an elbow injury from playing the violin too much. It was an overuse injury, like a pitcher or tennis player might get.

She remembered the drawings he made to help her understand how the tendons attached to a particular spot on her radius. He videotaped her playing so he could suggest modifications to the position of her arm. He had also given her exercises to help. Knowing that other musicians suffered from "musical injuries," her dad had researched ways of preventing these tendencies and given a couple of lectures to her classmates at college. Her friends always said how nice he was.

At breakfast, Liz and Rosella chatted about the weather for a while. Rosella missed the spring lilac festival in Rochester, so Liz showed her photos of some of the prettiest trees in Highland Park. With no apparent connection, Liz suddenly started to tear up.

She said, "I miss your brother so much. Spring seemed to be his favorite season. I remember him climbing up in a tree in our front yard in May with the branches just budding out. He would sometimes sit up there for hours. Sometimes, he would bring a notebook, and when he came into the house, he would read me the words that had come to him in the tree. Roz, do you remember that one tree with a natural seat in it? You two played on that since you both were very young. It was better than a swing—more like a saddle. I would bring your lunch out to you on a tray. You loved drinking a bottle of Coke perched up there. It was such a joy to look out the window and see you two talking and gathering little objects to scatter around."

Rosella said simply, "I miss him too."

Liz asked, "You know, we all don't talk about Roger much. Why is that? I have asked myself that so many times away from the place where the memories formed, it seems easier."

"I know, Mom," Rosella answered. "I don't talk about him much either. Sometimes, when Cal or I say something that sounds like what he would say—we look at each other and smile, but that is as far as I can go."

"Last week, a young man came into Redbud Music with his guitar. He looked a lot like Roger. As soon as I saw him walk through the door, I fled to the back room and asked Helen, my helper, to wait on him. Then I sat back there and shook." She turned toward her mother and asked, "Is that normal? When should things feel like they could be normal?"

Her mother lowered her head and said, "I don't know. I only know I never want to forget your brother. Some days, and rarely really, I will wake up, and it's halfway through the day before I think of him. You would imagine that would make me feel better, but I feel worse when that happens. The guilt. Why was he the one to die at such a young age? Why not me, who has lived so many years?"

Liz continued, "You know, I went to the bereavement sessions that hospice offered about a year ago. I knew I had what they called 'complicated grief.' I recognized it from seeing it in patients. I knew what it was called, but that didn't make me feel any better. The leader of those groups was good. No doubt about it. She encouraged us to tell the story of our loved one's death."

"There were about five in the group. No one else had lost a child. Every week, the time would come for me to talk about Roger, and I couldn't. Tears flowed, and my voice left me. At one meeting, an art therapist came as a guest. She brought all kinds of paper, paints, colored pencils, aprons, and plastic for the floor."

"This art therapist asked us to think of one word to describe the person who died. Just one word. The first word that came to my mind about Roger was 'alive.' You know how he was so full of life, so excited about everything, and so kind. The therapist then asked us to translate that word onto the paper in whatever form it took.

"Well, as you know, I am not an artist, and the thought of creating a painting scared me, but this therapist said it didn't matter what we drew or painted. Just put anything down on the paper. So I found all the brightest colors in the bunch—I mixed up crayons of bright blue, red, yellow, orange, and green, and I splattered some bright watercolors on the blob and finally outlined the whole mess with a border of colorful magic markers. The color leaked through to the other side, but the therapist said that didn't matter.

"Next, as people finished their artwork, she asked us to turn the paper over. She said, 'Now fold the paper in half, and in half again, and once more fold that half in half.' By this time, the blank section of the back of the paper was only an eighth of the size of the whole. 'Now,' Ann said, 'think of a word or two that describes how you feel on your worst days of grieving. Maybe it's sad, or shame, or guilt, whatever you feel on those days. And I want you to depict that word by writing, drawing, or painting it. But I want you to write it with your other hand from the drawing you did on the front. When you're finished, unfold the page and stare at the front side. See if you can find the corner of the page that you wrote on in the back.'"

Rosella was rather surprised her mother was telling her all of this. For most of Roger and Rosella's life, their mother was this invincible, enviably strong woman. Rosella listened intently as Liz went on.

"That exercise seemed dumb. While I was writing the words on the back, I questioned my sanity, but I took the paper home and tacked it to the mirror in my bedroom. Every morning, I looked at the bright colors that represented 'alive,' and, as if by some miracle, the black ink of the words 'guilt' and 'sad' faded. I would have to squint to see their backward imprint in the corner."

Liz continued, "The next time I went to the bereavement group, when it was my turn to share, I talked about Roger. I talked about his illness, about you going through the transplant with him, about the long months of worry. I cried as I described all this, but I managed to speak. The other people, some of whom had become my friends, sat silently. When I finally stopped speaking, I was afraid to look up—afraid to see the looks of pity or afraid I would have sent someone back into the throes of grief. But one by one, each person sitting in the circle said, 'We love you, and we wish we had known Roger.' For the first time in a long time, that night, I slept straight through."

Rosella knew of only one thing to do, and she got up from her chair and held her mom's shoulders. They cried together for a bit until the odd positioning became uncomfortable. As they settled back into their places at the table, Cal entered the room and poured a cup of coffee.

He said quietly, "Excuse me, and I am sorry to be eavesdropping, but I heard what you just said, Liz. That was beautiful. It helped me to hear what you said and did. I miss him too and am so glad I got to know him."

Cal moved toward Rosella and wrapped his arms around her as she sat. There was a calm peace amongst all three. The dog, Hannah, in need of breakfast, signaled the return to reality by bringing her empty bowl to Cal.

That evening at the FNE, the usual guests enjoyed the time together. Judy and Jerry were engaging and informative in their talk about the clinic. What they had done for over twenty years with the clinic was quite amazing, and while they didn't come to fundraise, Rosella noticed several people handed them money at the end of the night to help with patients' expenses. As expected, the conversation about the Amish patients was interesting. Besides Beth and Joe, most of the group knew very little about the community, even though, at one point, everyone had been behind a slow-moving horse-drawn buggy driving around the area.

New Life was working on getting more of the Amish children vaccinated. This was a big problem as there had been an outbreak of pertussis and measles in several Amish groups nearby. Jerry and Judy had worked to gain the trust of the Amish bishops by providing care for so long at the clinic. While the male leaders were the final deciders of whether immunizations were allowed, the mothers had a lot of influence. Students working out of New Life arranged small meetings with some sympathetic mothers to discuss vaccines and the diseases they prevented. The health department in that county had made special accommodations to be available to administer vaccines, even offering to do home group vaccine clinics.

Jerry said, "Like many things we try, it doesn't always work as planned. We had little luck with this project. The community was never convinced that vaccines were necessary. They wanted to rely on their own medicines and felt that exposure to the disease was the natural way to build resistance." He continued, "That was sad because one child—a toddler—actually died from pertussis that year. But there are other parents who choose unwisely, and their children suffer, so I can't specifically blame the Amish." The non-judgmental attitude of these healers always impressed Rosella. In her mind, she couldn't be so forgiving.

The evening ended relatively early, as talking about these topics had been exhausting. Even Cal, who usually listened closely but spoke infrequently, appeared tired. Cal's comments were often the most succinct and profound of the entire discussion. Rosella wished she could be more like him with her interjections, but she usually got so involved with the conversations that she felt she was babbling.

Looking around at the guests as they packed up and headed to their cars, she was pleased and especially happy that the group had accepted Tresne so completely. The young person was relaxed in this setting and had added much to the conversation tonight. They were staying here at Rosella and Cal's, so they, along with the couple and Liz, sat around the fireplace after the others had left.

Cal poured everyone some of his favorite bourbon. This month, it was Basil Hayden. Cal was a connoisseur of bourbons, and it was one reason he had been happy to move to Kentucky. He and Rosella had taken tours of nearly every one of the Kentucky distilleries, and they both enjoyed a nip in these intimate settings.

The intimate group quietly swirled their glasses, breathing in the complex mixture of odors. Tresne was unfamiliar with bourbon when they first met Rosella, but this being their fourth or fifth visit, they were developing a discerning taste for the liquor. Liz had always liked the taste and sometimes would sit at a bar in Rochester, savoring the taste of a good bourbon. When Liz drank alone like that, she felt very hip and forgot the constraints of being an upstanding physician. The Elmwood Inn, within walking distance of Liz and Larry's house, was her favorite place to lose herself.

After a while, the bourbon glasses were empty, and Liz headed to the guest bedroom. Tresne prepped the couch for an overnight snooze. Rosella saw Tresne and Liz talking before the guests arrived earlier, and she was pleased to see them hug each other good night.

Saturday morning always started slow. Cal or Rosella would get up to attend to Hannah, but they both liked sleeping in on this non-workday. When Rosella eventually picked up her phone, she noticed a missed call from Ava and a voice message.

It went, "Hi Rosella, this is Ava. I am sorry I didn't make it to last night's gathering and sorry I haven't been coming to my lessons. I can explain better in person. Would you have time to get together to talk or maybe take a walk?"

Rosella immediately called Ava back and told her she didn't need to feel bad about missing things. She knew Ava was busy doctoring. Rosella went on, "My mom is visiting, but tomorrow, I am driving her to the airport in Lexington. Would you want to drive over with us? We could talk, and I would like you to meet my mom."

Ava hesitated slightly but agreed. She added, "Would you mind if I drove? I like to drive."

Rosella, who wasn't the greatest driver, was relieved and quickly agreed. "See you in the morning," they said together.

Ava arrived at Rosella's exactly on time. She liked to be punctual (though her medical duties often made her late) and would pace around in her kitchen until the clock showed the precise time she had calculated to leave so as not to be too early or too late. Since her commitment to playing the guitar more, she often practiced scales while she waited to depart.

Ava felt she had to do this mindless waiting because she knew if she started on a task in the half hour before needing to leave, she would lose herself in the activity and be late. It had always been like that. When she was young, her mother often had to set an alarm to remind Ava to stop reading her book. Otherwise, she was so absorbed she noticed nothing else.

Ava noted that Rosella's mother looked much like her daughter. Lithe, tall, graceful, with an ease in meeting people.

When introduced outside the car, Liz gave Ava a big hug and said, "I'm a hugger." Ava usually reflexively thought (not out loud) to say, *Well, I'm not a hugger and wonder why the hugger always prevails.* But being enveloped by Liz today, Ava sunk into the embrace and felt an odd connection. Liz said, "I am so happy to finally meet you. Rosella has told me about you and your practice. I want to hear more."

They headed to the west, and until they passed the next highway exit, their conversation was business-like. Liz sat in the front and asked about Ava's practice. When Ava revealed she had done her family practice residency in Rochester and had rotations at Strong Memorial, Liz interrogated her further on dates, which service she was on, and who had been her attendings and preceptors. Surprisingly, Ava had not intersected with Liz during those three years of her time in Rochester, but they knew many of the same doctors. Ava hadn't been back to Rochester since finishing the program, but she knew the city itself had changed, and Liz confirmed.

From the back seat, Rosella asked,

"Did you ever go to any of the musical offerings in Rochester?"

"Oh yes, I loved going to the free concerts at the Eastman," Ava responded.

"Did you ever see any of the local bands?" Rosella queried.

"No," Ava declared, "I never went out to see that kind of live music. I never saw your band."

Ava had read the article in *Rewind* about R and Me, but she had never brought it up with Rosella.

Liz said quietly, "The R in their band name was for my son Roger. Did you know he died?"

Ava nodded, "Yes, Rosella told me. I am so sorry."

Liz went on, "It's OK. I was telling Roz, that's what we call her, about how long it has been since I could say, 'It's OK.' The pain is still there, but lately, I have been able to talk about it."

Ava looked in the mirror at Rosella, who smiled back at her, silently sending the message that she and her mom were there to listen to whatever Ava needed or wanted to say.

Ava began, "I know what you mean about the pain. My mom died about a year ago."

Liz placed her hand over Ava's on the stick shift, "I am so sorry."

Ava continued, "That's why I wanted to talk to Rosella. She told me one day about losing her brother and how hard it was and how training for triathlons had been her therapy."

From the back, Rosella said, "Yes."

Liz asked, "What was your mother's name, Ava?"

"Margaret," Ava whispered. "She died in a car accident. Someone ran through a red light, and she was hit broadside. The doctor said she died instantly."

Liz and Rosella both declared, "That's horrible. We are sorry."

Ava went on, "It was horrible. My whole life, nothing like that had ever happened. I always, up till that point, felt like I was lucky; there were no deaths or tragedies. My dad was in the car and was severely injured and nearly died, and he was still in the hospital when we had her funeral. It was a difficult time. Still is."

Only road noise penetrated the silence of the car.

"I have kept a lot of my feelings locked up since she died, but I don't think that's working. My mom and I had a unique relationship. She always pushed me to be perfect and work as hard as possible. And her pride in my accomplishment was kind of embarrassing. I don't know why. Maybe because of her high hopes for me, I never really had a deep conversation with her about who I really was. Oh, I am sorry, this is not like me to spill so much out."

Liz encouraged Ava by saying, "Go ahead. We're listening, and we want to hear."

Ava went on, "The last time I saw my mom, we argued. Not really an argument, but something. I don't even remember clearly what it was about, but I ended up going to something without my parents because I was embarrassed for them to go. I think I was still thinking like a teenager. Even though I was over thirty. I wish we had talked more, that I would have had more time with her. That I could have told her thank you and really meant it."

Rosella asked, "So you feel regret? So did I. Roger and I were as close as two siblings could be. I wished I had told him so much more than I did. I wish I could have shown him how much he meant to me before he got sick."

Ava took a deep breath. She said, "Thank you for letting me say this. I know there is more, but I feel like I need to let it out slowly. What you said, Rosella, about how you felt after your brother died is exactly how I felt after my mom died. Like there was a hole in my heart, and I wanted to do anything to replace that pain with a more agreeable emotion. Fear even. It is just now that sometimes I can replace it with happiness or a little piece of joy. It is taking a lot of time."

Liz spoke up while watching out the window.

"Right after Roger died, my friends and acquaintances said how sorry they were and asked what they could do. When they saw me, a look of concern would come over their faces. For a while, I felt like losing him was a shared experience with these friends. But then, I noticed those people moved on. They forgot. As the months went by, routine activities replaced the tragedy in their lives. They didn't live a life with a son no longer in it. Even with my husband, Roger's father, our loss was perceived differently. Even with Roz, I couldn't know exactly how much she was hurting. Nor could I have offered much comfort had I known. In the end, people go through dying alone, and survivors go through grieving alone. But talking about what it feels like has helped me; I just learned this. Ask Roz to tell you about my artwork sometime. Thank you for trusting us with this conversation."

Rosella spoke up from the back seat. "Mom, I want to tell you something."

Liz turned in her seat to face Rosella. "Go ahead."

"I wish you hadn't asked me to play at Roger's funeral. You know how I froze and ran out of the church? I think that experience has made it hard for me to recover. I am not blaming you, but I wanted to tell you."

Liz gasped and teared up, "You know, Roz, I have thought so many times what a bad idea that was. I wish I could take those days back and do things differently. I was not in my right mind. I am so sorry. I don't know what else to say."

Rosella said, "It's OK, Mom."

They were almost at the airport by this time, and the group fell silent. Ava pulled up at the departure lane and hugged Liz goodbye. She watched as mother and daughter walked in through the airport doors arm in arm. She thought, *Rosella is so lucky to still have her mother.*

<u>Ad-Ad</u>

Notes for *Inside Taber's: A Study of the Medical Dictionary* by Dr. Ava

I have written thousands of prescriptions, and I did not know that "add" or "adde" is a prescriptive abbreviation meaning "let there be added." And, oddly, similar to the condition known as Addison's Disease —failure of the adrenal glands and insufficient production of steroid hormones. I have only seen one confirmed case of this while often considering it in my differential diagnoses.

The "adeno" section of Taber's is very tiresome. The word, from the Greek "aden," means glands. A gland is an organ that secretes things, such as breast milk from the mammary glands, lymph from the lymph glands, and a lubricating sebaceous substance from the tarsal glands in the eye. There are a lot of glands.

What I learned by slogging through the adeno sections relates to stains. Every other week, I go to the Tumor Board at my hospital. Here, the surgeon who removed the tumor sits next to the pathologist who examines the tumor, who stands next to the radiologist who guesses by x-ray where the tumor lies and how far it has spread. Next to them are the medical and radiation oncologists who make comments about how best to treat this tumor and its host. Finally, usually squeezed into a back corner, I sit with my Palliative Care badge. The hospice doctor occupies another back-row seat. Both of us know we will see many of the patients in the future but are rarely asked to contribute insights into their "active" treatment.

Enough snide comments about the role of palliative care services in cancer treatment. It is getting much better. The insight I had about stains relates to the many slides of special stains that the pathologist projects. The cells take up the stains (or not sometimes) because they are "adeno"— glands. There is space for them to take up stains. Anyway, that's a pretty rudimentary understanding of what happens that I can understand.

Yesterday, somebody asked me about their tonsils, in particular, some material they had found in their tonsils. That can be called a tonsillolith. Interesting, but the reason it came up in the As was "adenoids." Adenoids are lymphatic tissue that forms a prominence along the wall of the pharyngeal recess of the back of the throat, closer to the nose, as opposed to the tonsils, which are actually a "mass" of lymphoid tissue just below this area. I wonder when a prominence becomes a mass.

Chapter 15: The Medicine Closet

Ava pulled out of her drive Monday morning with wipers flying. Rainy and snow days meant many patients wouldn't make it into the office. The hills around Berry Hill made for a dangerous drive. There were many more snow days for school children here in Kentucky than in Michigan. When Ava first moved to Kentucky, she couldn't understand why school was canceled so often, but after making a few trips to homes on these back roads, she completely understood the dangers of driving a school bus up the hollers.

Thinking about hollers always made her think about the differences between people who had grown up in this area and those who had been "transplanted" here. How they pronounced the word "hollow" was a good indicator of where somebody was from. The locals said "holler"—pronounced like a term for shouting. The new people said "hollow"—rhyming with follow. There were a lot of words that Ava had gotten used to hearing pronounced differently from in Michigan. "Appalachian English," some people called it. Adding an "er" to words ending in "a" like "potater" or the oft expressed "tobaccer." Ava liked the way people pronounced these words, and when she read scholarly journals about why such dialects came to be, she was reminded of the musical lyricism of this speech. Listening to her patients every day, she had come to enjoy their speech's unique twists and turns. She felt offended when comics or smart alecks made fun of them.

Today, she drove much under the speed limit, remembering her near miss from not long ago. She thought back to the near collision as she passed the junkyard. That was the day she knew she wanted to slow down. She guessed that her decision to read more *Taber's* and play more guitar were good things but still felt that something else was wrong in her life.

When she arrived at the office with plenty of time to prepare for the day, she reviewed Lawrence's lab work. It was not good. She thought through the workup he would need and what these findings probably meant—that his liver was failing. She also rehearsed what she would say to him on the phone. Knowing that he lived alone up a holler, she decided to wait till after the storm in a day or so to inform him of the results. Why add more worry to his day?

She always chafed when doctors adopted this paternalistic attitude —withholding information because they thought it would be better for a patient—but in this case, she excused herself. Plus, she acknowledged that she was not capable of telling him the news just yet. She didn't want to cry on the phone.

While she was collecting these thoughts, one of the nursing assistants came to her desk.

She said, "There's a boy with a laceration in room 1. He was trying to get out of the house with his family this morning and bumped into something in the yard. Their house was in danger of being washed away by the rain. His mother is with him."

Ava asked the assistant, Stephanie, without looking at her, "Did you clean it up?"

"Yes," Stephanie responded rather impatiently, "And it will need stitches."

Ava said, "OK. I will be right there. Can you find out when he had his last tetanus shot?"

Closing out Lawrence's labs, she hung her stethoscope around her neck and headed for room 1. Inside was one scared boy, Josh, about twelve years old, and his mother, Bonnie. Ava had never met them before but knew other family members.

They both had wet hair and wet shoes. Momentarily, a path of mud distracted Ava. Bonnie had a large purse in her lap and removed an official-looking green card when she introduced herself to Ava—the immunization record. Ava sighed with relief and marveled at the mother's organization to pack out the small card during a likely hasty escape.

She asked, "How are you doing? I understand you had to leave your house this morning. And now this, you have had quite a morning, heh?"

Bonnie nodded her head and said, "Yes. It's the third time this year we've had to leave in a hurry. At least we know what to pack after two practices."

She tried to laugh, but the chuckle was half-hearted.

"I don't know what he scraped his leg on, but my husband has some old lawnmowers in the front yard, and I think some piece on those must have done it." Bonnie continued, "He's all up to date with his shots, and here is his shot record. He had his most recent one just last year."

Ava looked at the record. The mother was right; Josh had had his DtaP—tetanus, diphtheria, pertussis—shot just last year when he turned 11. Luckily, he did not need another one today. Ava turned to Josh and asked, "How are you doing?"

Josh quietly replied, "OK."

"Did you get bit by a piece of metal? Those things can be pretty mean."

Josh ventured a smile, but he still didn't look very relaxed.

Ava asked if she could see his leg. Josh reached for his mom's hand. "OK."

Ava put on gloves and raised the loose bandage covering Josh's left shin. She found a straight-line laceration about halfway down on his shin. The wound was nice and clean and had even edges. When she touched it gently, the edges pulled apart, and she could see it was deep. Her assistant was right; it would need stitches. If this had been in a different, more visible area, she might have suggested steri-strips or even glue, but with an active boy who probably would be out running by tomorrow, she decided to place a few sutures.

"Well, Josh, that is a pretty nice cut you have. Do you mind if I help keep it looking nice by hemming it up a little?"

Josh looked questioningly at her.

"Does your mom do any sewing? Like, does she make quilts?"

Josh said, "Yes. She and Mamaw made a quilt for me as a baby."

Bonnie added proudly, "He still sleeps with that quilt every night. We packed it when we left this morning." Josh looked sheepish.

Ava continued, "Well those little stitches your mom and grandma make, that's what I will do to this cut. Add a few tiny little threads that will keep it together."

Josh looked more apprehensive.

"Hey," Ava said, "do you want your mom to go get your quilt, and you can lie down and rest while I fix up your cut?"

Josh looked at his mother and nodded.

Ava went to the door, "While your mom goes to get that, let me ask Pat to come in and keep you company. You must know her son—you're probably in the same grade at school. Do you know Andrew?"

"I know Andrew Lewis and Andrew Hogg."

Ava gave him a thumbs up. "Andrew Lewis, that's her son. Hold on just a minute." Ava asked Pat to help her in the hallway, and she and Bonnie walked out as Pat entered. She knew Pat would relax the boy, making the entire operation easier.

Ava asked Bonnie how she was doing as the exam room door closed.

"OK, I guess. I'm worried about what we'll find when we get back to our trailer. Last big rain, the creek came up in our yard, and we lost some of the kids' toys. Today, they say it may be worse. My husband stayed at home to save whatever he could. Like I said, this is the third time this year. I don't know how many more scares I can take."

Ava didn't know exactly what to say except that she was sorry. She knew enough about life here that just moving to higher ground was not an option for many people. Almost all of Ava's patients were lower income, and moving a trailer or finding a more desirable home site was out of reach for many.

She asked, "Who will you stay with until the creek goes down?"

Bonnie replied, "My mother-in-law lives up on the hill, so we can stay there. But that's not always the easiest thing, either, if you know what I mean."

Ava nodded and smiled. She recalled meeting Bonnie's mother-in-law once, knew that she was very religious, and guessed she might be a challenge to be around for long.

She gestured toward the back and said, "Well, let me get my supplies, and you can go get the quilt. I'm eager to see it myself. I'll meet you back in the room in a minute." With that, she headed down the hall to the medicine closet/room.

Ava selected the lidocaine and a suture kit from an array of choices. She enjoyed sewing lacerations up and, every year, ran a suture clinic for third-year medical students.

Back in the exam room, Ava handily injected the anesthetic in Josh's leg while Pat entertained him, and he clutched his quilt. Having him distracted this way, he barely flinched when she placed the tiny needle. She quickly sutured the wound with eight interrupted stitches and told him he was all done. He couldn't believe she was already finished and looked down at his leg like it might have been amputated.

He hopped off the table, a relaxed and carefree kid. Pat gave Bonnie instructions on when to return and a bandaging schedule. Ava told Josh how good he was and asked if he would like to stop at the treasure box on his way out.

"Sure," he said. "Can I pick out something for my baby sister?"

"Of course," Ava said and looked at Bonnie.

"His sister is with my mother-in-law," Bonnie said while Josh was in the room. When he was out of earshot, she added, "Hopefully, Mother will let them keep the toys."

Despite arriving at the office early, this emergency had set her back on her schedule by about twenty minutes. She fleetingly thought about patients' complaints related to waiting for a provider. They were upset if they were waiting too long, but if they were seen and the provider seemed rushed and wasn't excited about spending extra time with them, they were upset. Luckily, Ava's patients knew that while she sometimes ran a few minutes behind, she spent a reasonable amount of time with each patient and never rushed them out.

The rest of the morning and early afternoon were surprisingly busy at the office. Patients were coming in despite the storm. By 3:00, though, the rain continued, and the office manager suggested closing the clinic so all the staff could get home before it got worse. Everyone was in favor of that. The nurses, assistants, and front office staff quickly finished their work and headed home. Ava still needed to do some charting, so she was in her back office typing and closing out files.

Her colleagues headed out and told each other to drive carefully. Ava thought of the last time she drove in heavy rain and ran off the road. Pat walked into the office and sat down.

She asked Ava, "Are you OK? Will you be able to drive home? I can have my husband give you a ride home if you want. Or you can spend the night at our house. You know it's just up the street."

"No, I am OK. I think I can make it home. I will definitely not take the back roads. The highway is the way for me today."

Pat asked again, "Are you sure?"

"Yes," Ava reassured her. "I'm sure."

"OK," Pat said. "Then I am off. Do you need anything?"

Ava said, "No, I'm good."

The office became eerily quiet with the sudden departure of the staff. Ava was about to leave herself when she noticed the bottle of lidocaine sitting on her desk. The health accreditation commission had just visited the clinic, and that was the one demotion they had received when inspectors found some half-used lidocaine bottles out in the open. They were told they needed to be locked up in the medicine room.

This room also held a small supply of drug samples that could be dispensed as trials for patients and the medicines used for codes and emergencies. Since the inspection, maintenance rigged up a locking system to a room previously used for cleaning supplies. That's where the lidocaine was kept now. Ava thought about the rule and decided to follow protocol and return the bottle where it belonged.

She got up from her desk, holding the bottle, to make a quick trip to the medicine room. She punched in the code and swung open the door, keeping her foot in the door as she leaned in to replace the lidocaine on a nearby shelf. With the recently reconfigured room, the maintenance crew hadn't figured out a way to keep the lock from engaging when the door shut, and there wasn't a way to unlock it from the inside.

As Ava reached toward the shelf in the dark room, her foot tripped over a box lying on the floor. The instant she tried to regain her balance, her back foot slipped out from holding the door, and it shut with a bang. She lunged for the door, but it was too late, and the heavy door clunked shut.

The office manager explained the situation in the staff meeting just days before and warned people to be careful. Ava was trapped inside with no food, water, or toilet. "*Oh boy,*" she sighed.

Ad-Ag

Notes for *Inside Taber's: A Study of the Medical Dictionary* by Dr. Ava Hogan Levine

Consider the phrase "ad nauseum," which literally means "of such degree or extent as to produce nausea." I may not be so flippant with that term now that I think about it. What would it be like if one suffered from aerophobia—the morbid fear of a draft or of fresh air?

There are two columns of after-somethings, from after-action to after-vision. Most everyone has experienced an aftersensation when we still feel like we are on a swing, boat, or pogo stick after that action or stimulus has stopped. What causes that? Are our vestibular systems so gullible or malleable that they conform to any position change so easily? And how long does it take to experience an aftersensation? I notice it from a swing after the shortest time—maybe ten or twenty swings. The aftersensation that lasts the longest for me is when I have been snorkeling in the ocean. That feeling of the swells of the waves seems to stay with me when I go to bed and long into the night—yet another interesting question.

A good deal of physiology teachers have demonstrated Kohnstamm's phenomenon. This is an "aftermovement"—a persistent and spontaneous contraction of a muscle after a strong contraction against resistance has ceased. For example, when I stand in a door frame, pushing my arms up and against the frame, then move forward away from the walls, my arms abduct involuntarily and are elevated by the deltoid muscle. That's a cool experiment to show kids.

I am reading through the list of agents, which is by necessity long since an agent is defined as something that causes an effect. How can "riot control agent" be sandwiched between "oral hypoglycemic agent" and "sclerosing agent" in a medical dictionary? The only explanation is that some riot control agents, e.g., tear gas and pepper spray, can cause a medical condition. But so do guns, and the only "guns" in the "G's" are "Gunn's dots" (white spots on the retina of the eye) and "Marcus Gunn Syndrome." This syndrome, fascinatingly, is a congenital condition where a permanently partially closed eyelid, ptosis, opens briefly when the mouth is opened, or the jaw moves to one side. Also known as "jaw winking,"—the condition can be acquired like after Bell's Palsy. There seem to be more exciting words when I venture out of the As.

Chapter 16: Big Changes

Rosella lay next to Cal in their double bed. She stared at the ceiling but thought furiously about her conversation with Tresne earlier in the day and about her conversation with her mother. She couldn't explain why she felt excited when she thought of the covered bridge.

She said to the dark air, "What do you think?"

Cal, half asleep, murmured, "What?" He was used to Rosella carrying on half of a conversation in her head before speaking out loud, but this question completely took him off guard.

"What are you talking about?" he repeated kindly.

"What do you think about my not playing?" she said, continuing her internal thoughts. "Have you ever understood it?"

Cal took a moment. From experience, he expected her to say more.

As predicted, Rosella asked, "Do you think there is any rational reason to have stopped performing?" Cal again remained silent, knowing this was a personal inquiry.

"Do you think any good has come from it?" Rosella continued. "Tell me what you think, Cal, from a personal perspective and as a philosopher."

This was Cal's cue to respond. But he wasn't sure what to say. For years, he wondered what good it had done for Rosella to decline every invitation she was offered to play in public. He longed for the days of sitting in an audience and watching the faces of those around him sink into the music. The cheering after a song ended was as uplifting to him as it was to the band. While being private, he also liked the proximity to fame accorded him with his status as a member of a band family.

Cal started off, "From a philosophical perspective, "good" could be thought of as 'right.' The right way as opposed to an evil way if one thinks of the two as opposites. This refers to times when someone has a choice between two directions. Aristotle. So, is the good you ask about related to your own personal good or a public good?"

"I think we both would agree that there has been no public good that has come from your decision to stop playing in public. And if you had been given a choice without any other considerations, then one could say you took the wrong course—the not-good course."

"This was the choice you made for your own personal good, and only you can decide if that was the right course. I believe it would have been hard for you to perform without your brother, and emotionally, it may have torn you apart." Cal realized he was lapsing into professorial mode.

He softened his voice, "On the other hand, did you stop performing because you thought you didn't deserve to benefit from that aspect of music? Maybe, because Roger died, there was a piece of you that felt you did not deserve to continue doing what you loved."

Rosella rolled over to look squarely at Cal.

"But I wasn't able to save him," she said shakily.

Cal reached for her and said, "You couldn't have saved him. He had biology working against him. Not anything more magical or more changeable than that."

Cal knew he sounded harsh speaking this way, but Rosella had blamed herself for so long. He hated that she felt responsible for Roger's illness. And he thought she should ease up after all this time. When she started doing triathlons, he saw it as a breakthrough from her grief, and it did seem to lift some of her sadness. But she carried this guilt always.

Cal went on, "Think of my friend Moe and his wife Diane. She had the same kind of leukemia your brother had. Do you blame Moe for letting Diane die? Of course not. He did everything he could. Just like you did."

Rosella was quiet for a couple of minutes.

"You know," she expressed, "when I stopped doing triathlons last year, one of the reasons was that I didn't feel the need to go through all the suffering of training any longer. As if what I accomplished finishing the races really was enough to remember Roger, and that, maybe, in a way, I decided I didn't deserve to punish myself physically any longer. You are saying that I don't deserve to deny myself my music."

Cal replied, "Yes, I think that is what I am saying. I remember how much you loved being in front of an audience and taking them along on the ride. You were good at being attuned to people listening. Even in our living room, when friends came over, you knew exactly what to play and how to phrase things. That's a gift."

Rosella nodded in agreement. "I did love that."

Cal went on, "Your brother was the instrumental whiz; he really was a genius, but you were the heart of the music. You gave it color."

Rosella laughed, "Are you saying I couldn't play very well?"

Cal reassured her, "No, not at all. I'm just saying that what you added to the mix was soul and humanity."

Rosella relaxed and said, "I suppose you're right."

She went on to tell him about Tresne's conversation. She explained, "They mentioned recording in a covered bridge up north of here, and for the first time in a long while, I was excited and could almost hear myself playing. I imagined what music would sound the best and how to arrange a couple of songs that would be perfect for that setting. I thought about how some of my students could be involved as well. I was excited about it—I am excited about playing there."

Cal said, "I'm glad." Their conversation released a tension that had been simmering under the surface for a while.

They held each other closely, enjoying how their minds and bodies responded. That evening's love making felt boundless.

Awakening late the next morning, Rosella found a note from Tresne on the kitchen table next to a pot of freshly made coffee.

> Had to leave early. Thanks for all your hospitality. I saw a spark when we talked about the covered bridge. Let me know what you are thinking. I am all in.
>
> Love,
>
> Tresne.

For the rest of the morning, Rosella could hardly focus on the Redbud Music invoices she was trying to balance. She was thinking of the music. She took her favorite guitar from its case and tuned it up. With Hannah by her side, she played through some chords and tried out a few melodies. She thought about all the songs she knew. None of them seemed quite right for her mood, so she hooked up her looper and made syncopated beats and chord progressions until her fingers started to go numb. She would need to build up calluses if there was to be more playing. Cal listened with one ear and a satisfied smile.

Rosella was relieved that yesterday's bad weather and rainstorms had stopped before Tresne traveled back to Cincinnati. She also thought about Ava and her mother's accident. She thought about the difference between a sudden death and an expected death. And remembering her conversation with Cal from the night before, she wondered if there would have been even more guilt or "what ifs" had her brother died in an accident. She never asked Ava if she was angry at the other driver. Did the other driver die? Those were questions she might ask if ever the time was right.

Rosella made a home visit to the sister of the patient that Ava had seen last week. She went there every couple of weeks, and the girl, Amy, was progressing well on her guitar. She and Amy usually sat at the kitchen table and worked on her lessons. There wasn't space in the living room with all of Daniel's equipment, and their mom was usually tending to Daniel in that room.

Out of the corner of her eye, Rosella could see Daniel making jerky movements. Sometimes, his arms moved like he would hit his mom, Lisa, who only laughed and tickled Daniel. What a great attitude she had. Other times, Lisa concentrated hard on hooking Daniel's feeding tube up to a bag of liquid. Despite Rosella not wanting to stare, she couldn't tear her eyes away from what was happening in the other room. Amy proceeded like this was all normal.

One day, Rosella asked Amy, "What is it like to have a brother who takes so much of your mother's time?

Amy answered, "Sometimes I get mad at her because she never has time for me. I love my brother and would do anything in the world for him, but yeah, I wish he wasn't sick."

Rosella took a chance and said, "I had a younger brother too. He wasn't sick when he was young but got sick after we grew up. It's different when you are all grown up. But I can see what you are saying. Your life would be different if Daniel weren't so sick."

Amy nodded and said, "I know it makes my mom sad. I think that's why our dad left. He couldn't handle it. I am madder at him than at anybody else."

Rosella just wanted to hold the girl, but instead, she played some minor chords on her guitar. The chords, like the blues, were so sad that they actually made her feel better.

She said, "Have you practiced your A minor and E minor chords?"

Amy said, "Yes, I have been working on them. They're easy."

Rosella said, "Play those two chords while you tell me how you are feeling." Amy looked at her oddly. She had never talked or sung while she played and wasn't comfortable combining the new activities.

Rosella said, "Go ahead, just talk while you are doodling around with those chords."

Lisa and Daniel had moved to the bedroom, and other than hearing a few loud giggles from the back room, Rosella was pretty sure no one would hear Amy strumming in the kitchen.

She prodded Amy more, "Just try; I'll even walk into the living room if that would be better. It's hard to sing in front of someone."

Amy nodded, "OK." Rosella walked into the front room and started to put her guitar in its case.

She noted Amy's case propped up in a corner.

There was a very generous doctor who donated instruments to students whose families couldn't afford to buy one. While the doctor remained anonymous and Rosella had never revealed her identity, she did mark the cases with a distinctive symbol. It was a straightforward image of a hand holding a heart. She usually stamped it somewhere that was not too obvious. She could see the stamp on this case in Amy's house.

At least fifty other donated instruments were scattered around the area, given away by this one person. Rosella remembered reading about an instrument drive for people who had been displaced by a tornado. More than 500 instruments were collected in less than a month, and everyone who lined up to receive one said that being able to play a banjo or mandolin again would be the best balm to losing their home.

Rosella could hear a faint voice from the kitchen as the A and E chords alternated. It was so soft that Rosella couldn't make out the words. She waved goodbye to Amy as she left, and the girl gave her a nod, never interrupting her song.

Rosella checked in at Redbud Music and found the shop humming with activity. An after-school group was setting up their mics. The group used computers, electric keyboards, and a beatbox to produce pretty good "deep house music." She couldn't help herself from tapping to the tunes.

Her assistant, Helen, was helping someone buy strings for a guitar. Another woman was waiting to be helped, and Rosella introduced herself and asked, "Can I help you?"

The customer was older with gray hair and seemed a bit timid. She said, "I wondered if you have any acoustic amps?"

Rosella motioned toward an area of the store with sound equipment and said, "Yes, we have several kinds. What would you be using it for? Just for practice or for performance?"

The woman seemed hesitant and a little embarrassed.

"I just play in my house but want to try different things. My friends have said it's fun to loop and play along with myself. Is that crazy?"

Rosella laughed and touched the woman's shoulder, "Absolutely not crazy. You'll love what you can do with a looper and maybe some reverb. What instrument do you play?"

The woman again seemed hesitant, though Rosella could tell she was loosening up a bit.

She answered, "I play the nyckelharpa."

Rosella exclaimed, "Wow, I have never met anyone who plays the nyckelharpa. We have an old one on one of the shelves, and I've tried to play it, but it's so complicated, I never could."

The woman said, "I am from Sweden, and many of my friends in high school played. I moved here many years ago but have never found another nyckelharpa player in all these years. I miss playing duets with my friends."

Rosella led Ingrid away from the amps and to a shelf with old accordions. She stood on a nearby stool and reached to the back of one level to pull out a long instrument. It looked a bit like a violin, except with pegs and many more strings. Attached with a loose string was a bow about a third the size of a violin bow.

Rosella presented it to Ingrid. "What do you think?" she asked. "Is it playable?" Ingrid took the heavy piece and plucked a couple of strings. It was woefully out of tune, and dust flew.

Ingrid said, "It is beautiful but needs tuning. I think it could be played."

"All of the pieces are there," Rosella explained. It was made by a music enthusiast who once lived here. He made and played dulcimers and told me that since he was Swedish, he tried to make this nyckelharpa. He passed away a couple of years ago and donated this one to the shop.

Before he died, he said I was to give it away free to anyone who came in asking for the obscure instrument. You are the first person."

Ingrid said, "Why don't I teach you to play, and I won't have to buy the looper and amp? I've heard about you in *Rewind*. My son is a musician and reads every issue of the magazine. I know you will catch on to playing it very quickly."

Rosella was a little skeptical that she could learn to play this thing, but she said she would give it a try. They arranged to meet next week for Rosella's first lesson. Ingrid told Rosella she would need to get new strings, though. When she left, Rosella went to her supply catalogs to find some, and of course, there were many sources. She was happy to see that Amazon did not sell them.

Even as Rosella looked again at the ancient-appearing instrument, she thought about the covered bridge. The spark of music was returning to her in full force. She walked over to the electronic group and listened for a good half hour. Seeing the joy on these kids' faces made her wonder why she had denied herself this gift these past years. But just as she thought this, she knew it could have been no other way. Her grief would not have allowed her to enjoy music like this until now.

She also watched the door for Ava. They had arranged last week to shift lessons to Tuesday late afternoon to have a little more time. She was surprised Ava hadn't arrived yet as she was almost always early. She considered what music she might suggest to Ava that could also pull her out of her grief. There were some groups she had listened to on YouTube that combined sorrowful lyrics with upbeat background music. Even this electronica sound might be therapeutic.

Last week, a harpist came to Redbud Music for something, and Rosella talked to her about where she played. The woman, named Trina, was a "music thanatologist." Trina was in a hurry to get to the hospice house but promised to come back and talk to Rosella about the field.

Rosella Googled the term and found information on the Music-Thanatology Association International (MTAI) site. Thanatology is a musical/clinical modality that unites music and medicine in end-of-life care. Using a harp, voice, or other instrument, music responds to a patient's physiological needs.

Rosella remembered the last few days of Roger's life. She asked him what music to play from his vast music collection, but he wasn't interested in hearing anything. Rosella thought she understood. When she listened to familiar music, she focused so intently on how the sounds were made and what would be the next note or chord. It took all her attention. She thought Roger didn't want to concentrate so hard on the music. But what a "music thanatologist" offered would have been perfect. Music that was not intended to distract but rather bring comfort and was unscripted.

Returning to the covered bridge idea, Rosella had an idea for the feel of the music she would play. And she had an idea of which bridge to start with. It was an unused one that led over to an old church with a cemetery on its grounds. The thought of a cemetery was a bit scary, but Rosella felt a strong instinct that this needed to be the setting for her return to performance. She found her phone to text Tresne and her notebook to start jotting down some words and phrases for the song. She had the melody in her head already.

24

Chapter 17: Trapped

Ava looked around the room, taking inventory. Her first thought was *that this was a small space.* Her next thought was, *Will I be able to breathe in here?* She looked at the gap under the door and breathed slightly easier. She assumed there was enough air exchange, but she could already feel her heartbeat speeding up and moisture in her armpits. *Take deep breaths and relax,* she told herself.

Realizing she still held the bottle of lidocaine, she turned toward the stacked shelves. In a shallow tray were the other bottles of partially used lidocaine. She made sure to put this one with the others labeled with epinephrine. She arranged the eight bottles in lines and carefully replaced the tray in its place. Her mind was on the edge of panicking about being in this room for an unknowable amount of time, hours likely, but she began to make a list in her mind. This simple action calmed her a bit. First, she would carefully examine each area in the small room and decide what she could use for comfort and what she could learn from the product.

Under the shelf of lidocaine bottles was the crash cart, which was wheeled into the storeroom at the end of each clinic day and restocked. Although the apparatus had a plastic lock, she felt justified in breaking the lock to look. She would do that later.

On a separate tray on the second shelf were several boxes of Narcan. These nasal types could be easily grabbed and used in an emergency.

Last week, the clinic hosted a Harm Reduction Team that used the office to educate the public about using Narcan and distributed free boxes to anyone who took the training. There were several left, which the group had said could be given to family members of substance users who came to the office. Ava knew this would be hard for her patients to admit. Despite widespread coverage about drug use and overdose deaths in her area, there was still a lot of embarrassment or shame in talking about what was happening to a daughter, son, or parent.

She wondered if it wouldn't be a better idea to have the Narcan out in more accessible places where someone could take a box without being so obvious. She had read that some hospitals had started placing these reversal drugs in waiting areas and stairways for immediate access if a person was found unresponsive. But, like putting condoms in bathrooms, this would normalize the treatment. There had been no public outcry about placing AED units everywhere. But sexuality and drug use carried much more stigma.

Distracted, Ava thought about her disappointing efforts to convince the mayor of Berry Hill to support a needle exchange program in the town. These health department-sponsored programs would do more to bring addicts in for testing, avoidance of diseases, and hopefully eventual rehab than the attitude of shaming them. It was an uphill challenge to sway opinions, especially with the heavy religious emphasis on sin.

Next on this shelf were the syringes filled with heparin and saline. Ava registered that they were pretty close to each other and ticked that off as something she could rearrange while stuck here. At the top of this shelf were paper supplies: toilet paper in big rolls, paper gowns folded flat, a few real gowns, and a couple of blankets. These would come in handy for sleeping.

Beside these shelves were two compact refrigerators: one for medicines like insulin and vaccines, the other for the lab specimens and reagents. Someone had picked up today's labs, so at least Ava was not sharing the room with urine and stool samples.

Beside this area was a small sink and an autoclave. A few wrapped sterile instruments were packed in a steel kidney basin. What an odd name. Ava assumed it was named for the shape of a kidney bean. She would have to check that in *Taber's* when she got out. The panic resumed as she rephrased her thoughts to *if she got out.*

A neat pile of easy-to-reach 4 X 4 gauze packs and nesting plastic kidney basins. Finally on that side of the room were the portable oxygen tanks used when patients walked or wheeled in needing oxygen. The office usually switched patients who were on continuous oxygen over to the clinic's tanks, so their precious personal tanks would last till they got home. Only a few of her patients used the portable shoulder-held devices that ran forever. The oxygen-conserving devices.

The opposite wall held brooms, a mop with a bucket, and some cleaning cloths. These couldn't be all the cleaning supplies for the clinic, but they must be used for quick cleanup. Ava turned the bucket over and sat down. She thought again, *Oh boy.*

There wasn't much in this room. She repeated no food, no water, no toilet in her head. She also didn't have a phone since she had left it on her desk when she dashed into the room to replace the bottle. And she didn't have her watch. Why did she choose this one day to leave her watch at home on the dresser? Because the strap was irritating her wrist? So, she didn't have a way to tell what time it was or how long she had been in here.

She noticed a blinking red light from the smoke detector in the corner of the ceiling. Fleetingly, she thought this could be a way to track the minutes. Figuring that her heartbeat was about sixty beats per minute when relaxed, she felt her pulse while watching the red blinking. There seemed to be no connection between the beats and the blinks. After counting to sixty a few times, Ava abandoned this idea.

She formulated a strategy of organizing the shelves first. Then, she would make a palette with the blankets and use the paper products as pillows. After every task she planned, she would lie down for a period and try to meditate. Already, she was feeling a wave of panic at being here, possibly until eight o'clock in the morning—over twelve hours.

The next thing she would work on would be opening the crash cart and reading through the ACLS manual and cheat sheet she knew was there. She was due to recertify for ACLS next month, so this would be productive. She would also pretend she was running a code with different scenarios, as she knew she would have to do for the ACLS class. She figured these activities would take at least a couple of hours. After that, she didn't know what to do. Maybe someone would return to the clinic for some unexpected reason, and she would escape.

Organizing the shelves took less time than she had imagined. There wasn't much to organize. Since the most recent accreditation inspection by The Joint Commission—everyone at the office still called them JC-AHO—there were no more drug samples allowed in the office. Ava had always shunned the drug reps who brought goodies and free lunches while they promoted their newest products. She read through the material they left, even if she wouldn't take up patient time to see them, and tried not to be influenced by the studies sponsored by and probably biased towards the promoted drug. Being objective was a constant battle since advertising was everywhere—TV, magazines, billboards.

She made her palette and sat in the lotus position, trying to meditate. That was impossible. Her mind came back to this trapped room with every breath. Even repeating the Om sound she had learned at Yogaville did not help. She remembered a time she went into a sensory deprivation tank at a spa for an hour. She floated in an Epsom salt solution that took away her sense of touching any surface. The reason she had tried it was because some of her patients talked about how it had helped their aches, and another said it was good for her depression. The difference between this involuntary isolation/deprivation and that experience was that she had soothing music playing through headphones and knew she could push a button and be released at any time. The experience in the tank had been relaxing, but this was not.

Her stomach began to rumble, and she recalled skipping lunch, hoping to leave the office early. Luckily, she hadn't drunk much water today so the lack of a toilet might not be a problem for a while.

She broke open the flimsy lock on the crash cart and pulled out the papers and laminated drug sheet. This might not have been the best idea to decrease stress, as running codes and thinking about running codes was always an anxiety-producing experience. At the time, Ava projected calm, but anticipating the experience always caused fear. She knew ER doctors who thrived on this kind of adrenaline surge, but not her. She put the manual back in the cart and shoved it back into place. She would study for the course another time.

Listening carefully in the silent room, she thought she heard the clinic's back door open. The door would have been a couple of hallways away and close to fifty feet from this room. She jumped up, pounded on the door, and called out, "Help!" in the loudest voice possible. She also kicked the door and grabbed the mop handle to amplify her pounding. She paused to listen and heard no other sounds.

She surmised that the lab courier had stepped inside the back door to grab the lab specimens from inside and had left already. Like Ava had planned to do earlier, this person usually held the door open with his foot while he quickly gathered the specimens and finished within seconds. She stopped pounding and sat back down on the bucket. It would be a long stay here, and figuring that the courier usually came at five or six, maybe earlier today because of the storm, she had only been trapped here for at most three hours.

Waves of panic started to rise in Ava. She could stifle them if she sat very still and took deep breaths, but after a few moments of heavy breathing, she felt like the room lost its oxygen. Logically, she knew this couldn't happen, but she felt the room air grow stale.

During her residency, she took a scuba diving course and went to the Florida Keys with her friend to dive. As she descended with the master, she felt this same kind of rising panic. There was this imbalance; she didn't know which way was up or down, and she felt like the water above her was crushing her. She tried to concentrate on observing the fish and coral in front of her, but this sense of panic would not leave. She had never dived again. Even the thought of being under 10 feet of water made her uncomfortable.

She also began to think about the concept of time. A few years before, she had been very interested in the definition of time and the association of time with energy. She had this idea that time expanded with the amount of energy expended in that unit of time. It was a bizarre concept, and the physics people she knew made fun of her idea. She had come to this query because she found that when she was concentrating on an activity, time seemed to move slower, and when she was nonchalantly engaging in something, time moved faster. Maybe it was her perception of time. She read an article that measured time perception in subjects experiencing a life-threatening event. The study determined that the slowing of time, which is often talked about during frightening events, was more of a factor of recollection rather than perception. In other words, when asked later, people thought the time was prolonged compared to what others thought. "Duration dilation."

Why was she thinking of this now? Her mind came back to the present situation, which was not quite life-threatening but somewhat frightening. She compared herself to people stuck on elevators or in a stairwell. Now, being stuck on a capsized boat at sea would be life-threatening. She thought of all these comparisons to calm herself, but it wasn't working. She watched the blinking red light in the corner, trying again to measure time with it. She tried singing but again became fearful of using up too much air.

Finally, she slumped onto the upturned bucket, put her head in her hands, and started to cry. Not just cry but sob. A sobbing where she could hardly take a deep breath.

Her grief seemed to take in everything—her mom's death, her divorce, her near accident, and then this. She couldn't stop her sobbing.

When her mother had been killed, she cried often and easily, but she couldn't remember sobbing at such a depth. Now, she cried because she would never see her mother again. More than a year had passed, and she had finally grasped the weight of this reality. The great magnitude of her mother dying. The essential fact of losing someone. She would never talk to her again on the phone nor receive a letter from her. She didn't believe in an afterlife or heaven, so she couldn't "make believe" she would see her mother in some other setting.

If she ever had children, her mother would never see them. Margaret would never see her only daughter in a healthy relationship. And much to her horror, Ava began to imagine what the last few moments of her mother's life had been like. Ava had not been with her. She was not able to hold her hand, say it was going to be okay, or offer any comfort. She wasn't able to do these things for her own mother while she was able to provide this comfort to hospice patients she barely knew who lay dying. Margaret died alone on a dirty street in the middle of an intersection.

For a long time, she cried until the front of her shirt was wet. She wiped at her eyes, but the tears kept flowing. She could stem neither the pain nor the tears. Nothing seemed real. She thought truly the only moment she wanted to slow down was the time it would have taken to be by her mother's side on that Labor Day Saturday. That would have been the only time that mattered.

"Go ahead and cry, let it out. This is what you need." She remembered saying this so many times to people in pain. To people who had just lost a relative or their health. In this closet, imagining someone saying those words to her did not help. She was alone, and her heart ached. And for the first time that she could remember, it was okay to let herself feel something. Anything.

In time, her respirations slowed, and she could take a deep breath. The sounds from deep in her chest changed from uncontrollable wailing to weeping, and at some point, there was no sound—just silent tears.

She lay back and didn't notice that her paper towel pillow made crackling noises and the makeshift pallet was nothing more than a sheet. Ava fell asleep. She awoke disoriented, with a bit of drool at the corner of her mouth. The overhead fluorescent light flickered, and she rose to extinguish it. Her body craved more sleep.

Just then, she heard voices. Human voices. At first, she thought she might be having an auditory hallucination, so she listened breathlessly. Yes, these were voices calling her name.

"Dr. Ava, are you here?"

"Where are you?"

Ava ran the three steps to the door.

"I'm in here," she yelled. "In the medicine room. I'm stuck here. Help me."

Now she recognized one of the voices as Pat's.

The doorknob turned, the lock released, and the door opened. Pat and a tall man looked in with apprehension.

"Oh, I am so glad to see you," Ava gasped. "Thank you, thank you, thank you!"

Pat held the door wide, and Ava rushed to the fresher air.

"What happened?" Pat asked.

"I was putting this bottle of lidocaine away, and the door shut on me. I've been trapped in there for hours, I think."

Pat explained, "I was worried about whether you had gotten home okay, so I called your phone, and no one answered. I kept calling, but no one picked up. I called the hospital because I thought you might have had to go in, but no one had seen you there. That's when I got worried. My husband—oh, this is my husband, Tim. Tim, this is Ava."

Ava bowed, and the two shook hands. Pat continued, "I told Tim we had to check on the doc. So, we drove by the clinic and saw that your car was still parked out back. That's when I knew something was wrong. We didn't know what we would find here. I thought maybe a dead body, or that you had fallen, or something had happened. Anyway, we just rushed in and started calling for you."

Ava gushed, "I am so glad for you. Thank you so much for checking on me. You might have found a dead body in this room if I had to stay in there all night. It was terrifying. I am sorry to get you out like this. Is it still raining?"

Pat said, "No, it stopped several hours ago."

That's when Ava looked at the wall clock in the lab and saw the time was one o'clock. She said, "Wait, is that one o'clock in the morning or the afternoon? I'm confused."

Pat responded, "It's after midnight; it's one o'clock in the morning. Tim didn't get home until very late, and I was afraid to come into the clinic by myself, so I had to wait until he got home. I am sorry; I should have come sooner."

Ava still felt confused and disoriented. She sat down in one of the rolling chairs and looked around. It felt like she had been in the room forever. Then she remembered how much she had to pee.

She said, "Can you excuse me? I have got to use the bathroom. Will you wait until I get out?"

Pat said, "Of course."

Once she released about two gallons of urine, Ava felt much clearer-headed. She threw water on her face and noted her drooping, red eyes. Pat and Tim were waiting for her when she came out of the bathroom.

Pat said, "OK, so you are not driving home tonight. You will stay with us. We have an extra bed, and you will go there and sleep as long as you need to."

Ava started to say no and protest, but she could see her attempts would be futile. Instead, she said, "OK, just let me get my things."

Her phone had twenty missed calls from Pat and a few other unanswered text messages. The display showed 1:15. She still couldn't grasp the time. Pat insisted they would drive Ava to the house, and Ava was to leave her car parked at the clinic. Ava followed instructions quietly. The boys were asleep when she arrived at their house, and the guest bed was made up with a cozy comforter.

Ava asked Pat, "Do you have anything I could put my contacts in?"

Pat said, "Yes, of course, I'll get you some solution and a case."

Ava's eyes were beginning to burn. She told Pat, "Thank you so much. You don't know how much this means that you saved me. And it means a lot that you were thinking of me and worried about me. I haven't had anyone worry about me since my mom died."

Pat gave Ava a long hug, and Ava melted into it. The body-to-body contact was more exquisite to Ava than anything she could remember.

Once settled into the room, she removed her contacts and plunged into her world of feeble vision; she lay down. After a few minutes of getting comfortable and enjoying the fresh scent of the sheets, she fell into a sound sleep. Something had happened in the medicine closet she couldn't explain.

Light streamed in from the west when she awoke, and as she reached for her phone, she saw the display again at 1:00. She assumed p.m. There was a note slipped under her door from Pat that said,

> Sleep as long as you like. Your appointments have all been canceled for today. There are biscuits in the kitchen. Call me when you are ready, and I will come pick you up. Don't be in any hurry.
>
> Love, Pat.

Ava felt like she was getting another hug from Pat.

25

<u>**Ag-Ag**</u>

Notes for *Inside Taber's: A Study of the Medical Dictionary* by Dr. Ava

On to Agent Orange, a horrible defoliant used in Vietnam and thought to have caused either Lou Gehrig's Disease or a similar fatal neuromuscular disease in many veterans. I have had patients with this disease; most were not Vietnam veterans, and it is not a pleasant condition. Patients watch as they slowly lose all muscle function. One man could only blink his left eye.

Here is a much more uplifting word—"agerasia." Pronounced like nothing I could rhyme it with, it means the youthful appearance of an old person. Nice word. I see a lot of patients receiving chemotherapy who have "ageusia"—"the absence, partial loss or impairment of their sense of taste." When everything tastes like cardboard, no wonder people lose weight.

Here is a fascinating concept—agglutinins. The definition is "an antibody present in the blood that attaches to an antigen present on cells or solid particles, causing them to agglutinate or clump together." Very simply, antibodies are the immune system's patrol force. They float around in our blood vessels, watching for trouble. The antigens are trouble. They could be a deadly bacterium that has penetrated our defenses, a toxin, a drop of the wrong blood, or a slew of potential or actual attacks.

The antibodies attach to the antigen, ideally making them less of a threat. However, sometimes, the clumped complex creates an even bigger problem. That's why certain microorganisms or even drug reactions can cause symptoms ranging from a rash to blood in the urine to death. Like many things related to the complexity of the body, sometimes some alterations can cause a disease, such as cold-antibody disease. This is what's fascinating. Of course, not for the one in a million Americans developing this disease yearly. In these people, the usual low number of "autoantibodies" —antibodies triggered by an element of the person's own body—is much higher. For the cold variety, they agglutinate or clump at temperatures below 32-37 degrees Fahrenheit. This can cause blue fingers, blue hands (remember acrocyanosis), fatigue, anemia, and enlarged spleens. All due to these complexes being trapped in the spleen's filtering mechanism. The whole phenomenon reminds me of the body as a test tube.

26

Chapter 18: The Defenses Weaken

Ava called Pat, and she was there within minutes. They drove back to the clinic, where Ava was teased a bit about her night in the closet.

Stephanie said, "Heard you had quite a night."

Ava responded, "Oh yeah, it was a blast."

Dr. Frost joined in the fun. "I heard you stayed late to rearrange the closet. You didn't have to do that."

Ava just said, "Uh-huh. Glad I could provide everyone with a good laugh."

She felt shaky, and when she walked by the medicine room and saw someone from maintenance working on the lock, a shudder ran through her. Glancing over at the clock in the lab, the first one she had seen after her release, she felt even worse. An uncomfortable chill ran up her back. She wiped a thin layer of sweat off her upper lip and quickly moved away from the area.

Pat said, "We have taken care of all your patients today. Some were rescheduled, and others were cared for by Dr. Frost." Pat continued, "You can just go home and rest today. I am sure you got little sleep at our house last night with all of our noise."

Ava disagreed, "No, I slept like a log."

The office scheduler, Linda, came from the front and said, "If you want tomorrow off, too, we can call your patients and let them know."

Ava looked around at the sympathetic faces. She hated being the center of attention. "No," she said. "I'm fine. I'll be here tomorrow, no problem. Plus, I must see those people because I'm off for the next two weeks. I need to see them before I leave."

Dr. Frost joined the group and added, "I can see them if you want. Just tell me what they need. I know a couple already that I saw on your list."

Ava shook her head and said again, "I'll be here. Don't worry about me." She felt more uncomfortable with their notion that she couldn't do it. With these words of finality, she headed back to her office.

Sitting down at her desk, Ava took some deep breaths. She knew she wasn't OK, but suggesting that she couldn't handle whatever was happening was not something she did, especially in her professional role. She would have to power through this feeling. Her mind remained foggy as she looked over the lab reports from Monday. She remembered she hadn't called Lawrence to inform him about his labs. Thinking about this sent another shudder through her. She didn't think she could make that call. Maybe she could ask Dr. Frost to call him and take over what to do next.

She caught Betty between patients in the hallway and asked for a minute.

"I hope I didn't sound rude. What I said earlier about being able to see my patients," she started.

"No, not at all. I understand," Betty said.

Ava went on, "Could I ask you to take care of one patient, though?"

"Of course," Betty responded.

"It's Lawrence. He's the man who had a liver transplant and recently has had signs of recurrent liver trouble. His labs are not good. His bilirubin is up, enzymes are high, and platelets are falling. He will need a workup and probably a referral back to the transplant clinic. I can't call him and tell him this bad news. Plus, I will be away, and I thought maybe you could manage his care?"

"Yes, I can do that. As soon as I finish up here, I'll look over his chart and try to call him a little later. Do you know why he might be back in failure?"

"I think he started drinking again. He lives alone, no one cares about him, and I think he has given up. His only interactions are with us when he comes for his appointments."

"OK," said Betty. "No problem."

Betty pulled Ava off to an alcove away from the flow of traffic.

"You know," Betty said in a lowered voice, "you have been through a lot in the past day. Pat told me about your near car accident a while back. It's normal to be a little shaken. Being stuck in that room for so many hours must have been scary."

Ava nodded, but she felt a lump in her throat as big as a walnut (again with the food similes) and knew her voice would betray her. Betty placed a hand on Ava's shoulder and said soothingly, "If that had happened to one of your patients, you would tell them to take it easy and not push to return to normal so quickly. You know the phrase, 'Physician, heal yourself.'"

Ava nodded.

While Betty talked, Ava became more uncomfortable with all the "handholding" and special accommodations. When Betty mentioned patients in a similar situation, Ava recoiled slightly and thought she was stronger than others. She could handle stressful situations—she had done it all her life—and never cut back to care for herself.

But then a distant recollection came to her, almost like a message: "You are grieving for your mother. It's OK to be kind to yourself. Relax and go home." Ava turned to look over her shoulder at where the voice came from. No one was there.

Rather than say any of this aloud, Ava drew back from the hand on her shoulder, steadied her voice, and told Betty, "I think I will be alright. I'll get home and take a long shower, wash my hair, and get something to eat. Long showers always revive me. I'll be back to my normal self by tomorrow. Don't worry about me."

Ava left the clinic and drove at a comfortable speed on the highway. She entered her house to find nothing different from when she left the morning before. Still, she felt like she had been gone for weeks. She took a prolonged shower—so long the water turned cold. She put on her most comfortable sweatpants and relaxed into her glasses. She called her brother, but he didn't pick up again, so she left a voice message to call whenever he had a chance.

She thought about the previous day and still felt unreal. "Maybe I'm in shock." This felt a little like the feeling she had just after hearing about her mother's accident. She was exhausted. She slipped under the covers and tried reading a boring novel. She reread pages repeatedly, and soon, her eyes drooped, and she fell into a fitful sleep until the alarm went off in the morning.

Ava's eyes popped open to the neon display of her clock radio as the news began at 6:00 a.m. Like at the clinic when first released, she was confused if this was six p.m. or a.m. After realizing it must be morning because of the light streaming through her window from the east, she felt heavy and panicked. Her breathing sped up, her hands began to sweat, and a sense of dread overcame her. She forced herself to turn over and get up with great effort.

Taking another long shower helped a bit, but she felt the same uneasiness as she dressed in her work clothes and picked up her stethoscope. *Maybe some food and coffee will help,* she thought to herself. But nourishment and caffeine didn't change her vague sense of unease. She purposely tried not to remember her time trapped in the closet, especially the crying.

She again used the highway to work and arrived just as the clinic opened. Her patients were scheduled on a tight time frame, as she had tried to get as many in as possible before she left on vacation. Thinking about vacation, she remembered that she planned to leave work on Friday afternoon and drive to Lexington to stay overnight for a very early flight to Belize the next morning. That thought brought even more discomfort. She thought she might have to cancel a commitment for the first time ever.

She found it difficult to attend to patients because her mind was not focused on what they were saying. She could see their mouths move but not hear the words. She asked them to repeat themselves several times, and she would refocus successfully for a few minutes. She checked and rechecked every prescription she wrote that day and even asked Dr. Frost to confirm the dose of one pediatric antibiotic dosing. She was not working with full brain power.

Ava hoped that no one noticed and that she wasn't making any mistakes. Luckily, her instincts and habits helped her get through the day of mainly seeing routine problems. She was wiped out by the end of the day and sat in her office chair for nearly half an hour before heading home. All the staff, especially Pat and Dr. Frost, had been nice to her, bringing her lunch and offering to help with anything she needed. She did appreciate this and offered thanks profusely.

That evening, she went to bed early and slept fitfully at home. The next morning, she had the same reaction to seeing her clock and decided not to wear her watch, as she had begun to get anxious when she saw the clock face.

The thoughts of her Belize trip and what was involved made her increasingly nervous. She thought seriously that she would have to cancel the trip. Seeing patients was even more challenging than on the day before. At lunch, she decided to cancel and emailed her friend, Linda, asking her to call back. She summarized the circumstances. She thought Linda might be able to understand this inconvenience better if she sent the email first rather than announcing it over the phone. Before Ava left work, Linda said it was okay for her not to come. They had an extra provider for Ava's volunteer weeks, and they would be fine. She was going to call Ava that evening, she promised.

The route she chose to get home tonight was the back road. She said to herself that she had to get over whatever was happening to her and that she thought revisiting the area of the near accident would help. It didn't. As she approached the gravel lot, the pond, the concrete pillars, the bridge—her hands shook, her heartbeat pounded in her ears, and she nearly missed the next curve. She pulled over in a safe spot down the road from the pond and tried to calm herself. It was hard.

"Maybe this is what people experienced when having panic attacks."

Immediately, she went through her usual treatment plan for patients with panic attacks. Counting to ten, paper bag breathing, therapy, maybe even some medicines. With each suggestion, she dismissed them, thinking they couldn't help.

Just then, her brother, Ted, called and apologized for not being available the last few days. He had been out of the country with work and could not get phone messages. He asked what was going on. Ava sighed and related the events of the last few days. Ted was quiet on the phone as he listened to the detailed descriptions of the actual events.

When Ava finished her story, he asked, "So, how are you feeling now?"

Ava was surprised Ted had asked about feelings because that wasn't something her family discussed. She answered, "I feel pretty bad in a way I haven't felt before. I don't feel like I can control this pressure, this anxiety. I don't know exactly what to do".

Ted asked, "Well, what matters to you right now?"

Ava thought about this question. It was a twist on the questions she had been asked all day—How are you doing? How are you feeling? She answered, "What matters to me right now is returning to my normal functioning. I don't like this weakness of my body, as if I have no control over what my body is doing."

"You probably need to see a therapist or someone who could help you with this heaviness. I don't know what to tell you. Didn't you see a therapist once before?"

"Yes, about a year ago, but now that fellow has become a monk and no longer sees patients."

"Is there someone else you could see? You must know some psychiatrists or counselors. Can you make an appointment?"

Ava felt like Ted was giving her good advice. She knew anyone would tell her that, but hearing it from Ted, who, like her, didn't often express his feelings, was more persuasive. They talked about their dad a little and agreed to speak again soon.

Ava went to the hospital's patient portal. She rarely saw a doctor, preferring to self-diagnose and treat herself when something was awry. Looking through the mental health providers, she recognized a few names, but when she attempted to make an appointment, their schedules were booked for over six weeks. She knew from referring patients that this was the typical wait time. She had always found it frustrating.

Unless someone was suicidal or homicidal, the wait time to get mental health care was ridiculous and ineffectual. For so long, mental health worked along a medical illness model that functioned well for illnesses like pneumonia and heart attacks but less perfectly for disorders of the mind. Most problems with depression or anxiety were not as temporally apparent as these medical problems. The treatments were not about taking a pill for seven days or going into the hospital for an operation. Ava sighed and felt even more helpless.

In the meantime, Rosella had begun to worry about Ava since she missed her appointment and had not called or texted to explain. She decided to stop over at her house and knocked on the front door at about seven p.m. on Thursday evening. Ava answered after the second knock and looked distraught.

"Come on in, Rosella," Ava said. "Would you like some tea or a beer?"

"I'll take a beer if you have one," Rosella answered as she entered the house. "How have you been? I missed you at your lesson on Tuesday."

Ava turned around hurriedly to face Rosella. "Oh, I am so sorry I forgot all about it. It's been an awful week. I completely forgot about the lesson."

Rosella reassured her, "It's fine. No problem. I was just worried and thought I would check up with you. What happened this week?"

Ava relayed the week's events for the second time that evening and ended with the same refrain: She didn't feel like herself and wasn't sure where to turn.

Rosella listened and sat with Ava while they both drank a beer. She gave no advice or helpful strategies for dealing with the panic. She did say, "I am sorry you are feeling that way. What you describe sounds horrible. I am thankful I haven't felt that way. Sometimes I would get nervous before a show when I was younger, but nothing like what you describe."

Rosella took a sharp breath and exclaimed, "Oh! I am sorry. That sounds terrible. I didn't mean to say what you are feeling is so strange. I have had a few friends with panic attacks who describe it just as you said."

Ava reassured her, "It's ok. I have never had these before this week. However, now that I think of it, I might have had one at a meeting last week when I thought I would be late. Weird, I just now thought of that."

Rosella said, "I can ask my friends what has worked for them. Would that be okay if maybe one of them called you?"

Ava said, "Really, I would rather you not. I feel embarrassed about this, especially since I am not functioning as a doctor. Can I let you know if I want to talk to any of them?"

Rosella said, "Sure, of course."

They finished their beers while talking about less important stuff. Rosella invited Ava to her FNE gathering in a couple of weeks, and Ava said she would try to make it. She would be in town since she had canceled her trip to Belize. They hugged when Rosella left and promised to keep in touch.

Ava was utterly wiped out as she prepared for bed. Tonight, though, she had the idea of covering up her clock radio so the sight of the time wouldn't stress her out in the morning. She wanted to be able to get through Friday since it was the last day before her time off.

The strategy worked until she glanced at another clock in the kitchen while eating breakfast the next morning. Again, this realization of the time and whether she would have enough time to get to work and spend time with all the scheduled patients sent her into her worst attack yet.

This time, she felt dizzy and noticed her chest was hurting. She felt like she might be dying. Was she having a heart attack? Her medical mind went through all the reasons why this was unlikely—her age, fitness, no family history—but she couldn't stop herself from considering it, and this made her symptoms even worse.

After lying down and deep breathing, her chest stopped hurting, and she relaxed, but the thought of driving to the office sent her into another mini spasm. Reluctantly, she picked up the phone to call the office and ask them to cancel her patients. She talked to the head nurse and relayed instructions to tell certain patients while feeling a drain of energy and concentration. After hanging up, she slept for at least a few hours, and when she looked outside, the sun was high in the sky. Something had to give. This was not how Ava controlled her life.

Getting up out of bed to fix tea, Ava noticed the *Taber's Cyclopedia* beside her desk. It had been a couple of weeks since she had read anything out of it, but she picked up the heavy volume. She looked at the entries on the page marked by her bookmark. As coincidental as this was, her bookmark was on page 144 with the heading of "anus" to "aorta." On the left-hand column was the entry "anxiety." Defined as "a vague, uneasy feeling of discomfort or dread accompanied by an autonomic response: the source is often nonspecific or unknown to the individual: a feeling of apprehension caused by anticipation of danger. It is a potential signal that warns of impending danger and enables the individual to take measures to deal with the threat." *Wow*, Ava thought, *what is the threat I am afraid of?*

The entry continued with a "patient care" section, which included everything Ava would have used to calm a patient down. For once, when reading *Taber's*, Ava didn't feel this section was as personal as needed. Reading through the suggestions for the provider to maintain a "calm, caring, quiet and controlled atmosphere" did not make Ava feel better. She flipped to some of the SEE entries. "Anxiety disorder"—here was mentioned, "panic disorder with or without agoraphobia or simple phobias." Ava didn't think she had agoraphobia—she wasn't afraid to go out. She recognized that seeing a clock this morning had triggered the most recent attack, and thinking about seeing patients within a specific time frame was scary and maybe could be considered a "threat." She looked up phobias.

"Any persistent and irrational fear of a specific object, activity or situation that results in a compelling desire to avoid the feared stimulus." SEE: *Nursing Diagnoses Appendix: Phobia Appendix.*

She was beginning to realize that this book needed an owner's manual to use. Where was the Nursing Appendix? Finally, sorting through the over 700 pages of appendices, she found the list of phobias. There were three full pages of kinds of phobias—two columns on each page with a font of six. By quick count, she estimated this added up to over 300 specific phobias. Wow.

Reading through the long list took her mind off her anxiety and made her chuckle at the varied objects people could be afraid of. And the names of the different phobias. As she looked at the list, she vowed never to judge someone who suffered from one of these because now she knew how they felt and how uncontrollable it was. "Fear of being naked-nudophobia." "Fear of crossing bridges—gephyrophobia." She knew someone who had this. He feared he would unexpectedly turn his wheel and drive off the bridge.

Some names did not need a definition, and Ava thought they weren't very imaginative. "Decido-phobia," "symbolo-phobia," "venereo-phobia," "mythophobia." Most were surprising. "Levophobia—fear of the left." "Dextrophobia—fear of the right." "Onomatophobia--fear of hearing a certain name." There were a lot of phobias.

As she perused the list, her eyes stuck on "time"—chronophobia. On page 2,479. Upon looking this term up on Google, she found this explanation:

In Greek, the word chrono means time, and the word phobia means fear. Chronophobia is the fear of time. It's characterized by an irrational yet persistent fear of time and of the passing of time. Chronophobia is related to rare chronomentrophobia, the irrational fear of timepieces like watches and clocks. Chronophobia is considered a specific phobia. A specific phobia is an anxiety disorder characterized by a powerful, unwarranted fear of something that presents little or no actual danger but instigates avoidance and anxiety. Usually, the fear is of an object, situation, activity, or person.

Thinking about how she was feeling and her new fear of seeing the clock, she wondered if it was possible she had chronophobia. When she studied further, risk factors for this condition were people told they have limited life expectancy, prisoners, and people who have experienced a trauma that might involve being in a space for an extended period. One of those fit her recent experience.

"Chronophobia," she thought. "Interesting." Diagnosing herself made her feel better momentarily, but soon, her incapacitating anxiousness returned. She still didn't know what to do about it. And how to get out of a panic attack if they recurred. This process of trying to wrestle with her brain was tiresome.

She went back to bed and welcomed sleep. Her last thought before slipping into unconsciousness was remembering the play-acting scenario at Yogaville. The assignment was to convince a "hydrophobic" person to cross a flooded road. She remembered how good Sara was at talking people through their panic. Maybe she could speak to Sara. Ava felt a tiny ray of hope thinking of this plan. She also had the briefest image, as if in a dream, of herself weeping in the medicine closet.

27

<u>Ag-Ag</u>
Notes for "Inside Taber's: A Study of the Medical Dictionary"
by Dr. Ava

I am curious about agitation as defined here: "Excessive restlessness, increased mental and physical activity, especially the latter." Taber's says agitation is especially common in the elderly, in patients with dementia, and in patients with organic brain syndromes.

Why does the compromised brain respond with agitation or an inability to sit still? The same response I have to boring meetings that last more than an hour. Near the end of a person's life, they often have this same behavior, coined "terminal restlessness" by palliative/hospice specialists. (Surprisingly, not in Taber's under T.) Frequently, in my unscientific survey, women who are in and out of consciousness at this stage tend to repeat a hand motion similar to doing crochet or needlepoint. Men tend to grab for catheters and tubing and hold on tight. I don't know the significance of these gestures. Regardless, it is interesting to question why the brain responds this way.

The brain is an amazing and complex organ. A demonstration of this is how many words are used to describe the absence of a brain function. "Agnea"—the inability to recognize objects; "finger agnosia"—inability to identify fingers of one's own hands or others; "auditory agnosia"—inability to interpret sounds; "acoustic agraphia"—inability to write words that are heard; "optic agraphia"—inability to copy words; and last example "amnemonic agraphia"—inability to write sentences, although letters and words can be written. The list could go on.

Presumably, an afflicted person could have more than one of these absences, but imagine that the brain is so compartmentalized that one area directs the hand to copy a word separate from the area that writes words de novo. Amazing.

28

Chapter 19: Help From Afar

Sara and Ava had kept in close contact since the Yogaville retreat and saw each other when she was in town, but Sara was still living between Kentucky and New York—two months in one spot and two months in the other. She felt she couldn't abandon her patients in New York and was taking a long transition between the states.

When the two friends talked, they shared stories of patients and their challenges. Recently, Ava had treated a young man who came to the office complaining of vague physical symptoms. Ava hadn't thought there was anything seriously wrong with him, but when she walked into the hallway, his girlfriend came around the corner and motioned for Ava to follow her to an area where they could talk without being heard by the young man.

The girlfriend was concerned that the man was depressed. He had recently lost his job and was having difficulty finding another position. The girlfriend said he had been depressed once before when they first met, and he had taken antidepressants at that time, which helped. She was asking Ava to do something. Ava instructed one of the nurses to ask the young man to return to an exam room. The girlfriend had asked Ava not to mention she talked to her because the man might be upset. This made it difficult for Ava, of course.

When Sara and Ava talked about this case, Ava asked her what her approach to such a situation would be. Ava further clarified that the young man denied feeling depressed and would not admit to any life stressors when asked about his life.

Sara agreed it was a difficult situation.

She said, "This brings up the issue of 'who is the patient.'"

Same as the whole problem of giving out medical information to someone who is not the patient. Ava recalled another patient's family member who insisted the actual patient, her father, was suffering from severe pain. The actual patient did not complain of pain, but the daughter insisted that he cried and moaned all night. Later, Ava saw in the "Court News" of the local paper that this daughter had been arrested for drug possession. She had probably been using her father to get pain medicines. That time, Ava hadn't fallen for the scheme.

"With mental health conditions," Sara explained, "it was a little different, and the accounts of family members were important. Ideally," she added, "you should try to get them both in the room together so you have the consent of the patient to hear what the girlfriend has to say. Most important is to find out about suicide or homicide tendencies. Did the man have a gun?"

Ava regretted not asking about a gun. She did not own a gun, and her father, the warden, had never owned one. Her family were not gun owners. When she asked patients about firearms, she always felt uncomfortable because of her lack of knowledge and inherent bias about gun ownership. In this case, the patient and his girlfriend never came back to the clinic. She did wish they had returned for a follow-up. Thinking about her mistakes while handling the encounter kept her up for a few nights.

Ava called Sara the day after falling asleep, thinking of her with hope. Sara listened to the retelling of Ava's recent days. Ava knew she had Sara's complete attention even on the phone and could visualize her sitting and listening calmly. Ava ventured her suspicion that she might have chronophobia.

While still maintaining respect, Sara laughed at the suggestion of chronophobia. She had never heard of this type of phobia. Ava did not feel dissed. With Sara's laughter, she realized the situation's humor. Sara asked, "How have you tried to deal with your panic attacks?"

Ava replied that she knew what she should do—breathe, relax, let her body go limp—but she couldn't break out of the moment of bodily tension. Sara asked if there were any mental health providers she could see. Ava related how long a wait it was to get into any counseling unless she went to the ER.

Sara said, "It would be better if you talked to someone in person, but I can try to help over the phone. I won't be back in Kentucky for two weeks."

Ava sighed with relief to hear this and felt some of her desperation fall away.

Sara asked Ava, "What else could be bothering you? Sometimes, the sudden appearance of panic attacks can be your mind figuring out a deeper issue. Is there anything else you may be processing?"

Ava had the same brief recollection of crying in the medicine closet. She felt a pang in her chest—a pressure. For a moment, she thought she might be having another panic attack.

She replied to Sara, "Maybe it has to do with my mother dying."

Sara was not surprised at this admission. She knew Ava's mother had died. One night at Yogaville, Ava talked about the accident. Even then, Sara had been struck by how little emotion Ava showed when talking about the tragedy. Her recounting of the specifics was told as if it had happened to a patient, not a relative.

From her experience with clients, Sara knew she couldn't blurt out, "Of course, it has to do with your mother." She had to let Ava come to this realization herself.

Sara wanted to be with Ava in person. She could feel her great suffering through the phone lines.

She asked, "Are there any friends in Kentucky you could talk to? With whom you feel comfortable talking about your mother?"

Ava was quiet at the other end of the line, then said, "Maybe I could talk to Rosella. Her brother died. One time before, I talked to her mom and her about grief. It seems like a long time ago. My friend, Gwen, is also always willing to listen."

Sara asked, "How about your family? Can you talk to them? Do you and Ted or your dad ever talk about your mom?"

"We did once. One night after my dad's birthday party. That's the only time."

She went on, "They're like me. We don't like to talk about it."

Sara said, "It might help to talk about your feelings. Just a suggestion."

"Yeah, maybe. It's just so painful", Ava countered.

All Sara could say was, "I know."

Ava added, "I wish my mom were here. She could tell me what to do. She would know how to help all my family. She was the one who kept us all sane. But that's crazy. She's not here. Never will be."

Again, Sara wished she could be there to hug Ava. Being so far away, she didn't want to press Ava further, but an idea came to her to call the people who were close. She remembered the name of the music store, Redbud. Surely, there was only one Rosella who worked there.

Concluding the phone call, they agreed that the next time Ava felt an anxiety attack building, she was to call Sara, no matter the time of day. Sara also recommended Ava look into some self-help books about phobias. She knew that Ava was the type who would research and learn everything to be learned about phobias and anxiety, so she directed her toward reputable resources. They ended the conversation with a promise to talk every day.

Ava knew how to make healthy choices and appreciated that, in her present mental state, she could motivate herself to take action. She showered, dressed, and went out into the woods for a walk. This alone made her feel better. While outside, she forgot all about time and only considered what day it was when she realized she had two full weeks of no commitments with her unexpected cancellation of the Belize trip.

She still avoided looking at timepieces and had covered or taken down all the clocks in the house. After a tuna fish sandwich lunch, she sat down to read more of *Taber's*. The book was comforting as long as she didn't consider how many more pages she had to read. It flashed across her mind that reading about chronophobia had possibly saved her sanity. While covering her clocks seemed strange, it made her feel better. And reading about all the phobias somehow made her feel normal, like she wasn't so different from her patients.

<u>Ai-Ai</u>

Notes for *Inside Taber's: A Study of the Medical Dictionary* by Dr. Ava

AIDS is the next multipage entry to appear. What to say about "Acquired immunodeficiency syndrome?" The frightening disease seems to have been tamed by "modern medicine," at least in developed countries and in people who have health insurance, good nutrition, some degree of medical sophistication, and access to an AIDS/HIV clinic. More on this when we get to the H's.

Air and airways take up many entries. And really, life comes down to "the airway" as the basic necessity of existence. Without an open airway, a person can die within seconds. I think the absolute best example of this is in the movie, "Field of Dreams," where the doctor/baseball player rushes over to save the boy choking on a gumball, thus ending the man's dreams of being a baseball player. That's a poignant scene.

In patients near the end of life, their airway is a significant factor in the sounds they make, the positions they prefer, mentation, life, and their deaths. Of course, in CPR and Basic Life Support, all rescuers are taught that the airway is the A of the ABC—the first thing to think of to save a person's life. And nearing death, it is usually the last organ to shut down. Kidney failure can cause a person to go into a coma, but the final factor is that the airway collapses when someone is in that deep of a coma. Heart failure or lung failure does the same as people tire from the work of breathing and as the acidity level in the blood rises. They become unconscious; again, the airway is the final common denominator.

I have intubated (placed a tube into the airway) of many people, from newborns to elderly. So, let me talk about procedures briefly. Most procedures involve invading a bodily cavity or puncturing a barrier or wall of the body. Take, for example, a spinal tap, also called a lumbar puncture. A small diameter needle is inserted in the lower back, and, with careful care, it travels in the small space between the bony structures (vertebral bodies) of the lumbar spine into the space that spinal fluid flows in. We use it to determine if a patient has meningitis or a spinal fluid infection.

There is a feeling when the needle punctures the cavity (in this case, the spinal fluid space) that is so fulfilling, so satisfying. It is just a whisper of a sensation but usually signifies that you have hit the target. Almost immediately, fluid begins to flow through the needle, and to me, relief courses through my body. Entering this cavity, which is so well protected, takes very little strength but immense prowess. The same feeling comes from successfully doing a bone marrow biopsy, drawing blood, or using a needle to draw off fluid from the chest or abdomen. I have never punctured an eyeball, but it might be similar. Even when intubating a patient, when the tube is in the correct place, there is a sensation as it passes through the vocal cords. Something spiritual.

Chapter 20: Group Therapy

While Ava was sitting, staring, and thinking about things in the afternoon, there was a knock at the door. Gwen and Rosella stood outside, one holding a picnic basket, the other a bottle of wine. Ava invited them in.

"What is happening?" Ava asked.

Rosella replied, "We brought lunch to enjoy the beautiful day with you."

Gwen added, "We haven't seen much of you lately and missed you."

Ava was surprised but happy her friends were checking on her. She found three wine glasses and cleared off the table on her porch.

Rosella asked after they had exhausted the topics of weather and wine, "So, how have you been?"

"OK, I guess. I still have these panic attacks. I talked to Sara this morning. She's helping me get through them. It's been nice to have some time off."

Rosella took a breath and admitted, "Yes, we know Sara is helping. We each talked to her this morning. She called us to check on you. She said she wished so much she could be here but couldn't fly down right now."

Ava was again surprised that Sara would have called her friends. She also wondered how that had occurred. But she was glad to know they all cared.

After each woman had drunk a glass of wine, Ava said, "I guess I need to tell you more about my mom. She has been on my mind." The wine seemed to have loosened Ava up; she felt less guarded in her words and actions.

"You both know my mom died in a car accident about a year ago. It was the hardest thing that has ever happened to me. I couldn't stand to even think about it. When I did, I couldn't function. This never seemed strange until just lately. Now I remember that when I was trapped in that closet, I was sobbing. I finally realized that my mom would never be with me again."

She trembled. Both Gwen and Rosella moved their chairs closer, and each put an arm around Ava. Their firm enclosure comforted Ava.

She said, "I was weeping for all the things my mother will miss in my life. All the things she will miss in my brother's life. All the pain my father has gone through. It's hard to explain how deep that pain goes."

Saying these words felt good—like a dam had broken. Ava sobbed. The arms around her tightened, and she felt the others' heartbeats in the closeness. She could handle the pain more easily than when she was alone in the closet. All three women stayed like this for several minutes, breathing together, in sync.

In time, the group hug felt awkward, and the three separated, laughing at finding their arms were numb. The mood of the group was different. More relaxed. More intimate.

"I feel better. Thank you," Ava finally declared.

Rosella kept herself from saying anything about her grief but connected with Ava's pain and release mysteriously. Gwen thought of how lucky she was to have her own mother and vowed to tell her how much she loved her more often.

31

<u>Ak-Al</u>

Notes for *Inside Taber's: A Study of the Medical Dictionary* by Dr. Ava

Here is a word I have never heard. "Akee"—a tropical tree, the unripe fruit of which, if ingested, can cause severe hypoglycemia. Does this fruit act like insulin, or does it somehow block glucose breakdown? Very interesting.

Medicine is rampant with abbreviations, so much so that there is a list of banned abbreviations on each hospital chart. Regardless of how confusing they can be, here is one that's new to me but may become my mantra: ALARA—"as low as reasonably achievable." When would this be appropriate to report in a medical record?

Albumin and its derivatives are the next large section, and frankly, I was relieved to come to albuterol finally. The albumin level is the first lab I look at when seeing a terminal or chronic illness patient. Albumin is so important and so sensitive to changes in eating and illness. What is it? It is "one of a group of simple proteins widely distributed in plants and animal tissues. In humans, the principal function is to provide colloid osmotic pressure, preventing plasma loss from the capillaries." In other words, it keeps the stuff—fluid, blood, water—that's supposed to be circulating through veins and arteries inside that vessel. When you wake up with dark circles under your eyes, that has to do with osmotic pressure. The same forces contribute to swollen feet and ankles at the end of a hard day.

People with low albumin can't keep their fluids in place. And patients who aren't eating have lower than-normal albumin levels.

Recently, after fifteen-plus years of eating a vegetarian diet, I returned to a carnivorous existence. Taber's tells me I will now be ingesting albumin, which is of higher nutritional quality than I formerly ate—animal source vs. vegetable source. I can't tell the difference.

I love this book. On page 67, there are two red-boxed warnings. One is a "caution" about isopropyl alcohol—"toxic when taken internally" and the other about rubbing alcohol–"it is poisonous if taken internally." There are no such cautionary diversions in Webster's. The Cyclopedia is part medical jargon and part mentor, and a personality shines through.

32

Chapter 21: Time Starts Again

Gwen, Rosella, and Ava finished the bottle of wine and said their goodbyes. Ava was closing the outside door when her phone rang. It was Sara.

"Did your friends come by?" she asked before Ava could say hello.

Ava wondered what she would have said a month before about Sara recruiting people to come to her house like that. Today, she could feel only grateful.

She told Sara, "Yes, they just left. Thank you for sending them. We had a good talk. I think I feel better about my mother."

Sara said, "Good. That's all I was checking up on. I will leave you alone, but I'll call you tomorrow. And I wanted to let you know I will be back in Kentucky next week. I'll stop by when I arrive."

Ava felt relieved to know Sara would be back soon. She said, "That's good news. I look forward to seeing you in person. Thank you for all that you've done."

Ava walked into a room of her house that was rarely used—a kind of den. Although there was a reading chair and a small loveseat in this room, it was not a room she went in unless she had visitors. Looking around the room, she noticed an old-time clock on the floor in a corner. Many months ago, she had bought the clock at a flea market because it reminded her of a similar one her mother had in the house where Ava grew up. Ava had found, though, that the ticking kept her awake at night, and the loud chiming every hour was annoying. So, she'd let the clock run out and placed it out of the way in the corner.

Ava remembered the flea market where she bought it. She was returning from visiting her father in Michigan, and while passing this market on Route 75, she pulled in to stretch her legs and take a driving break. She often took a break here since it was the halfway mark of the trip.

The clock was nestled on a shelf in one of the back booths. It was only a few weeks after her mother's crash, and when she glimpsed the clock, images of her mother strolling around antique stores came to Ava. Her finds always delighted Margaret. She often went with her best friend Rosemary to estate sales and antique stores and brought home beautiful pieces. Sadly, Ava didn't share her mother's love of old things but now that she was gone, the old items took on a special meaning.

The clock was a windup, with a pendulum that hung down and Roman numerals on the face. It chimed every hour and needed to be wound more often than Ava could manage. Its hands were frozen at 7:30. As she sat staring at the clock and considering all these memories, she realized she was comfortable. There was no panic looking at this clock. If anything, she was feeling more relaxed. Weird.

Seeing the clock made her think of home, and she thought of her father sitting there alone. Though she called him about once a week to check in, they mostly talked about nothing in depth. Today, she felt a powerful urge to talk to him about her mom and her love of antiques. When she dialed, he answered on the first ring.

"Hi, Dad," she said.

"How are you, Ava?" he replied. "What a surprise for you to call me in the day. Is everything OK?"

It was rather unusual for Ava to call during the day..

"Yes, everything is OK, Dad. I was thinking about how Mom went to all those antique stores and brought home things."

"Yes," her dad replied, "she loved shopping at those places. I never enjoyed it myself."

Ava said, "But you never discouraged her. That was nice."

"I guess," her dad said in a lowered voice. "Now, I wish I had gone with her and shared her enthusiasm."

"Hey, Dad, do you remember having clocks around in the house?"

"Oh, yes," he said. "We had that enormous grandfather clock and two other wind-up clocks. Your mother had me wind them every Sunday evening before bed. I never could understand her fascination with the things. Your mom had a room in one of our houses where she tried to repair her friends' old clocks. Why do you ask?"

"Oh, I have been having some weird things happen to me with clocks. I was just wondering."

"What kind of weird things?"

Ava explained, "I just get nervous when I see a clock. It happened suddenly, and I don't know why."

"You know," her dad started, "I saw some things in the prison related to time. The guys who were sentenced to life told me they would get anxious thinking about time. There is an official term for it: 'Prison Neurosis.' I heard about it a lot. It was fascinating how it would show up at a certain point during their incarceration. Some inmates never complained, but others would get restless, unable to sleep, and have no interest in anything. It was sad. Who could blame a person for losing the will to live when it would be years of the same routine, no freedom, and so little stimulation? While I was warden, I had very few resources for helping those guys. We didn't have any psychiatrists. Back then, the guards were the closest thing to a counselor. They helped the best they could."

"What did you do about it?"

"Well, the key was prevention. We tried to schedule activities for the inmates, like art classes or yoga. We had a schedule for these events that we thought inmates could look forward to—something to connect them with a day or time. I don't know for sure if it helped."

Suddenly, her father said, "Wait. Did something happen before you started noticing this thing with the clocks?"

Ava admitted, "I was trapped in a room for a few hours. I wasn't going to tell you so you wouldn't worry."

To herself, she thought she would not tell him about the near accident.

Her dad said, "Oh, that might be why you are thinking about time. I read someplace that a traumatic, uncontrollable situation can cause problems, too."

Ava recalled how accurate her *Taber's* was.

Ava agreed, "Yes, I think that is what happened."

Her father sighed. "I wish your mother was alive. She would know what to say to you."

Ava assured her father, "It's fine. You've made me feel better. Just talking to you is nice. I also think I need to talk about Mom more. Would it be OK to talk to you about her?"

Her dad also said, "Yes, I would love that."

They talked a little more about the weather and hung up, promising to talk again soon.

After all the events of the afternoon, Ava was tired and laid down for a nap. When she awoke, she started reading one reference Sara had given her and prepared a delightful meal with a glass of red wine.

She was still focused on time and read more about time. She hit on the term chronemics. The study of how humans use and perceive time. She often did that. She could spend hours reading about one subject. This time, she related it to her condition. She thought about all the times it felt like driving out to a new patient's home for a house visit would take much longer than driving home from the house. She had talked to Judy, her nurse, about this many times. It was the perception of time rather than the actual passage of time. Concentrating on the directions and trying not to miss turns altered the perception. She also thought of times when she had used marijuana. Time seemed to slow down. Nothing she read confirmed or disputed this finding.

She also thought about her patients' complaints related to time. There were more heart attacks in the early morning and more asthma admissions at night. Anxiety also seemed to get worse at dusk, and patients with dementia who had "sun-downing" were worse, predictably, at sundown. Very interesting. As Ava prepared for bed, she noticed she had not had a panic attack all day.

Early the following day, Ava awoke in a sweat, and it took her a few minutes to reorient herself. She had awoken in the middle of a nightmare. In the dream, she had been reading *Taber's*, but with every turn of the page, she returned to the same page she had just read. The more desperate she became and the faster she turned the pages, she always landed on the same page.

She couldn't make out what entries were on the page she returned to, but she had this powerful feeling that she had to move ahead—the feeling that there was something very important in the next pages— something so important that it might mean life or death. She tried to skip ahead in the book and physically could not separate more than one page at a time. It was a strange dream.

Ava had a friend who purported to interpret dreams. Usually, when someone told this person their dream, she would ask, "What did the dream mean to you?" This didn't seem like a valid way to interpret dreams to Ava. Because she was already wide awake, Ava pulled out her phone and looked up the meaning of a dream about reading a book. Most interpretations talked about it being a sign of gaining knowledge or expressing oneself. A dream about turning pages was a good omen— it suggested that one would find the answer. None of these interpretations sounded legitimate for the dream Ava had. She got up and started reading some more of the actual *Taber's*.

As she reached for the book and felt its weight unexpectedly, she began to have what she now recognized as a panic attack. Her heart raced, and her breath sped up. She was first chilled, then began to sweat. Her mind panicked as before, and everything she had read in the books Sara recommended flew out of her mind. The only firm thought she had was remembering Sara said to call her anytime if she had another attack.

She dialed Sara's number, and after a few rings, Sara answered cheerily. Ava knew she had woken her from sleep, as it was still quite early, but Sara astounded pleasant as ever.

Ava just said, "I'm having another of those attacks."

Sara calmly told her they would get through this together. She asked Ava if she was near a couch or bed and if she could lie down. "Good," she said. "Lie down and get completely comfortable. Don't have anything pushing up against you."

Sara's voice was so soft and meditative Ava felt herself calming already.

"Now," Sara continued, "I want you to become aware of where your toes, ankles, and knees are. Go through every body part like that. I will wait here while you check every part."

Some minutes transpired, and Ava said, "OK."

"Now," Sara said, "I want you to pretend that someone who is not feeling very well lies down next to you. That person is feeling as panicky as you were. They can't relax. You want to help them. So, you say to them, 'I want you to watch everything I do and imitate me.'"

Sara goes on, "Now tell this person that by the time they finish, they will be totally relaxed. OK, now go ahead and go through a progressive relaxation. Clench your toes, then release. Tense your feet and relax them. Speak to this imaginary person with each step."

Sara remained quiet and could hear Ava's breathing slow as the minutes passed. Finally, she asked, "How are you feeling?"

Ava said, "Much better. That worked. It is so much easier to show someone else how to relax than it ever has been for me to tell myself to relax."

"Good," Sara said. "Now go back to sleep or just lie there, and I will talk to you later."

Ava was able to sleep and woke later in the morning feeling refreshed and optimistic. She showered, walked in the woods, and did some necessary house cleaning. She visited Rosella at Redbud Music. She thought being in the store would be relaxing, and she wanted to talk to Rosella again and follow up on the conversation from the day before.

Ava knew she couldn't be cured of her panic attacks that easily, but she didn't have the overwhelming feeling of despair she had just a couple of days before. The days off, the walks in the woods, and her friends and family's help had been therapeutic. She wished all her patients had the resources she had. And again, she flashed to the entries in *Taber's* about phobias. What would she have done if she had not discovered the name of her phobia? And went on with the feeling her fears and panic attacks would never get better. Is this what people felt who contemplated suicide?

While driving to Redbud Music, Ava reflected on what she had read in a book about panic attacks and anxiety. She was surprised to find that so much of what was described in the book applied to her, and she was mostly surprised that she had never thought of her upbringing in this way.

Her family never talked about their emotions. Although she and her dad cried at sad movies, sometimes her mom made fun of them for it. This sounded cruel, but Ava understood why. Her parents had a child who died just before Ava was born. She never found out exactly what he died of because her parents never talked about him. He was less than a year old when he passed away, and all Ava remembers was that she always thought he was in limbo because he was so young when he died.

In their house growing up, her family never talked about their grief. She just knew it was always there. Ava considered that this was why she was so driven to be in control of things. Many people who have anxiety, panic attacks, and phobias have had some sort of trauma. Ava wondered if she had a type of generational trauma from childhood added to the trauma from her mother's death. Her parents losing a child certainly was traumatic.

She did worry and was a bit afraid that she might have another panic attack. She thought clocks were her precipitant but wasn't confident something else might trigger an attack. By the time she arrived at

Redbud Music, she had almost talked herself out of going in. And she noticed with surprise that she was whistling. Rosella saw her from the window and waved, so Ava had no choice but to turn off the ignition and walk into the store.

Rosella greeted her friend with a hug. Ava noticed a new display case. Inside was a clock—a tall grandfather clock with Roman numerals on the face and a pendulum hanging down. Ava felt calm. It was weird how the sight of this timepiece was so different from looking at her watch or alarm clock.

She asked Rosella, "Where did you get the clock? I hadn't noticed it before."

"Oh, a customer came in the other day and traded it for a new guitar. He said it had been in his family's home, but he didn't have room for it in his house. I wasn't sure what it might be worth, but I liked it, and we had plenty of room. Do you know much about these clocks? It doesn't seem to want to run."

Ava stood and gaped at the clock. A mental image of her mother working on their wind-up clock at home came to her. She remembered the little workshop her mother had in the basement. When Ava or her brother entered that area, her mother always reminded them to be careful and shooed them out. There were springs and coils and little bottles of oil scattered around. Now that she remembers, there were several clock faces on a workbench, a variety of clock keys, and one or two pendulums. Ava was intrigued because she had forgotten all about her mother repairing clocks.

She said to Rosella, "I might be able to work on it. I know little about them, but my mother used to repair old clocks."

Rosella nodded and said, "Great. Come on back to the office and have a cup of coffee with me. How are you feeling?"

Ava answered, "Fine, I guess."

They settled around a cluttered desk in the back. Rosella drank her coffee from a mug with a beautiful hummingbird painted on the side. Ava's cup was squarish with the words Cool Beans inscribed on the side.

"So," Ava said, "how is everything going with the concert? Anything I can help with?"

Rosella sighed and said, "Can you help me write songs? I'm having writer's block. Nothing sounds right."

She said to Rosella, "I know some inspiration will hit you. Plus, can't you use some old songs?"

"Yes," Rosella replied. "I just wanted some new thoughts. Oh well, it will come. I've been a little distracted lately. Worries."

Ava gently probed, "What kind of worries? You don't seem like the worrying type."

Rosella took a deep breath and shared her concerns about the store's finances with Ava. She began, "Well, I talked to my accountant the other day, and Redbud is losing money. I might not be able to stay open if something doesn't change. Money from my touring days is running out, and the store didn't see a profit this past year. I'm not sure what I should do. I don't want to let Redbud close."

Ava weighed her words. She always thought Rosella could handle anything with a laugh and a smile. And she knew all the good Redbud did for the community. Suddenly, Ava had an idea.

She told Rosella, "Come with me." Rising from her chair, she led her back into the store, past the counter, and into the room with pianos.

"I noticed this new acquisition when I walked in," Ava explained.

It was an old-style Hammond organ with a double row of keyboards and a full-foot pedal set up. The speaker was housed in a small cabinet.

Ava slipped her shoes off and slid onto the wide bench. She said to Rosella, "Come join me." Rosella removed her shoes and eased herself onto the bench.

Ava began, "When I was very young, my first piano teacher was the organist in our church, and once a month, she would let me play the pipe organ when no one else was in the church. She sat next to me on the bench like we are. She worked the foot pedals while I played chords up top. The sound was stupendous. I have never heard anything so grand as those pipes resounding through the church."

Then she said simply, "Let's play."

Ava held down the start button and turned on both the organ and the attached Leslie speaker. The system buzzed with a quiet whir.

Rosella exclaimed, "I didn't know you played!"

"Yes, I do. So, you work the foot pedals. It's just like a regular keyboard."

With that, she began with a simple blues progression in C and then switched to the more somber key of E minor. The sound from the Leslie boomed through the store. Ava flicked it to tremolo, and the two were transported to a different place. Rosella skillfully added base notes with her feet, sometimes reaching across Ava's dangling legs to reach the higher pedals. They laughed as they played.

One of the employees came out from the practice room to listen. The two played in this kind of ecstasy until Ava flicked off the instrument, and the Leslie's whir ground to a halt.

Ava turned to Rosella and said, "We can't lose Redbud. And everyone around here knows that. So, start charging for the wonderful things you do."

Rosella nodded, still a little out of breath from the pedaling exertion.

She said, "Okay," but she was thinking of how this was the solution. She could charge small amounts to the groups that practiced, have people buy tickets to concerts, and even develop the open outdoor space behind the shop into an outdoor venue. The possibilities seemed endless.

She told Ava, "Thank you." Ava was pleased.

They slid off the bench and walked in stocking feet to nearby chairs to replace their shoes. Rosella broke the companionable silence. She didn't want to forget Ava had needed her help not long ago.

She said, "That was a good talk we all had yesterday."

Ava replied, "Thank you again. I needed to talk like that. You know, this time off from work has allowed me to relax. For once, I don't feel guilty about a vacation or worry about all the work when I return. I needed a break.

Rosella agreed, "Yes, you did. You can't do it all."

As they walked toward the door, Rosella said, "I hope you will be at the concert. You can meet my dad and my old band crew. There's a new fellow coming too. I want you to meet him. Raphael says he is very nice. And unattached," she added with a wink.

"OK," Ava said, "don't play matchmaker."

The two laughed. Rosella had some customers come in, so she broke off the conversation, and Ava lingered around the store. She felt more and more relaxed with each step. As she looked over at an autoharp, she thought of one of her older patients whom she saw at home with dementia. While he couldn't remember family names or everyday items like a spoon or fork, he could belt out a church song with the autoharp. Ava looked forward to seeing him again and listening to him sing. It was the first time she felt genuine pleasure at seeing a patient in a long time.

33

Am-Am

<u>Am-Am</u>

Notes for Inside *Taber's: A Study of the Medical Dictionary* by Dr. Ava

Another word with many sub-entries is "amnesia," which means a loss of memory. Reading this, I learned an error I've been making for years. "Anterograde amnesia is amnesia after a precipitating event or medicine, and "retrograde amnesia" is forgetting events that occurred before the precipitating trauma. I had those backwards.

In this section is a very humanistic treatment plan for treating post-traumatic amnesia. I was impressed. Amnesia seems to be a popular and successful theme for movies. Think of "Memento" and Adam Sandler in "50 First Dates." Onward, I am reading all the words starting with the prefix "amphi"—indicating on both sides, on all sides, double. There's amphiarthrosis, amphiaster, amphibious, amphiblastula, amphicyte. As I scan down the list, I wonder what is "amphitheater." Ha-ha. The word looked foreign in context.

The next word with lots of memories is "amputation." I have many patients with limbs or body parts removed. Somehow, I feel a mixture of sadness, curiosity, bewilderment, admiration. And esteem. I am so im-pressed with the people who adapt and the inventors/innovators who adapt prosthetics. And the surgeons who adjust their final cuts to accommodate sensible attachments of these artificial limbs. Really, it is all amazing. I worked with one young patient suffering from phantom leg pain. He still had pain in his missing leg. Over the months, he had a series of modifications to his non-native leg, and the two of us tried multiple other treatments. The most successful was "mirror therapy,"—where a full-length mirror is placed on the bed to reflect the remaining leg. Tricking the brain, sort of, into thinking the body still has two legs. Then there were the many wounds I treated on stumps because of ill-fitting prostheses or over-wearing. It is a fascinating field. And mind boggling to think how people can adapt to a new normal.

34

Chapter 22: Life Goes On

Tresne and Rosella talked nearly every night about the "Bridge Concert." There were so many details to work out—more things to think about than when Rosella just showed up to play a concert with the R and Me band. Before, her promoter had arranged all the specifics, and the band played. Now, these were things she had to do herself, including how to amplify the sound. Tresne was learning along with Rosella, and the two worked well together.

Rosella had come to appreciate Tresne over the time they had known each other. One day, Rosella told Tresne, "You know, sometimes I misgender you, and I'm sorry I do that. It's getting much easier, though, to use the correct word."

Tresne replied, "You're fine. I don't notice you saying anything wrong." They went on, "Do you know when I started using they, them, their?"

Rosella shook her head, "No."

"It was about tenth grade, and we had an amazing music teacher, Mrs. Vandenburg. She brought out the best in everyone, and going to her class was the highlight of my day. By that time, I was dressing in ambiguous clothing—I didn't want to be identified as either a boy or a girl. It just seemed disingenuous to me to choose one gender. I felt I was both or neither."

"Anyway, Mrs. Vandenburg recognized I was different. She might have noticed from the song lyrics I wrote or the artists I listened to. She was very perceptive. "

"On this otherwise uneventful day, Mrs. Vandenburg referred to me as 'they' when talking to another student. I heard the term, and it felt so much less jarring than being referred to by my original gender pronoun. It was like someone was giving me a hug. I liked it. Usually, when someone referred to me as she or he, I immediately thought I wasn't either. But with 'they,' I felt at peace."

"A month or two later, I changed my name to Tresne, so no one made assumptions about my gender. And when my parents were so upset, Mrs. Vandenburg was one of the few adults who understood. I am eternally grateful to her for her respect and love."

Rosella listened to Tresne speak and felt a strong desire to hug them. Imagining how her own childhood and adolescence were filled with love and support from her parents, she wished that could have been the case for Tresne. She also thought of how mature Tresne was despite their challenging circumstances. She was happy she had met the young person. She also noted that Rosella's friends who met Tresne were getting familiar with and gaining insight into differences—even the older people. Rosella was happy she had friends who could adapt to societal changes.

The month before, Tresne had been the featured speaker at the Friday Night Enlights session to talk about homelessness among youth. Having experienced "unsheltered homelessness" themselves, the discussion was extremely pertinent. Tresne worked with an organization in Cincinnati called True Colors United. This group worked on state and local policies to reduce and prevent youth homelessness. Rosella and the Friday night group learned that a crucial part of the effort was to reduce the return to homelessness once a person found a temporary or permanent home. Close to one out of five experienced unhousing again. Tresne worked with the team that provided these youths emotional, economic, educational, and practical support. They explained the system of a twenty-four-hour on-call service to work with emergencies and other challenges these people faced.

Tresne talked again of the difficulties they had gaining acceptance of their gender disclosure with their parents and how that discrimination often carried over to churches and schools, making it difficult for trans or non-binary youth to find support in the usual places. As part of that evening of discussion at Rosella's, the group had watched a film entitled "Proper Pronouns" about four transgender ministers in the South. The film was wonderful, and there was much discussion after it ended.

Ava attended that night and talked about hearing her doctor friend, Linda, lament how many of the asylum seekers at the border of Mexico and the US were trans and how they had been tormented in their home countries. Sadly, these discussions showed that these immigrants would not be guaranteed a better reception in the US.

Meanwhile, Rosella was seemingly busier in the store. More customers, more people coming for lessons, more musical groups gathering to play. She wasn't sure what had prompted the increase but suspected the article in *Rewind* was a factor, plus getting known in the community as a good resource. She was especially glad that some of the high schoolers who came to play after school had invited their parents to come and listen. On this day, several moms and dads stood or sat around listening to the kids jam.

Today's group was assembling electronica music and doing a pretty good job. Rosella noticed they had improved over the weeks of coming here, and she had learned about the mechanics of sampling and looping. She thought about possibly using a looper and other special effects for the Bridge Concert.

In eastern Kentucky, there was one thing that Rosella hadn't noticed before in places she lived—the strength of family connections. It was indeed a power that was hard to define or explain except by witnessing firsthand. And it wasn't just pride for a daughter or son's musical prowess. It was a genuine love for being part of the family. In New York City, she saw parents who went to extreme measures to advance their child's musical, acting, or academic trajectory—a kind of hyper-focus on improving and being recognized. The families here didn't seem concerned with fame. For many, music was a generational trait—like having blue eyes or blond hair. Or even as fundamental as having ten fingers. She saw much more genuine enjoyment in playing music here than in the city. Thinking about all of this made her heart swell. She and Cal often talked about what a gift it had been to move to Kentucky.

Cal talked about the same bond of family with his students. While sometimes students were absent because a family member was ill, just as often, they told Cal that their sick or dying grandparent had told them to go to school and not to ever miss because of them. Selfless love.

Rosella had heard Ava discuss this concept with some of her palliative care patients. The person might have been ready to die, but because their family wasn't prepared for that finality, the sick patient would endure futile treatments to placate a family member. Ava said it was hard to understand, and sometimes she lost patience with these complex and costly futile measures, but Rosella understood the motivation. Family was a powerful force.

Once the date for the Bridge Concert was set, Rosella started thinking about whom to invite. Of course, she wanted her parents there. She had talked to them about her performing again, and she sensed that this return to some normalcy buoyed them. Even her father spoke with more joy than she had heard since Roger died.

She wanted to invite her old band family. Raphael and his wife were coming, and Raphael was going to invite a friend whom he played music with now. Rosella hadn't met him, but Raphael talked about how talented but shy he was. The other people involved with R and Me would attend as well. While Rosella was excited for all her former colleagues to attend, it made her nervous about the performance.

When Rosella was alone with her thoughts, she still worried about playing in public. It had been a very long time since she cared how she sounded or chose music for others. When doubts arose, she talked to Cal or Tresne, and she thought again that Roger would have wanted this. It was indeed time for her to honor his memory differently than refrain from musical performance.

Rosella kept a closer watch on Ava and went to her house most mornings to have coffee. Ava still had trouble, and Rosella didn't pressure her to discuss anything. She just wanted to show Ava that she was with her.

Sometimes when she went over, Ava was still in her pajamas and looked like she hadn't slept well. On other days, she was dressed and vibrant. The third time Rosella invited her to the Bridge Concert, Ava finally committed to coming.

Ava asked if she could invite Sara to the concert. She said, "She will be in Kentucky that weekend, and I think she would enjoy the concert and meeting you."

"Of course," Rosella said, "the more the merrier. I would love to meet Sara. I talked to her on the phone when Gwen and I visited your house. She seemed like she really cared about you."

Ava explained, "She has helped me a lot with the panic attacks and other things. She's a very cool person. I think you would like her. I also think she might get along with Tresne."

"Oh," Rosella said. "Yes, I would like to meet her. Don't you sometimes call her when you're feeling bad? It's nice she will be moving here."

"Yes," Ava responded, "she has a way of putting me at ease. I'm not sure what it is about her, but she's one of those people who exudes calm. Like you."

Rosella asked, "Do you know why she moved to Kentucky?"

Ava said, "You know, I don't know. I think I remember her saying one of her grandparents was from Kentucky and that she enjoyed being able to hike and climb."

Rosella probed further, "Do you know if she is in a relationship?"

Ava answered, "I don't think so."

Rosella asked, "What about you? Are you interested in anyone here?"

Ava sighed and responded, "Nope. I haven't run into anyone that interests me. I guess I'm still gun-shy after Jack and all the trouble I had with the marriage. We'll see. I'm in no hurry. I enjoy being on my own, and right now, I have enough emotional issues to deal with."

Rosella nodded and said, "Yes, take care of yourself. And if you ever want to talk about your mom some more, I will be here.

Ava said, "Yes, that is what I have started to do with my father, brother, and friends. It wasn't natural to be impervious to how much that affected me. I might have gone on in this unhealthy way for years if I hadn't started having the panic attacks and the chronophobia."

Rosella considered momentarily and replied, "As if the panic attacks were just the tip of the iceberg for you. I'm glad you figured it out. Of course, that doesn't make the pain of losing someone go away."

Ava said, "Don't I know."

They began talking about Ava's guitar playing. Ava said she was glad to have time to practice, and Rosella could tell from listening that she had more confidence with the instrument. Before Rosella left, she gave Ava the details of the Bridge Concert so she could invite anyone she wanted. Ava thought she might announce the event at work as well.

As Rosella was leaving, she noticed the green *Taber's Cyclopedia* by the chair in Ava's living room.

"How is the reading going?"

Ava sighed. "I just discovered that someone else has read the entire thing and written a book about it. It's called *Taber's A to Z*. Last week, I tried to motivate myself by starting with the Zs and working backward. I was so frustrated with how slow the endeavor was taking. I'm unsure what I'll do now that I know it has been done."

She went on, "And, I was using my reading as a strategy to stretch time and take my mind off what I should have been dealing with. I don't know if I need to do that anymore."

Rosella simply said, "You'll figure it out." With those words, she headed for the door and waved at Ava as she hopped in her car to drive to Redbud Music.

Rosella thought about Ava on the short drive and considered how much more relaxed she appeared. She didn't look like a powder keg ready to explode. And Rosella remembered that when Ava came to her Friday night gathering this last time, she was early. This had never happened before.

Later in the day, Ava was relaxing at home when she again heard a knock on the door, and Sara burst in. The two friends hugged, and Ava invited Sara into her living room.

"Would you like some tea or coffee?" she asked.

"No thanks," Sara said. "I am still pretty wound up from my flight. I wanted to come here straight away to see how you were doing. So, how are you?"

Ava replied, "Doing much better. I'm handling the panic attacks. I'm sleeping through the night. I actually was able to help a friend with a problem. I am feeling pretty good."

Sara said, "That is great news. I am glad Gwen and Rosella were here. And again, sorry I wasn't close by. Do you have any plans for the day?"

"Well, let me show you something. I want to share something with you." With that, Ava led Sara into her bedroom. She went over to the dresser, taking a small jewelry box. She turned to Sara and asked her to sit down. Ava opened the box to reveal a small gray cloth bag with drawstrings on top. On the outside of the bag was a logo.

"Look at this. It was my mother's," Ava said.

Sara took the small bag and looked closely at the logo. The words Waterford Crystal were embossed in silver over a seahorse design. She loosened the drawstrings and reached inside to find a crystal seahorse brooch, only about the size of her thumb. Light reflected off the cut glass in rainbow colors.

Ava said quietly, "My dad bought it for my mother when we went to Ireland. She wore it whenever she dressed up. When she died, he gave it to me. He said he couldn't bear to see the pin without my mother. I've hidden it in a drawer for the past year for the same reason. I was going through my desk the other day and found it."

"It's beautiful. I love how delicate it is. The pattern on the body is something else. What's the significance of a seahorse?" Sara said.

"That's Waterford Crystal's trademark. They say it reflects on their connection to the sea. Seahorses have always fascinated me."

Sara asked, "Will you wear it?"

Ava smiled. "Yes, it will remind me of how much my mother meant to me and how much I loved her."

Sara walked over with the brooch in hand and gently pinned it to Ava's shirt. The crystal sparkled. She saw tears welling up in her friend's eyes. They hugged each other and said together, "It will be alright."

35

<u>**Am-Ap**</u>

Notes for Inside *Taber's: A Study of the Medical Dictionary* by Dr. Ava

Here is a very interesting term—"anastomosis," meaning 1) a natural communication between two vessels and 2) the surgical or pathological connection of two tubular structures. Here is one of the kinds that has to be highlighted: "magnetic ring anastomosis"—this is a device to hold two segments of a resected bowel together with increasing magnetic force. The device, which consists of two cobalt magnetic circles, is embedded in polyester and applied so the two segments are in the closest of proximities. After seven to twelve days, the outer layers of that section of bowel necrose, or, in essence, die, and the device is repelled and evacuated in the stool. I had never heard of this before, and just wow.

I now encounter a new phenomenon in the Cyclopedia—highlighted sections. Anemia is highlighted, and its sub-entries covering six more pages all have yellow shading. A brief white space and "anesthesia" and its sub-entries are highlighted for another five pages. There is an excellent diagram of "epidural anesthesia" on page 112. So illustrative that maybe a layperson could place an epidural needle—I just wouldn't want to be their first patient. Many words are related to "angio,"—which makes sense since the prefix means a combination of lymph and blood vessels. There are over five pages of angios but inexplicably no yellow highlights.

The antis are an extensive section, and wading through it, I feel antipathy. Everything looks interesting after this group. Anxiety is a big one.

Here is "free-floating anxiety"—anxiety unrelated to an identifiable situation or cause. I am fascinated by aphasias, even though reading about them makes me think I have one. They are very specific, further evidence of the complexity of the brain. "Nominal aphasia"—inability to name objects. "Optic aphasia"—inability to name an object recognized by sight without the aid of sound, taste, or touch. Interestingly, it was first reported by Sigmund Freud. It is not really an aphasia, but there is a term for the inability to laugh out loud: "aphonogelia." It is quite rare. One source I found reported only two cases ever seen in the literature.

36

Chapter 23: The End

When her two-week break was over, Ava returned to work. The clinic, the hallways, and her office were the same, but Ava was now different within this familiar setting. At first, she felt shaky, afraid of having another panic attack. But she was building confidence in knowing what to do, thanks to Sara and her suggestions. Ava was still hesitant to regard clocks but knew only digital displays caused her trouble.

One thing that Ava appreciated—"hunt the good stuff"—from her recent troubles was a new understanding of the suffering of people with anxiety or fear. In the past, she sometimes blamed the person and wondered why they couldn't get over whatever was bothering them as she would in the past. "Buck up, push through your fears." Now she realized she wasn't really "getting over things" and that "control" was an ill-defined entity. And when she thought of her mother—which she still did often—she said to herself it was okay. It was even okay to tear up about her mom and her patients.

From her first appointment to her last, she felt she was listening more closely. She found herself multitasking less often. Her habit of reading, listening, or listening with one ear while typing on the computer didn't feel right anymore. She saw it for the rudeness it was.

On her first day, Pat and Linda stopped in the hallway out of Ava's earshot.

Linda said, "It seems like Dr. Ava is doing better. She seems so much more her old self."

Pat added, "Yes, I noticed right off. She seems more alive."

Linda said more quietly, "And I haven't heard any whistling all day. Yay!"

Pat nodded and put her finger to her lips. "Let's hope that lasts."

Ava interacted with patients throughout the day in a congenial and maybe even collegial way. By the end of the day, she felt energized. She was not as tired as she usually felt after a full day. On her way home, she passed the site of her near accident with no hint of a panic attack.

One day, she told Pat that she thought she had chronophobia.

"What is that?" Pat asked.

"A fear of time," Ava responded.

Pat was incredulous and amused. "A fear of time? Like you are afraid of time? What in the world does that mean?" She was trying to suppress a laugh, but not very well. She went on, "I have heard of fear of spiders, snakes, and high places, but never the fear of time."

Ava explained, "Yes, I had never heard of it either, but it is a real thing. People fear the passage of time, I guess. Mine started after I was in that closet for so long. I started getting anxious when I saw a clock."

Pat was still smiling and shaking her head. "It just sounds made up."

Ava had not shared her "phobia" belief with anyone but Sara and her dad, and they both offered sympathy and understanding. She hadn't expected this type of response to her admission. But as she saw Pat laughing and muttering to herself, Ava realized it was a little funny. To be afraid of something she had no control over. An inevitable consequence of a continuum from the future to the present to the past. Unless multi-verses existed with alternative types of continuums.

The more Ava thought of this concrete definition of time, the more humorous her fears seemed. And the more unrealistic it had been to try to slow down time with reading or guitar playing.

She was confident that she would never denigrate someone else's fears or phobias, but watching Pat smile, she saw humor in her situation.

She remembered that her bedside clock was still covered with a cloth and that there were no other digital clocks in her house. She glanced over at the clock in the lab—the one she had first glimpsed upon being released from the medicine closet. Seeing the clock now, she burst out laughing.

She told Pat, "Yes, that clock over there scared me! That is funny." By this time, some other staff were looking at Ava and Pat with questioning looks.

While Ava laughed, she also felt a twinge of guilt about making light of a phobia. She wished to keep her realization separate from her professional consideration of people's fears. The two emotions were hard to mesh, but letting the levity take over felt easier and more pleasant.

She announced to the gathering crowd, "That clock over there was scaring me." Saying this out loud did sound ridiculous. But it also felt good to declare it in public.

The closest person, Dr. Frost, said, "Wow, what was it going to do to you?"

Ava replied, "I don't know. It was weird. But I think I'm not as scared now."

And with that, she walked over to the clock and made a big show of touching it. Other staff shook their heads as if they thought she might be bananas and went on to do their work.

Only Pat stayed and walked up next to Ava.

She said quietly, "I know what you mean. One time, I was afraid of goats. They scared me to death. I got over it when I had to rescue one from the neighbor's pool. No one else could understand why I was deathly afraid of the animals. I understand, and I'm sorry I laughed."

Ava said, "No, it's ok. That was exactly what I needed. Thanks so much for all you do for me." This time, Ava initiated a hug and thought, *maybe I'm becoming a hugger.*

For the rest of the day, Ava felt somehow lighter, as if a heavy weight had evaporated. She couldn't exactly identify the unfamiliar feeling, but the day sailed by, and she continued listening to her patients. She made a few jokes, and people laughed.

When she got home that night, *Taber's* was the first thing she saw on her table. She hadn't picked it up since discovering the other author's book about reading it. And since letting out her feelings about her mother.

Now, she saw the whole endeavor of reading it as funny, like an odd thing to do. She recalled the reactions of a couple of people she had told of her decision to read the book. They all wondered why she did that. Now, she could see their point. And she had the idea of finding the humor in the book, kind of as a signal in her life not to take herself so seriously. Why make life difficult?

But she knew, in a way, that her reading of *Taber's* had saved her life—or at least changed it so she could genuinely live it.

Sitting down after dinner with the book, a glass of wine, and her notebook, she pondered. All her life, she had observed events with a dichotomous mind, seeing things as real but also as fake. She remembered feeling this way at Yogaville when the teachers lit candles and incense to "summon good energy" into the air. Observing and participating in a cramped and uncomfortable lotus position, Ava was torn between seeing the mystery of such beliefs and the hokiness.

She thought about her self-diagnosis of chronophobia. In one part of her brain, she thought it was real and believable, but at another level, she wondered if it was made up—an illusion.

After some time with these conflicting thoughts, Ava was exhausted and decided it didn't matter that there was more than one way to see things. "Hunting for the good." She picked up *Taber's* and flipped to the Zs. Within seconds, she had found several hilarious words. When she looked up and saw the pendulum clock, she thought about asking Rosella if she could spare some room in Redbud Music for a clock repair area. It seemed like an agreeable companion to a music store.

Meanwhile, Rosella was preparing for the big Bridge Concert. All the details had been worked out, and the weather looked promising.

The friends she invited from out of town had all responded that they would be there.

She and Tresne drove out to the bridge two nights before the event. The bridge was wooden and spanned a river about thirty feet across at the widest. There was evidence along the shore of flooding, but the river flowed calmly and safely within its banks at this time of year.

Sturdy beams bisected the bridge's wood ceiling. The walls bore interesting graffiti. It was mostly kids' etchings or pairs of initials separated by a plus sign. Tresne and Rosella wondered if the couples who anonymously advertised their involvement were still together. They both laughed at some of the more humorous etchings.

The plan was for the two of them to arrive before the scheduled public event to record three songs inside the structure. It wasn't safe for a large crowd to gather on the shaky floor. A friend of Tresne was coming from Cincinnati to video record their performance. They didn't know what exactly they would do with the recording, but Tresne had a pretty popular Instagram site.

Tresne told Rosella, "You know, there's still a lot of people interested in R and Me. They would love to see this."

Rosella said, "OK, whatever you want to do with it."

She had enjoyed her obscurity for the past few years and knew that promoting the video and performing in public would be the end of that phase of her musical career. On the other hand, she wondered if a band without Roger would disappoint fans. The thought made her sad but not scared.

After the recording, Tresne and Rosella had arranged for a lineup of the various groups who played around at Redbud Music to perform for the public audience. There would be the all-girls electronica group, the Irish group, and another talented quartet. Even the harpist who had come into the store some time ago was going to perform. She had recently electrified her harp and did a lot of experimental work playing with a beautiful and talented singer.

Rosella would perform a duet with the woman who played the nyckelharpa. Rosella wasn't good enough to play the Swedish instrument but would accompany the woman with her guitar. Several final songs would be just Tresne and Rosella. Tresne would play an assortment of drums with Rosella singing and playing guitar or fiddle. In the end, Rosella used the old R and Me compositions. She never was able to write a new song.

The area in front of the bridge was perfect for the concert. There was a grassy area to the side for kids to run around and a flat area in front for people to sit on folding chairs, already set out haphazardly. The churchyard was wide open, with plenty of room to explore. The congregation supported the concert and agreed to sell snacks. Surprisingly, a local winery was going to sell wine. It was going to be an enjoyable day, Rosella kept telling herself.

On the day of the event, the sun gleamed. Temperatures were ideal for a late summer afternoon, and there was plenty of shade from the old oaks in the churchyard. The pre-concert recording in the bridge went well, and the sound engineer motioned a thumbs-up for every song. Tresne and Rosella recorded three good tracks and a couple more songs that needed work.

Then people ambled in for the concert. Some brought coolers and lawn chairs, while others had blankets and picnic baskets. The booth selling wine soon had a line, and the church's food booth also had a crowd of customers. Rosella greeted people as they arrived and helped some of the other musicians carry instruments and equipment over to the makeshift stage. Everyone was talking and socializing.

She recognized Raphael and his wife from a distance and ran over to hug them.

"It's been too long," each of them said.

A man she had never met and whom she assumed was their friend trailed a short distance behind them.

Raphael reached back to pull the fellow into the circle and said, "This is Ben, the guy I told you about that I play music with sometimes. Ben, this is Rosella, whom I have talked about so much."

The two shook hands and greeted each other. Ben was very handsome, with a tuft of brown hair that fell nearly over his blue eyes. He had a pleasant smile and an easy way about him. Rosella instantly liked him and noticed he had brought a guitar.

"Oh, you brought your guitar," she said.

"Yes," he replied, "I thought it was too hot in the car. I didn't know if there might be a time to pull it out and play."

Rosella exclaimed, "Of course! Yes, of course."

Just then, Ava walked up, and Rosella introduced her to the three newcomers. They talked briefly about Ava's time in upstate New York and made small talk about Kentucky and the weather. Rosella excused herself, saying she needed to get things ready to start, and Ava invited the New Yorkers to sit by her on the lawn.

Sara and Tresne had met earlier and seemed to be engaged in a deep conversation on the side of the stage. Ava was glad they were getting to know each other. She briefly entertained the thought that they would make a good couple. Thinking of that, she took a closer look at Ben, who was settling his blanket and cooler down near the group. He was good-looking and seemed at ease. Rosella had mentioned last week that Raphael thought he was shy, but Ava observed him talking easily to people. She liked him and felt her cheeks flush when their eyes met.

The concert began with introductory remarks from Rosella, who seemed a natural on stage. Tresne and Rosella played one opening song, which the crowd went wild over. Then, there was a succession of groups. Ava recognized the girl high school band from Redbud Music, and they sounded great.

Introducing the band, the lead guitarist of the electronica group announced, "This isn't our usual type of venue, and it won't be loud enough to make your ears bleed."

The audience laughed. A woman with a strange-looking violin came to the stage, and Rosella joined her with a guitar. The Swedish-accented woman explained the history of the nyckelharpa, and the duo played a couple of beautiful pieces.

There was a brief break, and Trina lugged her full-sized harp onto the stage. Ava knew Trina from the work she did with hospice patients. The music she and a woman vocalist made in this idyllic setting was truly heavenly. Everyone was stilled into silence, and when the pair finished, instead of interrupting the mood with loud applause, the audience waved their hands in appreciation.

For the final act, Rosella and Tresne returned to the stage. Rosella made a tearful speech about how this concert was dedicated to Roger, and Ava glanced over to see Rosella's parents crying but smiling. The pieces that Tresne and Rosella played were undoubtedly the most professional-sounding, and again, the crowd went wild.

People congregated around the different players and gushed with compliments. Ava hugged Liz and introduced herself to Larry with a hug. This time, she knew she had become a hugger. She enjoyed hugging.

As the afternoon turned into evening and the equipment had been packed, Rosella rounded up her special guests and invited all to come back to her house for dinner and drinks. Sara and Tresne rode together, Ava offered Ben a ride, and Raphael and his wife rode in the back seat of Liz and Larry's car. Cal had left the gathering earlier, and when the large group arrived, he had a delicious meal waiting. Everyone could fit around a long wooden table set up on the porch. The wine flowed, and there was lots of laughing and joking.

Ava looked around at the assembled friends. She had trusted Rosella and the others when she needed them most. They had drawn her in. She found she was no longer content to be just an observer. She wanted to be a part of this place and time.

37

Epilogue

Six Months Later

Ava stepped off the twelve-seater Tropic Airplane in Punta Gorda, Belize. The temperature was over ninety degrees, and she was already sweating. Whether from the heat or excitement, she didn't know. Her flight was much easier than she had imagined, and while skimming across the coast in a small commuter plane, she discovered she was enjoying the closeness of the sea. She had been invited to the co-pilot's seat when they left from Belize City, so she sat in awe of the view. Not once did she worry.

She saw Linda waving from behind the airport fence. Linda was a little browner, and her hair was a shade blonder, but she had the same open smile and calm manner. Ava grabbed her luggage and rushed to greet her friend.

The two hugged in a long embrace.

Linda said, "Welcome to Belize."

Ava gushed, "Thank you. Thank you. I am so glad to be here."

38

Afterword

<u>Ava's New Year's Newsletter: To All My Friends</u>

As many of you know, I have been reading *Taber's Cyclopedic Medical Dictionary* for many months. I wanted to share a few words I found funny to bring you cheer for this New Year. Best Wishes!!!

> Zelotypia
> Wharton's Jelly
> Prune Juice Sputum and Currant
Jelly Sputum
> Wet Brain
> Sunday Morning Paralysis
> Tarantism
> Sunflower Eyes
> Topothermesthsiometer
> Swiss Cheese Cartilage Syndrome

Word Salad—the use of words indiscriminately and haphazardly, that is, without logical structure or meaning.

Zelotypia—morbid or monomaniacal zeal in the interest of any project or cause.

Wharton's Jelly—the gelatinous intercellular material of the umbilical cord; it consists of collagen, mucin, and hyaluronic acid.

Wet Brain—an increased amount of cerebrospinal fluid with edema of the meninges; may be associated with alcoholism.

Tarantism—uncontrollable stupor, melancholy, and manic dancing attributed to the tarantula's bite.

Topothermesthesiometer—LONGEST WORD I COULD FIND IN THE BOOK. Device for measuring local temperature sense.

Acknowledgments

I want to thank my patients for allowing me the privilege of being present with them through some of the most life changing times. Gratitude to my colleagues for sharing knowledge and showing me examples of caring medicine. Thanks in particular to Judy Buelterman, palliative care nurse, who embodied love and warmth with all our patients. Appreciation to all the people I have worked with in medicine in the US and internationally who have dedicated their lives to helping. Acknowledging Ammon Shea and his book "Reading the OED: One Man, One Year, 21.730 Pages" that got me started on the story idea.

Thank you to the early readers of Ava Finds Time, (when it was originally titled Chronophobia Strikes or A Doctor Reads Taber's): Kelley, Ed, Cathy, Molly, my Morehead book club, Jeanette, Nichole from UpWorks. Thanks to Jerri Schlenker (author found under J. Schlenker) for resurrecting this manuscript, editing and helping me to publish. And thank you to my family- my parents, Ed and Helen both deceased, my brothers/sisters Ed, John, Kelley and Bobbie. Thanks to the three dogs, one still living, who conveniently slept while I wrote. Finally, thank you for the support of Egan Colbert and Capp Yess. Always on my mind.

About the Author

Dr. Ann Colbert has been a family and palliative care physician in Eastern Kentucky for four decades. She also lived and worked in Belize as a volunteer medical director of a remote clinic and spent time working in Africa and the US/Mexico border. She continues to work for health care equity and justice. This is her first novel but she writes commentary about medicine often and sporadically describes her experiences at anncolbez.wordpress.com. She lives with her partner and her dog in northeastern Kentucky.